CHASING THE 400

CHASING THE 400

Chase your dreams and make them come true!

Sheila Vance

SHEILAH VANCE

The Elevator Group Edition
The Elevator Group
Paoli, Pennsylvania

The Elevator Group Edition
Copyright © 2005, 2007 by Sheilah Vance.

Library of Congress Control Number:		2007900560
ISBN-13:	Trade Paperback	978-0-9786854-0-9
ISBN-10	Trade Paperback	0-9786854-0-7

Published in the United States by The Elevator Group.
(Originally published in different form by XLibris, Philadelphia, in 2005
under Softcover ISBN 1-4134-9174-X and Hardcover 1-4134-9175-8).

This book was printed in the United States of America.

To order additional copies of this book, contact:
The Elevator Group
www.TheElevatorGroup.com
610-296-4966
info@TheElevatorGroup.com

DEDICATION

This book is dedicated to:

- my mother, Ruth Vance, for her unfailing love, guidance, inspiration and support. All that I have done in my life is due to what you have taught me.
- my children, Hope and Vance, for filling my life with more joy and love than I could ever imagine, and for always believing in my dreams.
- to my late father, Robert T. Vance, Sr., whose spirit walks with me daily.
- to my grandparents, James H. Vance, Sr., and Elizabeth Weldon Vance, for their rich, loving legacy.
- to my aunts and uncles for teaching us the meaning of family pride.
- to my great aunt, Dorothy Caldwell, for instinctively knowing what I was doing and for giving me the information I needed.
- to my late aunt, Vera Vance, for guiding me to answer the writer's question: what if?

Love, Peace, and God Bless

CHAPTER 1

Vera Marshall stepped out of the Studebaker, straightened the seams on her stockings and smoothed her skirt. Jimmy Bennett leaned over, reached for the skirt and caught the hem.

"Haven't you had enough?" Vera snapped, moving her hips to the right, out of Jimmy's grasp.

"Never could get enough," said Jimmy, slurring his words and leering at her while resting his arm on the warm spot where she sat seconds before.

"Well, don't think you're getting any more," Vera said. "At least not this week." She flipped the mink boa around her neck and shoulder and turned toward the sidewalk. The dead mink's plastic eyes stared straight at Jimmy as he muttered "bitch," slammed the door and sped down Welsh Road.

Vera froze for a second as she thought about picking up that loose piece of sidewalk in front of her and throwing it like a long ball smack into Jimmy's back window. But that meant that she'd have to turn around, and she wouldn't give Jimmy the satisfaction, nor would she break one of her rules. She never watched men leave. She couldn't be bothered. She left them, and when she did, she never looked back. Now Jimmy Bennett let one taste too many of Johnnie Walker Red pass from his mouth to his brain and back through his mouth. She put him behind her as fast as he drove off. He was one more sorry piece of Ardmore that she'd be glad to leave behind.

Vera straightened her shoulders, lifted her head high, and walked up the steps to 479 slowly enough so that anyone on the street who wanted to see her ample hips switching in perfect rhythm could. She turned the handle on the door, and it opened immediately. With ten children going in and out all day, no one took the trouble to lock the door.

As soon as Vera stepped across the threshold, her mother, Emma, called out, "Shut the door." Vera laughed at how quickly Emma could feel a breeze pass through the front room, living room, dining room and into the kitchen. She thought that if her mother's skin was that sensitive, no wonder she had ten children. Every touch must have felt great.

Vera took off the red felt cloche with the purple feather and laid it on top of the mahogany china closet in the living room. The few times that her parents forced Vera to go to church, she always wore that hat. She liked the way the feather reached back to the end of the pew behind her and smacked somebody in the face every time she turned her head.

"Don't any of you kids think of getting up there and touching my hat," Vera said to three of her younger siblings gathered around the dining room table shelling and eating peanuts.

"Don't nobody want your old hat," said the youngest boy, Milton, throwing a peanut at her. Vera picked it up and threw it back.

Vera sashayed into the kitchen and announced, "I'm home, Mom." Emma bent over the sink shucking peas for dinner. She looked the same as she did most every day—hair center-parted, braids on each side touching the top of her shoulders, dark house dress fitting snugly around waist and hips, stockings three shades too light rolled down to her calf, mule-type slippers wrinkled from the pressure of 200 pounds. Emma turned around, took one look at Vera and shook her head.

"You'd better learn to put some clothes on," Emma said, waving a pea pod in Vera's face. "Blouse wide open, showing your bosom. Skirt split up the side of your leg. Little short jacket not even covering your behind."

"And don't think that skinny dead animal hanging around your neck is going to keep you warm," Emma said, sucking her teeth. "I could kill your Aunt Alfreda for giving you that thing."

"She knew what she was doing," Vera said, putting her hands on her hips.

Emma straightened up and moved her left foot back. "Even though you think you're grown," Emma said, "you're not. You're only seventeen, missy. And as long as you're still in school and in this house, you better not give me any back talk. When you finish school this year, you can go live where you want and do what you please, but you're not there yet, young lady."

Vera looked at Emma like she was crazy. She was grown, and Emma knew it. At least she did the things that grown women did, and she liked doing them. Ardmore was long past being too small for her. She couldn't wait until her class, the Class of 1955, finished Ardmore High School. Then she could move into Philadelphia with Aunt Alfreda. Two so-called "wild women" belonged together.

"Oh, Mom," said Vera, looking in the cupboard for something to eat, "you know I have a certain style, and I just have to show it." Vera laughed and wrapped her arms around Emma's neck, her usual way of apologizing for back talking.

"Besides," said Vera, "I gave Valerie my old winter coat because it's too small for me. My chest is still growing, in case you haven't noticed, and I could barely get that thing buttoned."

Emma chuckled. She was right. Vera's breasts were almost as big as hers, and Vera couldn't chalk hers up to giving birth to and breast-feeding ten children or being 75 pounds overweight.

"Maybe on Saturday we'll go down the Pike and see if we can find you a coat somewhere that'll cover your chest and your behind," Emma said.

Vera wrinkled her brow and shot Emma a look. "As long as it's not at that thrift shop," she said, "because I'm not wearing nobody's second hand nothing."

Vera couldn't even believe that a thrift shop operated on the Pike—the nickname for Lancaster Avenue, Main Street for the Main Line, suburban Philadelphia's wealthy and exclusive string of towns from Merion on the Philadelphia end to Paoli way out on the Chester County end. The Main Line included Ardmore, where the Marshall family lived in the town's working class colored section. Some of the most exclusive stores in the Philadelphia area operated on the Main Line, and it didn't make sense to Vera to throw a thrift shop up there.

"You'll wear what we can afford," said Emma, "and with all you kids, we can't afford much. Just because you're the oldest, don't think you have to get new clothes every time."

Oh, but I do, thought Vera. She wasn't known as the finest looking girl at Ardmore High School—colored or white—for nothing.

"If the clothes don't start out new with me, by the time they get handed down through four sisters to Caroline, there'd be nothing left," Vera said, as if that was perfect justification for buying the stylish new clothes that she loved.

"Get on out of here, girl," Emma said with a giggle. "You just won't give up, will you?"

Not now, not ever, thought Vera.

How could she give up when she knew that she could do better? Ten kids and two adults in a twin house in working class, colored Ardmore was fine for now, but not for always. From the moment her father, John, took her to one of those opulent Main Line estates where he frequently went on plumbing jobs, she knew that she had to do better. And she knew, just as well, that whatever she wanted, she had to get it for herself.

"Is Pop home yet?" Vera asked as she lifted up pot lids, smelling the collard greens and butter beans with ham hocks that Emma prepared for dinner.

"He's down in the basement cleaning his tools," said Emma.

"Where did he put *The Elevator*?" Vera asked. *The Elevator* was Philadelphia's colored newspaper. It came out every week, its motto splayed across the masthead in bold, one-inch letters: UPLIFTING THE RACE.

"On the sideboard. Where he usually puts it," Emma said.

Vera looked at the sideboard next to the basement door and didn't see the paper. Then she looked in the living room and saw her five-year-old brother, Mark, hitting her four-year-old sister, Lynn, with a rolled up newspaper.

"Give me that," Vera said, as she rushed into the room and grabbed Mark's hand just as the paper was ready to make contact with Lynn's head. Vera stuck out her other arm and put her palm directly in the middle of Mark's chest, keeping his flailing arms away from the newspaper.

"Don't even think of following me," Vera said as she gently pushed Mark into a nearby chair and walked into the front room. The same as she did every week when the paper came out, Vera sat down in the plastic slipcovered club chair that felt like she was sitting on marshmallows in a plastic bag and unrolled the paper. She flipped past the important news about segregation, the Ku Klux Klan and all of the colored firsts and turned to Section B, "Elevator Society".

Vera focused on the headline that spread across the society section's front page: "Mr. and Mrs. Donald Butcher Welcome Spring with a Champagne and Crocuses Soiree at their Mt. Airy Estate". The rest of the page was filled with photos of colored gentlemen in tuxedos and women in exquisite ball gowns toasting each other with champagne and holding small pots of blooming crocuses, the hostess' gift to each departing lady, said the caption. Vera studied every detail in the photos and tried to commit the names to memory. Then she turned the page and spent the next half hour looking at page after page of women in stunning cocktail dresses and suits and daytime dresses as fashionable as the Paris designer outfits she saw the white ladies wear on the Main Line.

The women displayed as colored society were the ladies of "the 400", an exclusive, informal collection of Philadelphia's black bourgeoisie, the talented tenth, the doctors, lawyers and other successful colored businessmen and their wives. This exclusive group patterned themselves after "the Four Hundred", the phrase coined in the late 1800's by New York socialite Mrs. William Astor and her friends to symbolize upper crust society—the truly worthy 400 people who could fit into the ballroom of Mrs. Astor's New York City home.

Like Mrs. Astor's Four Hundred, Philadelphia's colored 400 attended a seemingly endless round of balls, lunches, fashion shows and cocktail soirees. Mrs. Donald Butcher, Sr., given name Harriet, ruled the colored 400 which, in reality, had only about 50 people who were truly worthy. Donald Butcher made a fortune operating the largest colored funeral home in Philadelphia, and Harriet made a life running colored society.

The 400 applied the same philosophy to creating the pageantry of their social world as they did to their professional one—that they had to work twice as hard as whites to be considered half as good, and the 400 wanted to be considered not just good, but a credit to their race.

For white folks, the Main Line was the epitome of high society; for colored folks, Philadelphia was. White families used Daddy's World War II and Korean War veteran's housing benefits to flee the city and settle on the Main Line. Vera had a plan to do just the opposite, except the only Daddy she planned on using had the first name Sugar.

CHAPTER 2

"You chillun wake up," John Marshall called out at 6 a.m. as he walked down the second floor hall, knocking on three bedroom doors to wake his children before he went downstairs for breakfast. "Let's get this assembly line going."

John ambled down the hall, his 5'4", wiry frame slightly bent over from years of carrying heavy plumbing tools and equipment. His tan cotton cap was in his hand, where it spent almost as much time as on his head. When he put the hat on, it made his long, wide ears stick out even more.

In the oldest girl's bedroom, the sound of John's knock on the door reached Valerie first since her bed was closest to the door. She switched on the light with one hand and tugged on the window shade with the other. The shade flapped against itself and the window, signaling to Vera and her other sisters, Stephanie and Patricia, that it was time to wake up.

As the oldest girl, Vera had the privilege of sleeping in the bed at the other end of the room, the farthest away from the door and all the hallway noise generated by the sisters, brothers, parents and assorted cousins and friends who seemed to be in the Marshall house as much as they were in their own. The position of Vera's bed had its advantages early in the morning because the noise didn't wake her on the weekend when she wanted to sleep. But that bed being in the back of the room had its drawbacks when she came home late at night and wanted to sneak in and not let everyone in the family know her business, at least not right away.

"Wake up," Valerie said loud enough so that the other girls could hear. She knew exactly how loud to shout since calling out the wake-up had been her job for over ten years. As the second oldest Marshall girl, Valerie felt like it was her responsibility to stay in the room until the other girls woke up and headed to the bathroom. Normally, the oldest girl would feel this responsibility, but Vera didn't. After years of being forced to take care of her brothers and sisters when they were awake, she didn't feel like it was her job to wake them up, and if Valerie wanted to take that job on, that was one less thing to tie Vera down.

"I hear you," Vera said as she pushed back the covers and stretched her arms above her head. Vera hated to wait for anything so, more often than not, she jumped out of bed as soon as she heard Valerie raise the shade. If she waited too long to get into the bathroom, her brothers and sisters would have used up all the hot water, and Vera couldn't stand anything that didn't feel warm and satisfying next to her skin.

"Good," said Valerie. "You know how much time it takes you to get dressed.

Vera put a hand over her yawning mouth. "Anyone who truly cares about her appearance needs time to make sure that she is perfectly attired," she said.

"Speak for yourself," said Patricia, rolling her eyes and shooting a dirty look in Vera's direction.

"I always do," said Vera as she gathered her towel and washcloth and headed for the bathroom.

Vera found the bathroom door closed. She knocked on the door and said, "Time's up, little brother" and leaned against the floral wallpaper lining the hallway, waiting for the door to open.

"I'll be right out," said Bobby, Vera's brother. She called him little, not because of his size—he was 6'1", although at 135 pounds, he was skinny—but because he was 10 months younger than her. Of all her siblings, Bobby was Vera's favorite. Most people thought that Bobby and Vera were complete opposites, but Bobby and Vera knew better. Just because Bobby was shy where Vera was flamboyant, and Bobby was self-effacing where Vera was self-promoting, and Bobby was an honor student where Vera was barely passing, didn't matter to them. For two months of the year they were the same age, so they considered themselves to be almost twins.

He understood Vera better than anyone else in that household overflowing with people. Vera had saved Bobby from many a bully until he learned to defend himself. And Bobby smoothed over more than a few rough spots when Vera's loud-talking self got her into trouble that her braggadocio refused to let her see.

"Good morning, Vera," Bobby said, chipper as usual when he opened the bathroom door.

"I knew it was you in there," Vera said. "You're always in a hurry to get to school."

Bobby laughed and said, "And you're always in a hurry to get the hot water before anybody else."

"Hurry up and get to that chemistry lab so you can cook up God knows what," Vera said. "Do they know you're in there experimenting when you're supposed to be cleaning up?"

"Mr. Texton knows what I'm doing," Bobby said. Mr. Texton was his chemistry teacher and the chair of the school's chemistry department. He hired Bobby to clean up what he didn't trust the janitors to take care of. Bobby knew the difference between chemicals that were left out because somebody was sloppy and chemicals that were left out as part of an experiment. Mr. Texton didn't mind if Bobby did his own experimenting every now and then, in fact, he encouraged it.

"Just be careful you don't blow anything up," Vera said, twirling her towel.

"Now you know, of all the people in that school, I know what I'm doing in a chemistry lab," Bobby said.

"I know, little brother, I know," Vera said. She meant it, too. Bobby loved chemistry and knew more about it than anybody at the high school. "Go ahead on with that chemistry because you'll need it. But all the chemistry I need to know is how my A will mix with Mr. Right's B. If I get the right combination, I'll get a reaction that will last a lifetime."

Bobby laughed as he walked back to his room, but he hoped that whatever reaction Vera concocted didn't blow up in her face.

Vera closed the bathroom door behind her. She filled the basin with hot water and thought about the tasks ahead. Since she dumped Jimmy, she didn't have a ride to school. No other colored boys in Ardmore drove to school every day, but she knew that she'd rather get corns on her toes from walking the mile to school in high heels than ask Jimmy for a ride.

And since she dumped Jimmy, she had to find a new boyfriend. That shouldn't be any trouble, she thought. Almost every boy at Ardmore High just waited for her to glance in his direction. She flirted with them all, no matter who was lucky enough to be her boyfriend at the time. She always believed in having a spare on line for occasions such as this one.

Vera washed off slowly as she thought about who might be able to keep her occupied for the next few months until she graduated and moved away. The only face that came to mind was Billy Patterson. Six feet tall, wavy hair, skin like butterscotch—yes, he would do. Never mind that he went with Regina Climers.

Billy always took his time talking to Vera if they happened to meet in the hallway or somewhere in the neighborhood. Once he even put his hand around Vera's waist to keep her from falling when she caught her heel in the sidewalk on Welsh Road, and he held it there longer than necessary and longer than polite.

Billy Patterson it will be, thought Vera as she walked out of the bathroom. Three siblings shot evil looks in her direction as she walked by.

"Don't worry," Vera said, flinging her towel over her shoulder. "I saved you some hot water."

Vera opened the closet door searching for just the right outfit. The dresses hung in the closet with barely two fingers' space between them, but Vera knew the exact location of every dress she owned. Fingering past five dresses, she found the one she wanted. Lipstick red, cut low in the front, neckline accented with white lace, form-fitting to her hips, capped off by six inches of pleats from her knees to mid-calf. She pulled out the third shoe box on the left and took out her red leather pumps, both stuffed with tissue paper.

Then Vera reached in her dresser and unrolled a glistening pair of silk stockings. She picked up a black garter belt with a red satin bow stitched on front and center. She laid all the clothes on the bed for inspection. Everything coordinated perfectly. Now she was ready to get dressed, carefully and neatly.

"Valerie, help me with this, will you?" Vera asked, turning around so her sister could reach the zipper.

"Mom's going to have a fit with this," Valerie said as she fit the hook on one side into the eye on the other.

Vera sucked her teeth and then sighed. "Nothing new and nothing that I can't handle."

After dressing, Vera picked up the brush on the dresser and brushed her shoulder-length black hair. She usually let her hair hang freely around her shoulders because most men she knew liked it that way. But today, she wanted her dress and her body to do the talking. She decided to put her hair up in a bun. When Billy saw her hair up, he'd want to convince her to let it down. She knew what she was doing.

CHAPTER 3

The dining room table already was half full. Emma walked from chair to chair, pouring milk, dishing out more eggs, and handing out toast. Milton, the one-year-old boy, still trying to learn how to make the spoon reach his mouth, left eggs in an ever-increasing pile on the table, threw down the spoon and grabbed the eggs with his hand. Cindy, the two-year-old girl, took a few eggs off her plate and then reached for Milton's. Milton splashed milk from his cup as he swatted at Cindy's hand.

Emma heard the click-clack of high heels coming down the wooden steps. She looked up at Vera, focused on her neckline, and slammed the bowl with the eggs down on the table.

"Get back upstairs and put on some decent clothes that cover your bosom," Emma said.

Vera wanted to laugh. Emma always was shocked by Vera's outfits, and everyday she told Vera as much, knowing that her protests about proper dress fell on deaf ears.

"It is covered," Vera said as she tugged at the neckline, trying to cover a little more.

Emma reared back and put her hands on her hips, wondering how stupid this child thought that she was. "Don't play with me, Vera, not today," Emma said. You come down here looking like a harlot from Sodom and Gomorrah. No daughter of mine is going out of here like that, at least not while I'm looking."

Emma waved the spoon around for emphasis. Milton, who thought she was playing a game, leaned over, tried to grab the spoon and landed his arm in the egg pile in front of him. "I'm drawing the line, Vera. Cover yourself."

Vera didn't really want to push Emma, but she wasn't changing her clothes. Not today. Too much was riding on this outfit. She tried the soft approach to calm her down.

"Now Mom, you know I have a reputation to maintain," Vera said. "Best dressed girl at Ardmore High School—white or colored."

"Nobody voted you best dressed," Emma said, thinking and then adding, "if they give such a crazy award."

It's working, Vera thought. "Nobody has to vote me best dressed. Everybody knows that I am. The white boys even say so. The white girls think so, but they won't admit it. And you see all the other colored girls around here, so you know I'm telling the truth."

Emma knew Vera looked better in her clothes than the other girls in the neighborhood, but that went to the point she kept trying to make to Vera: the Bible tells you not to be prideful and boastful. Sure, Vera looked better—in decent clothes—but she didn't have to revel in it.

"A little modesty wouldn't hurt you any, Vera," Emma said.

Vera opened her eyes wide as if she didn't really believe what she just heard. "What's to be modest about? What's modesty ever gotten anybody?"

Emma shook her head, straightened up and raised her hand like she was about to be sworn in to something important. "Help me, Lord," she said.

Vera then knew that she had gone too far. Before Emma could open her mouth with a punishment that Vera would have to find a way to escape, Vera said, "OK, Mom. I'll be modest. But if I change now, I'll be late for school," knowing that Emma wouldn't want that. "How about if I go upstairs and put a sweater on over this. Will that satisfy you?"

Emma brought her hand down. Not a complete victory, but progress. "That would be a blessed sight better than what I'm looking at now. I don't have any more time to fool with you today, Vera," Emma said as she picked up the baby, "so go on and get your sweater."

Vera turned on her high heels, smiled at the wall, and walked back up the stairs. The sweater would be easy enough to take off once she got to school.

The sun peeked over the horizon as Bobby walked through the school parking lot, past the only car there. As usual, Mr. Johnson, the daytime janitor, had already arrived. Bobby opened the side door that Mr. Johnson left unlocked for him. He turned on the lights in the hallways that led to the chemistry corridor and headed toward the last room on the right, the chemistry lab.

He switched on the lights and looked around. The tables were littered with the evaporating residue of spilled solutions, burnt matches, and overturned test tube holders—the usual mess. The night janitor only emptied the trash cans and swept or mopped the obvious messes off the floor.

Bobby walked straight to the teacher's desk, looking for Mr. Texton's note telling him which experiments were continuing, which were finished, and which chemicals needed changing, mixing, or turning. Bobby never knew that Mr. Texton gave him a fraction of the chores that he probably should have for the $10 a week salary. Mr. Texton wanted Bobby to have time to experiment or read the books or journals in the vast chemistry library.

Today, the water in the advanced chemistry class experiment needed changing precisely one hour after sunrise, a time Bobby noted by reading the tables in the *Farmer's Almanac* on Mr. Texton's desk. The old water had to be collected in a sterile beaker for examination under a microscope.

Bobby carefully pulled the metal pan out from under a collection of rocks decomposing in a chemical corrosive solution. He funneled the liquid into the nearest clean beaker, fastened on a cork, and labeled it with the date and time as Mr. Texton instructed. He filled the pan with water, carefully balancing it so that none of the water spilled out, and placed the pan back under the rocks.

Then he walked to each lab table and gently lifted the more simple experiments and wiped off the marble counter tops with a special solution Mr. Texton developed.

Chores finished, Bobby checked the clock over the door and saw that he had enough time to continue the experiment he started yesterday. He was trying to concoct something to make his family rich—a solution that plumbers could apply to copper tubes to strengthen them and make them less susceptible to holes and cuts.

"Carpenter poked another hole in the copper," John often explained as he headed out the door to a job. As John became more aware of Bobby's interest in chemistry, he told him that the person who could figure out how to strengthen a copper pipe would make a million dollars—and then some. Bobby figured that with as much as he knew about plumbing and chemistry, he had just as good a chance of making a million as anyone.

Bobby took the solution he mixed the previous day out of the beaker. He found a few sheets of graph paper and plotted the vapor pressure-temperature relation to determine which temperature would bring the solution to the boiling point. He didn't want the solution to boil, so he heated it to 10 degrees below the boiling point he plotted on the graph paper. When the solution reached the precise temperature, he added two grams of zinc chloride and waited for a reaction. Nothing. No bubbles, no nothing.

He tried to think of what went wrong. What would happen if he added hydrochloric acid? That combination would leave an excess of heat so that the reaction would occur, according to his notes. Bobby tapped the side of the thimble. A bit of the acid sprinkled down, and he waited. It didn't take long. The solution churned and turned green.

As he recorded the results of the experiment in his notebook, a bell sounded three times. School started in 30 minutes. The experiment would have to wait.

Bobby wiped down the counters once more so they'd be sparkling wet when Mr. Texton arrived. Five minutes later, Mr. Texton walked in, his white hair gleaming in the full sun that now poured in the lab windows.

"Good morning, Bobby," said Mr. Texton. He walked over and placed his briefcase on the desk. "Everything taken care of?"

"Yes, it is, Mr. Texton," answered Bobby. "Good morning, sir."

"And how's your experiment going? Making any progress?" Mr. Texton asked, taking off his glasses and chewing on the temple.

"I sure am, sir," said Bobby, and he described in detail what happened that morning, eyes wide and words coming out in rapid fire.

Bobby loved to talk chemistry with Mr. Texton, and Mr. Texton, who had 38 years of teaching experience to share, loved to talk chemistry with Bobby. Unlike most students, Bobby seemed to have a natural ability to understand how chemicals worked together and an eagerness to soak up all the information he could.

Mr. Texton was sure that Bobby would win the senior chemistry prize next year, and he wanted him to have it. He knew that Bobby would need every cent of that prize money to go to college, coming from a family of ten kids with a father who got enough work in his plumbing business to get by but not all that he could because he was colored.

As soon as Bobby finished describing the experiment, the second bell rang, signaling that home room started in five minutes. "See you in class later, Mr. Texton," Bobby said. He gathered up his books and walked to the door.

"All right son, see you this afternoon," Mr. Texton said, as students poured into the room.

Ardmore Senior High School was the biggest public gathering place in Lower Merion Township, even though the mansions that some of the students called home were almost as big. The building, constructed of brick in that yellow color usually found in a baby's dirty diaper, took up a square block at the corner of Montgomery Avenue and Church Road in Wynnewood.

Green grass as smooth as a golf course surrounded the building on every side. About ten percent of the 600 students who attended the high school were colored, and they all knew each other. Half of them were related to at least one other student in the school, most to two or three. All the colored students lived in the same neighborhoods in Ardmore, Bryn Mawr or Haverford, neighborhoods made up of mostly twin and row houses only blocks from the Main Line's most prestigious streets.

If two colored strangers met on the street anywhere on the Main Line and one person said he lived in Ardmore, the other knew that it was on Welsh Road or Spring Avenue or one or two other streets. If the town was Bryn Mawr, the streets were Prescott Avenue or Warner Road. And in Haverford, Buck Lane.

The Main Line streets were segregated, and even though the high school was integrated, it might as well have been segregated. Most of the white students grew up with privilege and colored household help, often their classmates' parents. The white students couldn't ignore the colored kids in school because the colored kids acted like they had every right to be there, which they did. But the white kids knew that they didn't have to socialize with the colored ones, unless of course they were the poor Italian or Irish whose working class neighborhoods were right next to the colored ones.

Most of the school clubs had an unwritten rule: "white only." The colored kids let the white ones go on because they had their own clubs outside of school, like the Top Men of Distinction for socializing, Club Imperial for basketball, and the Ardmore Youth Association for everything else. That was until Vera started at the high school.

"Don't let those kids bother you," John said. "You have as much right to be in that school as they do. I pay my taxes, now you go get an education."

When the hygiene teacher formed a modeling club, Vera showed up for the first meeting. No one dared tell her that the club was for white only. Of all the students at Ardmore High, they knew Vera wouldn't fall for that.

"If anyone is going to learn how to be a model, it's going to be me," Vera explained to the principal when the hygiene teacher called him to the club meeting room to politely escort Vera out.

"You make me leave, and I'll have Randolph Jackson up here so fast it will make your head spin," said Vera, hands on hips, unafraid of the principal or the hygiene teacher now hiding behind the principal.

Randolph Jackson, the only colored attorney in Ardmore, was the attorney for the Main Line Branch of the NAACP. Jackson fought discrimination like he fought the Germans in World War II—swiftly with an aim to kill the beast. The principal knew that there'd be no lull in combat with Randolph and Vera, so he told the hygiene teacher to leave Vera alone.

The modeling club met only a few more times after that. The other girls became jealous when they saw that Vera was the only one in the club with natural modeling ability. When Vera walked, everyone stopped and took notice. The owner of Chez Femme, the modeling studio in Suburban Square, Ardmore's collection of exclusive shops, visited the third class. She complimented Vera on her ability and used her as an example to show the other girls proper carriage. After that, Vera left the club.

She told Emma, "I wasn't learning anything from those girls about modeling, and I sure wasn't going to let them learn anything from me. Those folks couldn't give me any more than what God already did. And you know I don't stick around where I can't get at least as much as I can give."

As soon as Vera opened one of the double wooden doors at school that morning, heads turned. The white boys in one corner weren't even shy about it. Carlton Adamson tried to put his books in his locker while looking at Vera's behind, but the books hit the floor instead. Burton Humphrey looked straight into Vera's eyes and smiled. Vera smiled back, but kept on walking. The outfit she wore was for Billy, not for some white boy who couldn't do anything for her, or wouldn't because he was too scared to.

When Vera turned the corner to the hallway leading to her home room, she saw her target in the hall talking to Regina. Vera didn't have to walk slowly to get Billy to notice her; she naturally walked slowly so that *everyone* noticed her. And Billy did.

His arm hung over the locker, lightly resting on Regina's shoulder. As Vera came into view, Billy moved his hand, stood up straight and said, "Good morning, Vera." Vera stopped dead in front of Billy, looked him directly in the eye, and said, "Good morning, Billy." She turned to the left and said, "And good morning to you, too, Regina."

Regina barely parted her lips as she looked at Vera and said, "Hello." Suddenly, Regina thought the blue and white polka dot dress she wore that day looked immature and juvenile.

"You look nice today, Vera," said Billy, who stroked his goatee and grinned as he kept his most prurient thoughts to himself. "Red is your color."

"Why thank you, Billy," said Vera. "I always say, why not brighten the day with what you wear. Don't you agree, Regina?", asked Vera, thinking that Regina's dress looked about as bright as those dark, musty basements she saw on plumbing jobs.

Regina knew Vera was trying to insult her, so she just looked at her.

Vera ignored Regina, looked directly at Billy and said, "Well, I'd better be going now. Home room's about to start. I'll save you a seat, Billy." She turned around and moved her hips with a little more emphasis than usual, making sure that Billy got a good look as she walked into home room.

Billy turned back to face Regina, kissed her quickly on the cheek and said, "You'd better go on now, Regina. I've got some business to take care of this morning."

I bet, she thought.

Billy bumped into two desks and three students as he hurried to reach the empty desk next to Vera. Just as he put his rear in the seat, Vera dropped a book on the floor next to him. She slowly crossed her long coffee-colored legs as Billy immediately bent down to pick up the book. His face was about two inches in front of her finely toned calves. She swung her bright red high-heeled pump from side-to-side twice and then slowly moved her legs back closer to her chair.

Vera quickly dropped her hand down to the side like she was going to pick up the book. Her fingers lightly touched Billy's wavy hair instead. She knew it would feel soft.

"Here, Vera," said Billy, picking up the book before she had to lean down any farther. "I've got it for you."

I bet you have, Vera wanted to say.

Instead, she said, "Thanks, Billy. These little desks just don't have enough room for all these big books. I can't even stretch out like I want to without knocking something off," she said as she opened both arms, making sure a wrist went right under Billy's nose. She wanted him to smell the perfume she dabbed on that morning. Vera heaved her chest and stuck out her bosom in the guise of stretching out.

"I walked to school today, and my arms sure are tired from carrying all these books," said Vera, noting that Billy's eyes lingered on her neckline.

"I thought you rode to school with Jimmy," said Billy.

"Not anymore," Vera said. "I quit Jimmy."

Thank you, Lord, thought Billy.

"If you want somebody to carry your books home, I'd be glad to," Billy said.

"Oh, I sure would," said Vera. "But what about Regina? I thought you walked her home from school every day."

"Every day but today," said Billy.

And all I need is one day, thought Vera.

CHAPTER 4

Phyllis Daniels popped out of her seat like bread out of a toaster as soon as she heard the bell dismissing students from home room. She rushed out into the hallway, a lady on a mission. She was going to say something to Bobby Marshall today. She liked his looks the first time she saw him in chemistry class. She couldn't help noticing him because they were the only colored students in the class, but she was surprised to see him. Phyllis took all college prep courses, as fitted her station in life. Everybody expected a doctor's daughter to go to college. But nobody—herself included—expected the plumber's son to want to go to college. She expected him to want to be a plumber, but she was glad that Bobby wanted something different.

From the first day of class, Bobby's intelligence shone through. He raised his hand frequently and knew the answers to the hard questions that nobody else could answer. He always scored among the tops in tests, and Phyllis was impressed that Mr. Texton hired him to work in the chemistry lab. She knew the importance of those experiments.

Phyllis usually sat next to Bobby in class if she could. She was glad that Bobby sat at the desk next to her the first week of school when Mr. Texton paired the two people closest to each other as lab partners. When Phyllis didn't understand something, Bobby explained it. But she never understood why he didn't ask her out.

All her life, Phyllis' parents, Dr. Ned and Mrs. Noreen Daniels, told her that because of the way she looked, every colored man would want her. They told her that her light skin and long straight hair assured her a bright and comfortable future. Colored men want white women but can't have them, her mother and father always said, so you're as close as they can get.

Phyllis heard that light skin-long hair promise all her life, but she didn't believe it. None of the boys at Ardmore High asked her out. That exasperated her, even though she knew that her parents wouldn't let her go out with just any boy.

Her parents only let her date the sons of the 400. No other colored families on the Main Line met her parents' exacting specifications. Dr. Daniels was the only colored doctor on the Main Line. No colored dentists practiced there. And the colored lawyer and his wife didn't have any children.

"You're too good for that riffraff," Dr. and Mrs. Daniels always said, although Phyllis didn't think the other colored kids at school, with the exception of Jimmy Bennett, were riffraff. Phyllis knew that her brother, Ned Jr., felt like their parents did.

He walked around school like he was better than the other colored kids, barely speaking to them and sticking as close to the white kids as they let him. The other colored girls in school were polite to Phyllis because she was polite to them, but she only counted a few of the girls as real friends and none of the boys as boyfriends.

The other kids knew that Dr. and Mrs. Daniels looked down on them because their parents told them so, and their parents were right. Everybody in town knew that Dr. Daniels was only too happy to treat you and take your money, but he didn't have any other contact with the colored Main Line. His social clubs, church, and civic groups all were in Philadelphia, in the cocoon-like world of the 400.

He treated his patients with a businesslike politeness, but he didn't get too close to them and didn't want them to get too close to him. Noreen Daniels was worse. She kept her nose so high up in the air that everybody could describe the inside of her nostrils perfectly.

But as long as Dr. Daniels kept up his veneer of no-nonsense politeness and tolerance, the folks flocked to his office. He wasn't dumb enough to outright disrespect his patients, and his patients wanted a colored doctor out of race pride.

Phyllis wasn't interested in the boys that met her parents' approval; she wanted Bobby. He was smart, handsome and trying to improve himself. She didn't care what her parents said.

If she had to endure one more week of sitting next to him in lab without telling him how she felt, she would burst. She hoped that her parents would let her date Bobby if they knew he was going to college. It wouldn't be easy making them understand, but she would try.

Bobby already sat at a desk at the front of the room reading the next chapter in the chemistry book when Phyllis walked in. He didn't look back when she came in, but a couple of the other boys did. She draped herself in pink that morning because she thought it brought out the pink in her skin tone and made her look soft and sweet like cotton candy. She was right. She put on a bubble gum pink dress with a grosgrain bow that tied in the back. Instead of her usual ponytail, she let her hair hang out around her shoulders and used a grosgrain pink ribbon as a headband. She hoped that Bobby liked long hair as much as every man did, not that she had so many dates to know that for herself, but that's what her mother and father told her.

Her white lace socks had pink lace trim at the cuff. Her cheeks sparkled with a dab of "In the Pink" rouge, and her lips glistened with one coat of "Pretty in Pink" lipstick. Before leaving the house, she dabbed on Enchantment perfume because it came in a pink bottle.

She even made some noise by moving her chair back and forth, pretending to find a comfortable position, but Bobby still didn't turn around. All during class, she prayed that Mr. Texton would send them to the lab. Halfway into class, God answered her prayers.

"Head to the labs," Mr. Texton said as Phyllis grinned.

Bobby got to the lab table first because it was closer to his side of the room. As Phyllis approached, he smelled her perfume and looked up. He opened his eyes as much as he could, raised his eyebrows, and moved his lips into an admiring smile.

"Why, Phyllis," he said. "I hope this experiment doesn't mess up that pretty dress you have on."

"We'll just have to be extra careful," said Phyllis. She pulled her lab stool closer to Bobby than she normally did.

"You not only look good," said Bobby, "you smell good."

"Thanks," said Phyllis. "It's called Enchantment."

"That's a fitting name. You look enchanting," he said.

Feeling bolder, Phyllis said, "I hoped you liked it." Shifting on her lab stool, she said, "I wore it for you."

Bobby dropped the test tube he was holding, and it almost broke as it bounced on the counter he cleaned hours before. "For me?" he asked. "Why me?"

I can't believe he's that dense, thought Phyllis.

"Well," she said, hesitating. "If you're going to force me to say it, I might as well." She took a few gulps of air to fortify herself. "I've been sitting here next to you in class for over half a year now, and I've grown to like you."

"I like you, too, Phyllis," Bobby said matter-of-factly. He reached for the chemicals needed to start the experiment. "You're a nice girl."

Phyllis waited. Waited for him to say something else. To ask her out. But when Bobby continued measuring chemicals and reaching for beakers and test tubes, she boiled. Nothing. He's not going to say a thing, she thought. Here I am, bearing my soul, and all he says is that I'm a nice girl.

". . . And," said Phyllis, the exasperation in her voice begging him to fill in the missing words.

Bobby just looked at her.

". . . And," she repeated, this time waving her arms in the air for emphasis.

". . . And," Phyllis said again, raising her voice enough so that the lab partners at the next table looked up. "I just tell you I like you and you leave it at that," she said, head shaking in disbelief.

"At what?" said Bobby, this time carefully placing the test tubes down on the counter. "What do you want me to say?" he asked, looking Phyllis directly in the eye, as exasperated as she appeared moments earlier.

"I like you, Phyllis," Bobby said, "but what of it? I know your parents don't want you mixing with the rest of us. Everybody knows it."

Phyllis looked at Bobby wide-eyed. "You mean to tell me that you like me, but you've never said anything because of my parents?" she asked incredulously. "How come you never let me decide?" she asked, getting angrier now that everybody but her was deciding who she could and couldn't date.

"Because I thought it was pointless," said Bobby. "Your parents only let you date boys from the 400. Everybody knows that."

"Well, I'm old enough to make my own decisions as to whom I date," said Phyllis, bold enough so that she would believe that it was true. "And I want to date you," she said.

Bobby knew that he'd be happy to date Phyllis. She was pretty enough and smarter than most any girl he knew. He looked at Phyllis and smiled. "OK, so we'll date," he said.

Phyllis took a deep breath and thought, finally.

"Why don't we meet after school today?" she asked.

"I'd be happy to," Bobby said. He looked Phyllis directly in the eye and smiled back. "Now let's see if we can get this experiment going," he said, again reaching for the chemicals in front of him.

The bell rang marking the end of school, and the scramble began. The kids with cars lined up at the circular driveway in front of school to pick up the kids they drove home and to let the other kids see that they either had the money or, as in the case of Jimmy Bennett, the hustle to have a car. Some of the cars lining the driveway were brand new Packards used strictly for joy riding; others were beat up pickup trucks used strictly to get from point A to point B with a minimum of trouble and a maximum of prayer.

Billy picked up Vera outside of classroom 21. He told Regina at lunchtime that he had to discuss a special home room project with Vera after school. Vera dropped men as soon as looked at them, so Billy thought that if things didn't work out with Vera, he hedged his bet with Regina by giving her a good excuse. He thought that Regina was dumb enough or in love enough to buy his story.

Regina knew the truth because she knew Vera and she knew Billy. But when Billy lied to her, she just smiled and told him to let her know when they finished the project. When Vera dumped Billy, as she was bound to do, Regina would be there. Billy was too fine, and she had come too far with him to let him go in one day to the likes of Vera Marshall. When Vera dumped him, Regina would gladly lick Billy's wounds and in a way that would guarantee that he'd never leave her again.

Vera made sure that she carried as few books as possible when Billy picked her up. She didn't want his arms to get tired from holding books; she wanted him to use all of the strength in his arms to hold her.

"I'll take them," said Billy, as he lifted the books out of Vera's hands and put them in the shoulder bag he borrowed from one of his friends to free his hands for better things.

Vera gave Billy the books and put her arm around his as if he were an usher escorting her up the aisle at a wedding.

"You don't mind, do you?" asked Vera, knowing that he didn't.

"Not at all," said Billy. "It's an honor to have you on my arm."

Vera knew that was true.

As they stepped out into the courtyard, she looked around for Regina. While she had Billy, she didn't want to rub Regina's face in it. She never had any beef with Regina or any woman as long as they weren't interested in the same man. She grew up with Regina. They used to run up and down Welsh Road playing hopscotch and rolling down the four-foot slopes of grass that made up their front yards.

Taking Billy was nothing personal against Regina, and it certainly wasn't anything permanent. To Vera, it was just something to do to get her through the next few months until she graduated or until something better came along, which she doubted it would in Ardmore. Something better waited for her in Philadelphia; she was sure of that. Regina could have Billy back when she was through.

Vera and Billy walked past the crowd of kids and down the driveway toward Montgomery Avenue. Billy noticed Jimmy sitting on the hood of his car at the end of the driveway as soon as they cleared the mass of kids. He sighed; he didn't want to have to kick Jimmy's ass. He didn't want to have to fight over Vera so soon, although he knew that what Vera had was worth fighting for. Jimmy chewed on a toothpick and twirled a black fedora on his index finger, watching Vera and Billy as they walked. The closer they got, the more Billy hoped that Jimmy didn't kick his ass either. He knew that any man who had Vera even once would probably fight to keep her, especially a crazy man like Jimmy. He couldn't see how any man could walk away from her body and all of its pleasures without a fight. But maybe Vera would give him an out.

Billy tilted his head in Jimmy's direction and said, "Jimmy's over there. Do you still want to walk this way?" Billy hoped Vera would say no, but he knew that she wouldn't. Vera wasn't afraid of anybody. That's part of what made her so interesting.

"I'm not worried about Jimmy," Vera said, squeezing Billy's arm even tighter. She assumed that Billy wasn't either or that if he was, he wouldn't let on. She couldn't stand a punk.

They walked on.

Jimmy watched Vera's every movement.

When she got within three feet of his car, Jimmy called out, "Are you sure this is what you want, baby?"

"Damn sure," said Vera. She moved her arm to Billy's waist and kept walking.

CHAPTER 5

"It's so nice out today. Let's walk down by the creek," said Billy.

"That sounds fine to me," said Vera. She'd been down by the creek so many times that the animals didn't even run away from fright when she came around.

They turned onto the path to the woods where the creek was.

"I know a real quiet spot where we can talk," said Billy. "Over there," he said, pointing toward what looked to the unsuspecting eye like a tangled mass of trees and vines.

Great, thought Vera. My favorite spot. The ground was far enough from the stream to not be too wet, and there was a flat rock big enough to hold two outstretched bodies.

Before heading in through the trees and vines, Vera sat on a rock and took off her shoes. "Turn around, will you, Billy," she said. "I want to take off these stockings, too."

Billy gladly turned as Vera unfastened the stockings from the garter belt and put them in her pocket. She wasn't going to ruin her good stockings walking in the woods. Besides, if Billy was like most men, and she figured he was, he wanted to touch her warm skin, not her cold stocking.

When they reached the clearing, Billy pulled a blanket out of his bag. Earlier that afternoon he visited the nurse's office and "loaned" himself a blanket.

"Have a seat," he said.

"You sure are prepared," Vera said, settling her hips on the blanket. "I like that in a man."

"There's a lot here that you could like, Vera," said Billy, sitting down next to her.

"Why don't you show me?" said Vera, as she leaned over and waited to be kissed.

Billy opened his mouth and pressed his lips against Vera's with all the force that he could muster, force and passion that he never showed Regina. Vera reveled in the kisses. She wrapped her arms around his neck and ran her long fingers through his black curly hair as she ran her tongue all around the crevices in his mouth.

Billy knew how to kiss. She appreciated that. The way a man moved his mouth when he kissed the lips on a woman's face told her a lot about how he'd move his mouth when he kissed her elsewhere. Billy pulled Vera closer and then pushed her back on the blanket. He rested his hand on her thigh and then moved it up and down on the outside of her dress, finally pulling her full body under his.

He pushed the dress back on the blanket and gripped her rounded buttocks with his hands. Billy felt the skin on Vera's thighs and legs and pressed against her even harder. He slid his tongue down her chest until it rested between her breasts, which he cupped with both hands.

Not bad, thought Vera. Not bad.

Billy was so hard that Vera could feel that he was big enough to make her moan when he went in. He pressed against her, moving in a motion that promised that the moans would continue for a long time. She let him move around her for about 10 more minutes, enjoying every minute herself, until she said, "I think we'd better stop now and save something for later." Even she didn't give it away on the first date.

Sweat dripped down Billy's face, and his crotch bulged out of his pants.

"You make me feel so good, baby," he said. "I'm about ready to burst."

So what else is new, thought Vera.

"Well, don't do it here," she said. "Save some for later." Then she kissed him in a way that she knew would only cause him more distress.

"We've only just begun, haven't we?" she asked. She moved out from under him and pulled her dress down back over her butt.

"Yeah," said Billy, kissing Vera's neck. "We're just getting started."

Bobby met Phyllis in the hallway outside of her last class. "I thought your mother picked you up precisely 30 minutes after school let out every day," he said.

"Every day but Friday. Fridays she lets me stay two hours later to go to the library," said Phyllis. "Except today I hadn't planned on going to the library."

"So you *planned* this?" Robert asked, chuckling at the girl's spunk.

"I can't say I *exactly* planned it because nothing would have happened if it wasn't for you," she said, "but I sure planned on asking you."

"What if I said no, I wasn't interested? Didn't you think that was possible?" Bobby asked as they walked down the hall.

"Anything's possible," said Phyllis, "but I didn't think you'd turn me down even if you weren't interested. You seemed like too much of a gentleman to embarrass me."

Bobby laughed. "Well thanks for recognizing that, but how do you know that I didn't just agree to meet you just because you asked?"

"I don't know that for sure, but I'll find out in time," Phyllis said as they walked outside. "Besides, I haven't seen you with any other girl for the past few months. Not since Hazel Little."

"Ah," Bobby said. "You're very observant. Have you been watching me?"

"Let's just say that I've noticed you. It's hard not to. We're the only colored kids in our chemistry class. And of all the other colored boys in school, you're the smartest, one of the tallest and, I think, one of the nicest."

Bobby was glad that his skin was dark brown so that Phyllis couldn't see the blood rushing to his cheeks. Her flattery embarrassed him, but he liked it.

"Thanks," was all he managed to say. They walked on in silence.

"Since your mother is coming to pick you up in a few hours, do you want to just sit over on one of the benches and talk?" he asked.

"That's fine with me," Phyllis said. Bobby lightly touched her waist with his hand and steered her over to a bench underneath a massive oak tree. As the sunlight streamed down through the leaves, Bobby noticed how the light danced off Phyllis' face and brightened her eyes. Phyllis noticed how the sun highlighted the coffee color in Bobby's skin and brought out the angles of his high cheekbones.

The next hour passed quickly as Bobby and Phyllis talked about the courses they wanted to take next year, the colleges they wanted to attend and the careers they wanted to pursue. Phyllis' back was turned when her mother pulled up in her boat-size black Cadillac.

Noreen's mouth dropped open, and she adjusted her blue horn-rimmed glasses when she saw Phyllis sitting on the bench with a boy. None of the boys at Ardmore High met her standards for Phyllis, so Noreen knew that whoever that boy was, he wasn't good enough for Phyllis.

Noreen pounded on the car horn three times. Phyllis recognized the sound, turned around, waved hello, and walked toward the car. That boy walked over with her.

"Hello mother," said Phyllis, grabbing the top of the window that Noreen had just rolled down. "I'd like you to meet Bobby Marshall. He's in my chemistry class."

"Marshall?" Noreen said in a high-pitched wail. She reared her head back from the window and peered over the top of her glasses. She repeated herself. "Marshall? Isn't that the colored plumber's name?"

She looked at Bobby and said, "Is he your father, young man?"

Proud and polite, Bobby said, "Yes, ma'am. That's my father. John Marshall, the plumber."

Noreen turned her head away from Bobby so quickly that her glasses slid down her nose. She pushed her glasses back up, stared straight ahead and said, "Phyllis, get in the car."

Phyllis looked at Noreen for a few seconds and then hung her head in shame. Noreen was angry, and it was pointless to say anything to her. Phyllis felt Noreen's rejection of Bobby as deeply as if she rejected her.

Phyllis turned to Bobby and held his hand under the window out of her mother's eyesight. She looked him straight in the eye as if she could make her eyes speak an apology for her mother's rudeness. She squeezed his hand and said, "I had a good time talking with you. See you in class on Monday."

Noreen squeezed the steering wheel so hard that her knuckles turned white, which wasn't hard to do since her skin was about the color of pancake batter. She yelled, "Get in the car, Phyllis."

"Bye, Phyllis," said Bobby. He gave Phyllis a look that said: "I told you so." He managed to get out "Goodbye, Mrs. Daniels" before she rolled up the window tight enough to shut out the sound of his voice.

Phyllis opened the car door and slammed it shut.

Noreen drove off.

Bobby kicked a stone lying on the ground and walked home alone.

"Mother, how could you have been so rude," said Phyllis in that shrill, haughty voice that Noreen used when she tried to show somebody that she was better than them. "You didn't even say hello! All you did was interrogate him about who his father was."

"That's because I don't want you hanging around with that riffraff. How could you even think that we would let you see that boy. That . . . that plumber's son," said Noreen.

"So *what* if his father is a plumber. He can't help that," Phyllis said.

She added proudly, "Besides, he's going to college, and he's the smartest boy in our chemistry class."

"I don't care. I will not have it," said Noreen. She pounded the palm of her chubby hand on the steering wheel for emphasis.

"We raised you better than that. We've worked hard to get ahead and to have you children accepted into some of the finest families in the 400," said Noreen, shaking her finger only inches from Phyllis' face, "and you tell me you want to date a plumber's son."

"Never," she said.

"And if I ever hear of you being with that boy again, you'll be sorry, young lady. We'll take away all of your privileges and the little bit of freedom we gave you because you were growing up," she said.

Shaking her head as if in disbelief, Noreen said, "Well, I see right now that you don't know how to handle freedom."

"Ned," said Noreen to her son who sat in the back seat and smirked at Phyllis' dressing down, "I want you to tell me if you see Phyllis with that Marshall boy or any of that other Ardmore riffraff, do you hear me?"

"I hear you mother," Ned said. He moved forward and leaned his arms on the back of Phyllis' seat. "I can't believe that you wanted to get mixed up with Bobby Marshall anyway," said Ned. "There's so many of those Marshalls that you can't tell one from the other anyway."

"I can just picture it," he said. "An elegant dinner at that little row house crammed to the brim with 10 children." He leaned back and chuckled.

Phyllis whipped around to face Ned and practically spat at him. "It's not a row house. It's a twin house."

"Whatever," said Ned as both he and Noreen giggled at Phyllis even thinking that a twin house was better than a row.

Phyllis pushed Ned's weighty arms off the back of her chair and said, "You have some nerve talking to me about Bobby Marshall. I've seen the way you look at Vera. It looks like you'd like to get mixed up with her. Except she doesn't want to have anything to do with you, and who could blame her. You act like you're better than every other colored kid at school."

Phyllis turned around and folded her arms in front of her as if she said the last word and that's that.

Ned leaned forward and whispered right into Phyllis' ear, "We are better."

Noreen nodded in approval.

But just the mention of Vera's name made Ned squirm. The thought of her long brown legs, thick black hair, and voluptuous breasts made his temperature rise. Good thing his mother couldn't see the way he now adjusted his pants to hide their sudden fullness.

He'd like to get mixed up with Vera alright; what man wouldn't? She wasn't the kind of woman he'd take home to meet mother; she was the kind of woman who gave a young man just what he wanted, or so he'd heard.

But Phyllis was right. Vera only spoke to Ned if he spoke first, and she never lingered for the conversation he desperately wanted to make. And he didn't understand why. Everybody knew that Vera wanted money, and he had more of it than any colored boy at Ardmore High. Sooner or later, Vera would come around, he thought. Then he'd get what he wanted and go on.

Ned snapped out of it and said, "Vera Marshall is the type of girl who's only good for one thing."

"Well, whatever that one thing is, she doesn't want you to have it," said Phyllis.

Noreen shook her head and said, "I can't believe what I'm hearing." She pointed a perfectly manicured nail at Ned and said, "I don't want you messing around with any girls like that. No telling what kind of disease you could catch from her. Your father's a good doctor, but he doesn't have a cure for everything."

"Don't worry, mother. I'm not thinking about Vera Marshall," Ned lied. "And I'll keep Phyllis away from Bobby."

Noreen stopped the car and looked right at Phyllis. "Stay away from that riffraff or there'll be hell to pay, excuse my French. Have I made myself clear?"

Phyllis thought quickly. Noreen wanted an answer, but she wanted Bobby, and she was going to have him. Whatever she had to do to see him, she would. And nobody in her family would know about it.

"Well, young lady," Noreen asked, "have I made myself clear?"

"Yes mother, perfectly clear," said Phyllis. She turned her head to the side and looked out of the window for the rest of the ride home.

CHAPTER 6

In Monday's chemistry class, Phyllis looked up every time the door opened. She put her books on the seat next to her, to save it for Bobby. When he finally walked in, she motioned for him to come over and sit down.

Bobby walked over and set his books on the desk. "Hi, Phyllis," he said. He leaned close to her and whispered, "How did everything go at home? I thought about you all weekend."

Then why didn't you call me, was Phyllis' first thought. Her second thought was that Bobby didn't need to know that her mother yelled at her all the way home and that her father yelled at her all weekend. He only needed to know that if they were going to date, it had to be in secret.

"I was on punishment all weekend," said Phyllis.

Bobby cut in before Phyllis could say anything else. "I knew your parents didn't want you seeing me," he said. Too bad, he thought, because it could have been good. She was a nice girl and good looking, too.

"I guess we'll just have to be friends," he said.

"I want to be more than friends," said Phyllis. She touched Bobby's arm. "I still want to date you."

The girl sure is persistent, thought Bobby.

"How can we date when your parents said you can't see me?" Bobby asked. "It's not like we can even get together in school. I'm sure your parents got your brother looking over your shoulder."

Tears welled up in Phyllis' eyes. "I don't care what they say," she said. "I like you, and you said you liked me."

Bobby patted Phyllis' arm. "I do like you Phyllis," he said.

"We'll just have to work something out," Phyllis said. "I'm willing to find a way if you are."

She touched his hand and said, "I couldn't bear not being with you."

This girl must really like me, Bobby thought. He dated girls before, but never seriously and never anyone who was willing to catch hell from her parents for him. He always liked Phyllis, always thought she was pretty, always admired her intelligence and willingness to study hard and excel in school even if some of the other kids teased her about it. Nobody teased him because he was one of the boys from the neighborhood doing good; Phyllis definitely wasn't one of the girls.

What the hell, thought Bobby. If Phyllis was willing to try, so was he.

Bobby put his hand on Phyllis' shoulder. "Don't worry," he said. "We'll find a way. It might take some doing, but we'll do it. I won't let you go that easy."

Phyllis smiled and laid her head down on the desk in relief. That battle was over, but now the war began.

Bobby and Phyllis met at lunch to go over their schedules and figure out if there was anytime during school that they could get together without Ned finding out. They knew they could eat lunch together every day because the juniors and the seniors had different lunch periods. But if Bobby and Phyllis ate together every day, the other kids in school would know they were dating, the gossip would spread, and Ned would find out.

"We could always say we're eating together because we're studying chemistry and lunch is the only time that we can get together," Phyllis said.

"That'd work for a few days," said Bobby, "but most of these kids aren't that gullible. And when their tongues start wagging, you better hope that you're not on the tail end."

Bobby didn't worry about his friends finding out about Phyllis because he'd tell them anyway. His friends, brothers and sisters, and first and second cousins all had to help him keep the rest of the Daniels in the dark.

"I'll pick you up after English and walk you to math," Bobby said. "You said Ned has gym then, right?"

"Right," said Phyllis.

"So he'll be on the other side of the building," said Bobby.

He looked at the rest of the schedules, comparing times and places. "That seems to be the best we can do," he said.

Phyllis sipped her milk and said, "That's good enough for me."

"I mean that's the best we can do in school," said Bobby. He put the schedules down and looked straight into Phyllis' eyes. "If we're going to date, we're going to date. We'll go to the movies, on walks, or whatever. We may have to sneak around to do it, but we don't have to do it alone."

"Of course we have to do it alone," Phyllis said. She wondered: maybe he isn't as smart as I thought. "That's what sneaking around means—you and me keeping our relationship a secret."

"No. Not just you and me. My brothers and sisters will help," Bobby said. "So will my cousins and my friends. They'll be our cover."

Phyllis looked at Bobby like she didn't understand. Bobby explained, "Say we want to go to the movies. You tell your parents that you're going with one of your girlfriends, except it will be one of my sisters or cousins or one of the other girls on my block. You'll go into the movies with them, and I'll be waiting on the inside."

"Good thinking," said Phyllis. Maybe too good, she thought.

"Have you done this before?" she asked.

"I haven't," said Bobby. "But Vera has. Hundreds of times."

That evening, Bobby called a meeting of all the Marshalls in the high school. There was one in each of the four grades, so Vera, Valerie and Stevie sat on the beds in Bobby's bedroom.

"What's going on, little brother," Vera said. She leaned back on his bed and kicked off her shoes. Waving her arm around the room, Vera said, "If you're calling us all together like this, it must have something to do with little Miss Phyllis."

Bobby laughed. "How did you know?"

"I can tell by looking when two people got something going on," said Vera. Shifting her body from side to side, she said, "There's a certain look in your eyes, a certain way that you stand, a certain smell about you. I saw you and Phyllis standing outside of her English class two days in a row."

"You can't hide it from me little brother," Vera said with a self-satisfied smirk.

"You're right," said Bobby. "But I have to hide it from the rest of the Daniels."

"Those high siddidy, high yellow, bourgeois ass holes," said Vera. "They think they're too good for us. And that Ned gets on my last nerve. I expect men to look at me like they'd like to tear my clothes off, but that Ned has the nerve to look at me *and* to try to talk to me. All that four-eyed weakling can do for me is to get out of my way so that I can find me a real man." Valerie and Stevie fell out laughing.

"Phyllis is the only one of those Daniels who has good sense," Vera said.

"I like Phyllis," said Valerie. "She speaks to everybody and doesn't act stuck up like her brother."

"So you want us to cover for you?" asked Vera.

"Exactly," Bobby said, as he paced around the room, "along with some of the cousins, like Sissy and Charlie. Valerie, I'll need you for the outside-the-movie cover sometimes. Sissy won't be able to make it all the time, and you look like her from behind."

"Why do I have to impersonate Sissy?" asked Valerie.

"Because the Daniels don't like any of the Marshalls, and they don't want Phyllis hanging around with you either," Bobby said.

"To hell with them," said Vera. "So what do you want me to do? They wouldn't believe that me and Phyllis were friends anyway. I like the child, but I ain't *like* her, if you know what I mean."

"I know what you mean," Bobby said. "We need you to divert Ned's attention at school so Phyllis and I can get together."

"You're asking for a lot, little brother," Vera said. She paced around the room and shook her head. "You actually want me to get with Ned Daniels? Who'd believe it? He's not my kind of man."

She waited for a minute and then said, "Actually, he's not a man at all."

"But," Vera said, "sure, I can divert his attention. I can get him looking in my direction just by walking by. And Lord knows, if I stopped to talk to him, he'd probably come in his pants right then and there."

"What a thought," said Vera. She laughed. "That sure would be a sight to see."

Over the next month, Bobby and Phyllis worked the cover perfectly. They went to the movies every week because Noreen thought that Bobby's cousin Sissy was Phyllis' new best friend. Bobby and Phyllis spent about fifteen minutes together after school every day.

Vera diverted Ned from spying on Phyllis by asking him for a few minutes of tutoring in math every day after school, even though she didn't need any tutoring. Vera eagerly learned math because she wanted to learn how to handle the money she was sure she'd make one day.

Ned didn't know that Vera knew all about multiplication, division and complex equations because Ned spent four years in the college prep math classes and Vera spent four years in basic business math. But Ned believed what Vera told him. It was good for his ego.

"You sure are smart," Vera told Ned one day. "How did you get such a head for figures?"

"It's easy. I was born into it," Ned said. Vera almost gagged. "My family's always had money, and they showed us how to handle it."

"Is that a fact?" said Vera, batting her eyes and feigning as much ignorance as Butterfly McQueen did when she played Prissy in "Gone With the Wind."

"Quite true. As a matter of fact," he said hesitating and coughing to clear his throat, "I wouldn't mind spending some of that money on you. Perfume, stockings, whatever you want."

Vera rolled her eyes. "I can buy my own perfume and stockings, thank you very much," she said. She leaned back in the chair, looked up at the ceiling and shook her head.

"Are you trying to ask me out, Ned? Because if you are, you should just come right out and ask me."

Ned didn't even realize that Vera set him up. "Well," he said, fidgeting in his chair, "if you put it that way, I guess I am asking for a date."

"Well," she said, mocking his tone of voice and the fidgeting that went along with it, "if you're asking, I'm saying no."

Too stupid to quit while he was ahead, Ned said, "Well, if you don't want to go out on a date, we can just get together."

How dumb can this boy be, Vera thought. "If I don't want to date you, why would I want to get together with you?" Vera asked. Then, in an instant, she knew.

"Wait a minute," she said. She threw her pencil on the desk and pushed her chair back so fast and furious that it fell over. She stood up and walked over to Ned so that she stood not an inch from his now cranberry-colored face.

"You think your money can buy something that I ain't selling, is that it?" she asked.

"Well, I thought you wanted money," he said.

Vera pulled back her hand to pick up some speed and slapped Ned square across the face.

"How dare you talk to me like that, you punk," she said.

Ned rubbed the outline of Vera's hand that made his red face even redder.

"Yeah, I want money. But I don't grovel for it, don't take shit for it, and don't spread my legs for it," Vera said as she picked up her books, turned on her heels and switched away.

What a woman, thought Ned.

CHAPTER 7

"Can't help you out any more, little brother," Vera told Bobby when she walked in the house that afternoon. She threw her books on the sideboard in the front room where Bobby was doing his homework. "That boy just worked my last nerve."

Bobby knew that it was only a matter of time. Vera never was very good about hiding her feelings. He admired her for that.

He put his pencil in the history book to hold his place. "So what happened?" he asked.

Vera repeated Ned's insults, word-for-word, not leaving out a gesture or an inflection. She moved about the room reenacting the scene, and Bobby had to calm her down as she told it.

When she finished, Bobby said, "What an idiot he is. I ought to slap him myself."

"Don't waste your time, little brother," Vera said. "I slapped him hard enough for the two of us."

She pulled her hand back and smacked it into the other one. "Wham!" she said, amplifying the sound of skin hitting skin. "That boy's jaw might not work right tonight." She laughed and plopped down into the big armchair, kicked off her shoes, and let her tired feet sink into the doughy ottoman.

Bobby paced around the room. "That joker's always messing something up, and just when Phyllis and I had this thing worked out."

He stroked his chin, raised his finger in the air, and said, "I know. I'll get cousin Margaret to meet Ned after school tomorrow. She doesn't have the looks you do, Vera, but she has that sweet Southern accent and that charm that a lot of guys fall for." Margaret was lace where Vera was satin, both beautiful to touch, but one was delicate where the other was smooth.

"She ought to keep Ned occupied for a while," Bobby said.

"Because if she doesn't, your ass is in trouble," Vera said.

The next day after school, Margaret took what used to be Vera's place, to the left of the front door. One-by-one, her friends gathered around her before heading home.

Margaret kept moving to the outside of the crowd so she'd see Ned when he came out. She didn't like him any more than Vera did, but in their family, when a cousin called, you answered.

After a few minutes, Ned walked out with a stack of books under his arm.

"Oh, Ned," Margaret called out as she walked in his direction. She only had to divert his attention for the few minutes it would take Bobby and Phyllis to walk out the door and around the corner undetected.

Ned heard Margaret's call and turned around. Then all anyone heard was metal crashing and glass breaking on Montgomery Avenue. Ned turned in the other direction, away from Margaret and towards Montgomery Avenue. He saw two mangled cars, but he also saw Bobby and Phyllis walking down the path to the woods behind the school.

Margaret continued to call out, "Ned, Ned, over here", but he ignored her. She wasn't Vera, and he saw something much more interesting.

Ned pulled his book bag over his shoulder and walked off down the path, taking care not to get too close to Bobby and Phyllis.

Bobby and Phyllis walked side-by-side for about 50 feet into the woods. The path grew less distinguished the farther they walked. At the birch tree carved up to its highest branches with JA & AH 4EVER, JD Loves VH, and other lover's initials, they turned to the right, walked off what was left of the path, and headed toward a spot overgrown with lilacs and azaleas and virtually undetected from the main path.

As soon as they walked about five feet off the path, Phyllis grabbed Bobby's hand. After a few more steps, Bobby lifted Phyllis off the ground and placed her on top of a rock that was flattened like a bench. He gently took her face in his hands and kissed her. Phyllis wrapped her arms around Bobby's neck and kissed him with all of the passion her 16-year-old lips could muster.

Ned, hidden behind the lilac bush, smiled when he saw Phyllis wrap her legs around Bobby's waist as she continued to kiss him. Wait until I tell Mother, he thought. Better yet, his sly mind schemed, Mother can wait. This is blackmail material. Ned watched as Bobby and Phyllis continued to neck.

Finally, Bobby lifted Phyllis off the rock and helped her down. They held each other for about five minutes and kissed again. Then Bobby picked up Phyllis' book bag, and they walked back to the path. Ned moved one foot behind the other, backing up slowly and quietly until the path cleared enough so that he could run away swiftly and without making too much noise.

Ned hid behind the great stone lion statue at the back of the school. He watched Bobby kiss Phyllis once more, stroke her hand lightly with his finger, and walk away. Phyllis walked back up the steps and to the library with a huge smile on her face.

At 3:50, Phyllis walked out of the library and over to the steps where Noreen arrived every day except Friday at 4:00. Ned was already sitting on the steps. He flashed Phyllis a broad smile that made him look like a swollen, muddy yellow Cheshire cat. Phyllis felt like slapping that grin off his face, for no particular reason she knew just then, but confident in the knowledge that the only thing that made Ned happy was someone else's misfortune.

But Phyllis didn't slap him. She just looked at him. The more she got to know Bobby and the other Marshalls and the rest of that Ardmore "riffraff" that her family complained of, the more she realized just how pompous and arrogant her family was. The Marshalls, their relatives, and all of their friends were nothing but kind to her. And she envied the closeness and the ease in the Marshall family—they harbored no pretensions that they were better than anyone else, although she could tell that they were raised to believe that they were as good as any body.

Their manners, their clothes, their posture and their friends didn't have to be perfect. No one got upset if the house wasn't spotless. The rooms in the Marshall house weren't untouchable to family and on display for guests who came with formal invitations. In the Daniels' house, people never just happened to drop by.

Phyllis never had been in a house like the Marshalls, with so much constant motion, so much laughter, so much love. The door seemed like a revolving one because if one of the Marshall children wasn't coming in or out, one of their friends or relatives was.

Phyllis loved to visit Bobby's street. Everybody's porch had an awning and mixed and matched furniture that never seemed empty. There were always people standing or sitting on their porches, their stoops or the sidewalk. Laughter and animated conversation floated up and down the street.

Phyllis' street was dead. No sidewalks invited people to stroll by, and large yards separated the houses. Neighborly conversations rarely occurred.

The Daniels' home was about as dead inside as the neighborhood was outside. Ned and Phyllis usually went to their respective bedrooms after school until Noreen called them for dinner. They'd walk into the dining room and join Ned Sr. as he sat at the table, hands folded in front of him, waiting for Noreen to serve him dinner. The routine never varied. Noreen served Ned Sr. first, then Ned Jr., and then Phyllis.

No one fought over the serving bowls like at the Marshalls where each child, even the youngest, knew that if he didn't get the food first, there might not be anything left by the time the bowl got around to him. At the Daniels', everyone knew who got what food when.

At the Daniels', the conversation flowed in an orderly manner and always under Ned Sr.'s control. Interrupting wasn't allowed, nor was raising one's voice above the proper level for polite conversation. At the Marshall's, you had to raise your voice just to be heard, and Phyllis loved it.

After dinner, Ned Sr. always retired to the den for one cigar and one glass of brandy, served in a Waterford crystal snifter that he purchased at J. E. Caldwell Jeweler's on the day that Pennsylvania railroad baron Warren Fitzgerald happened to stand right beside him purchasing 24 snifters for his summer home on Little Cranberry Island in Maine. Ned Jr. was allowed to sit with his father and finish his homework or, if Ned Sr. spoke first, Ned Jr. was allowed to speak with him. Phyllis was expected to clear the table and remain in the kitchen until she and Noreen washed and dried every dirty dish.

The routine never changed, Monday through Friday, every day the same—no warmth, no spontaneity, no fun. Phyllis found it harder and harder to contain her contempt for that way of life.

And now Ned, the embodiment of everything she hated, sat here smiling in her face.

"So did you learn anything new today?" Ned asked, the Cheshire grin still in place.

"What a stupid question. Of course I learned something new. That's what school's for," Phyllis said.

"What I think you learned today you didn't learn in school," said Ned. "Or did you?"

"I don't have time for your games, Ned," Phyllis said. She narrowed her eyes and pursed her lips. "What's that supposed to mean?"

Ned twirled a twig he found in the woods. "I think Bobby Marshall's been teaching you a thing or two."

"Bobby Marshall?" Phyllis said, putting on her best puzzled expression. "What's he got to do with anything?"

Ned threw the twig on the ground. "Don't act dumb. I saw you two walking toward the woods after school, and I followed you." He drummed his plump fingers on his book bag. "Wouldn't mother be interested in the things he taught you."

Phyllis' face turned scarlet with embarrassment, and then she exploded with anger.

"How dare you follow me, you little spy. You are so pitiful," she said. She threw her books down on the step. Ned scooted his behind away from Phyllis' books and wrath so fast that he scratched the seat of his pants on the gravel that littered the steps.

"I'm only telling you what I saw," he said. He leaned back and whistled now that Phyllis' hands were free of potential weapons. "And wait until mother hears about this."

"Wait, wait," Phyllis pleaded, her anger turning to fear. She held her arms out, palms facing Ned as if her hands could hold him back. "Please don't tell Mother. Why can't you help us?"

"Help you? You must be kidding," he said. "Why should I? Mother will reward me handsomely for this information. Why should I listen to you?"

"Because," said Phyllis, her voice shaking as much as her hands, "because I'll make it worth your while." No sister-to-brother appeal would work. Ned would only keep quiet if Phyllis paid some price.

"Oh, a bribe," Ned said. "I like that."

Phyllis whispered, "Whatever you want. Just don't tell Mother and Father."

"You drive a hard bargain," Ned said, "but I'm sure I can come up with something worthy of my silence."

Phyllis sat down on the step and put her head in her hands. "What do you want?"

"Come, come," said Ned. "Surely you can't expect me to come up with something so important so quickly. I need time. I need to sleep on it, let my finely tuned mind come up with something."

He chuckled like the Devil must do when he's made his bargain. "I'll let you know tomorrow. But in the meanwhile, don't push me."

At dinner that night, Ned said, "Mother and Father, guess what I saw after school today?"

Phyllis stopped her fork in mid-air on its way to her mouth and glared at Ned.

"What son?" asked Ned Sr. He swirled his prime rib in a puddle of gravy on his plate.

Ned paused and smiled at Phyllis. "This big accident on Montgomery Avenue. Tied up traffic for almost an hour."

Phyllis put the fork in her mouth, breathed a sigh of relief that no one could hear, and stared at her plate because if she looked at Ned, she knew she'd say something that might get her into trouble. Ned watched Phyllis until she lifted her eyes off the plate. When she looked at him, he smirked.

CHAPTER 8

The next day at school, Bobby waited outside Phyllis' home room to walk her to her first class. Phyllis hurried past the other kids going out the door, rushed over to Bobby and took his hand. As they walked down the hall, Phyllis said, "Ned followed us yesterday."

Damn that Margaret, thought Bobby; so much for Southern charm.

"And he's going to bribe me to keep him quiet," she said.

Before she could say anything else, Ned walked around the corner.

"Well, well, well," said Ned. "Two love birds walking hand-in-hand."

Phyllis quickly pulled her hand away.

"Don't try to hide it," said Ned. "After our little talk yesterday, I thought you would have learned, Phyllis." He tapped his toes on the floor as he stood directly in front of them. "I guess it must be love."

Phyllis raised her hand like she was about to strike Ned.

"I hate you, Ned," she yelled. "Why don't you just leave us alone?"

Bobby quickly stepped between Phyllis and Ned to stop them from coming to blows.

Ned shot back, "I just can't see you getting involved with any Tom, Dick or Harry—or is it Bobby—off the street." He pointed at Bobby and said, "You can do better than this." It took Bobby about two seconds to throw off that peacemaker role.

"Watch yourself, Ned," Bobby said. He grabbed Ned's shirt under his Adam's apple and lifted him a few inches off the floor. "One more word, and I'll throw you into those lockers," he said, tilting his head towards the lockers on the left.

The other students walking to their first class slowed down and looked over at Bobby, Phyllis and Ned. They quickly crowded around them to watch the fight.

Bobby just let Ned's feet touch the floor when Vera walked down the hall. She saw Bobby in the middle of the crowd, pulling on somebody's shirt. She figured that somebody was Ned because only one person could make Bobby so mad.

"Let me through," Vera said, pushing bodies from side-to-side to make a path. Some students who wanted a front row seat wouldn't move. "Get out of the way," she yelled and pushed even harder. Ned opened his mouth to say something, and Bobby pulled his arm back to swing at him. Vera pushed through just in time to grab Bobby's arm.

"Yo," said Vera. "Calm down." She held on to his arm tight as Bobby turned around to face her.

"What's going on here, little brother?" she asked Bobby. Oh no, she thought. Ned must have seen them. That damn Margaret never could do anything right with her country, Southern ways. Vera should have known: you can't send a girl to do a woman's job. She was the woman who was going to have to do the job, like it or not, and God knows, she didn't like it.

"What are you doing, Ned?" Vera asked. She moved her body between Ned's and Bobby's. She put both hands on Ned's chest as if she wanted to push him away, but she only wanted to keep him away from Bobby.

"I can take care of this, Vera," Bobby shouted from behind her. He tried to step around her to get to Ned, but she blocked him.

"Well here comes the vice principal at the end of the hall, and he'll have you all on suspension today if you don't cool off," Vera said. "If he catches you two down here fighting, he'll throw your two colored asses out on the street. That means you too, Ned, much as you don't want to believe it."

Paul Burton, Bobby's and Vera's cousin, watched the fight from the front row. He said, "I'll stall Mr. Stevens, Vera. You cool these guys down."

Paul pointed to a group of kids who gathered in the hall. "You all stand side by side and follow me," he said. Two rows of kids, five abreast, started walking down the hall. When they got close to Mr. Stevens, Edith Davis, at Paul's direction, slumped over and said, "Oh, God. I twisted my ankle."

Mr. Stevens couldn't ignore her, so he stopped, bent down and tried to help her. Paul motioned for the other kids to gather around. They formed a circle around Edith and Mr. Stevens to give Vera time to get Bobby straight. The kids could care less if Ned got in trouble, but they knew that if anybody in that fight was going to get in trouble, Bobby would. After all, he was only the plumber's son, and Ned's father's money still could buy some things, even from white folks.

"Ned, don't go getting all mad at Bobby and Phyllis," said Vera as she fingered his Adam's's apple and ran her hands up and down his chest. "You know that us Marshalls can't help but be attracted to you Daniels."

Vera knew that she sure must love her brother to even let those words leave her mouth.

"What do you mean?" Ned asked. Vera started tracing the outline of his ear with her fingers.

"I guess I have to come right out and say it," Vera said.

Bobby and Phyllis stared at Vera like they couldn't believe what she was doing.

"You know I like you," she purred.

"You like me?" asked Ned. His wide open eyes and arched eyebrows showed nothing but surprise.

"Sure I do," said Vera. She moved close enough to Ned so that her breasts almost touched his chest. He moved back.

"You insult me, smack my face, tell me never to speak to you again, and now you tell me that you like me?" he asked, incredulously.

"That's just an act," Vera said. "Haven't you ever heard of a girl playing hard to get? I play it all the time."

"So that's what's been going on," Ned said, looking like a cartoon character with a light bulb that just went on over his head. His giant-size ego tricked him into believing that Vera could treat him like dirt and still want him.

"Leave Bobby and Phyllis alone and come walk me to my class," Vera said. She wrapped her arm around Ned's. "They have their romance. Let's have ours," she said as she led him down the hall.

Before Ned knew what was happening, he and Vera had walked by Mr. Stevens, who was attending to Edith's ankle. By the time Mr. Stevens finished with Edith and looked up for Ned and Bobby, they were long gone.

When they reached Vera's first class, Ned asked, "Does this mean that you want to start dating me?"

"I've wanted that for a long time," Vera said. She almost choked on her words. "When can I see you again?"

"How about tomorrow night?" Ned asked. "We can go to the movies."

"Oh," said Vera, gliding her hands down his cheek. She whispered so softly that Ned could hardly hear it. "I can't wait."

After school, Vera waited outside, but this time it was for Bobby.

"Get over here, little brother. We have to talk," Vera said. She grabbed Bobby's arm and pulled him over to the stone wall.

"You owe me one big," she said.

"I know, I know," said Bobby. He laughed. "Thanks for stopping me from beating Ned and getting thrown out of school."

"I've got that jerk thinking that I like him," Vera howled. "Can you believe it?"

They fell out laughing so hard that other kids started looking and pointing.

"I sure must love you," Vera said, hitting Bobby on the arm. "I figure that if that jerk starts seeing me, which would kill his parents, he won't tell them that you're seeing Phyllis."

Bobby asked, "You'd put up with him again so I can see Phyllis? It's not like just talking to him for a few minutes after school. You're actually going to be alone with him and act like you like him?"

"Sure. No problem. It's not going to be for that long anyhow. I'll see him for a while, but I'm not going to waste any more time on him than I have to. I'll fix it so that he won't bother you and Phyllis anymore, trust me. Just give me a little time," Vera said, nodding her head.

"Thanks, Vera," said Bobby. "I don't want to stop seeing Phyllis now."

Vera shook her head and said, "Don't worry. You won't have to. I have to show that snot-nosed Ned that when you mess with one Marshall, you mess with them all. And the boy's got to learn that you don't mess with the Marshalls."

CHAPTER 9

"Where should I pick you up?" Ned asked Vera as they stood in the hall after home room the next day.

"At my house, of course," she said. Ned looked around and lowered his voice so none of the students passing by could hear him.

"But I'm not supposed to be dating you," he said. "I'll get in trouble if my parents find out."

What a punk, Vera thought. About to graduate from high school and still afraid of his parents.

Vera raised the volume of her voice enough to sound indignant. "Don't you pick up your other dates at their houses?" If he ever had any dates, he'd know the answer was yes, she thought. "Well, I'm no different," she said, trying not to laugh, because she was as different as any girl he could ever get to go out with him. "I may be more independent, but I still expect to be treated like a lady.

Ned pursed his lips and shifted from side to side.

"Oh, alright," he said. "I'll pick you up at your house, but we have to be careful."

"Don't worry," said Vera. "I know how to be discreet."

When Ned drove down Welsh Road, he was astonished at the crowd of kids sitting out on their porches. He never spent much time in that neighborhood, but that day it looked especially lively. Every house with a porch had at least three or four kids sitting up on it. He parked the car and walked towards Vera's house. He thought that every eye on the block followed him. He was right. Vera asked the kids on the block to sit out that night to be witnesses in her scheme to get Ned. They jumped at the chance to help.

Ned walked up the steps to Vera's house. He nodded hello to the five kids sitting on the porch of the twin house that was attached to Vera's and then to the six kids on the Marshall porch.

"Vera's inside," said her sister, Valerie. "Wait right here, and I'll go get her."

Ned stood on the steps there in awkward silence, looking straight ahead or at the ground as everyone around him talked and laughed. He didn't speak to these kids in school beyond saying hello when he had to and he wasn't going to start talking to them now. They figured the same thing and went on talking and enjoying the warm May day among themselves.

Ned rested his hand on the railing and patted his foot in obvious discomfort. After about ten minutes, Vera appeared. She wore a pink dress with pea-size mother of pearl buttons up the front. Ned thought about undoing those buttons one by one. Vera thought: touch me fool and you die.

She looked up and down the street and smiled at how the other kids turned out. Ned could never deny to his parents that he picked her up. She kept him standing outside long enough so that the kids could walk by and get a good look at him. She wanted him to feel as uncomfortable in her neighborhood as he tried to make everybody in her neighborhood feel for just being alive.

"Hello, Ned," said Vera. "Let's get going."

Ned quickly followed Vera down the stairs.

"Wait," she said. "A gentleman always helps a lady down the steps, and I love a gentleman."

Vera wrapped her arm around Ned's and paused for a minute so every body on the street could see them arm-in-arm.

Before Ned arrived, she made sure that the parking spaces directly in front of her house were filled so Ned had to park at the end of the block. She promenaded down the block as if she wanted everyone to see her new man. She wanted them to see him, all right, but she'd jump anyone who called Ned her man.

As she walked by porch after porch, kids called out, "Looking good, Vera." "Don't hurt him, girl", and "Go ahead, now." Ned burned with anticipation as Vera responded to every call with a "Hey, Carla." "How you doing Edith?" "Whatcha know good, Paul."

When they reached the car, Ned got in as fast as he could. Vera paused, smoothed her skirt, and adjusted the tilt on her hat—all to kill time. She bent over slightly to give Ned a good view of her behind before getting in. He grinned and imagined himself pressed up against Vera's firm flesh and almost forgot that he was in a hurry to leave.

He came to, rushed around to the driver's side, settled in and burned rubber as he sped off. "So much for keeping our date a secret," Ned said. "It seems like all the colored kids in the school were out on your block today. Now they all know."

Vera waved her hand in the air as if she was dismissing him. "I don't have any control over other people, Ned," she said. "I asked you to pick me up at my house like any lady would. I didn't know that it was going to be such a beautiful evening, that everyone was going to want to sit out on their porch."

She gently touched his arm. "But if dating me makes you uncomfortable, you can turn around and take me back home. She stuck her lips like she was pouting, but fully aware that Ned would never let her go now that he thought he had her.

"I'm not taking you back anywhere," he said. He leered at her over the rims of his quarter-inch thick black horn-rimmed glasses. "We're going to have a wonderful evening."

Impossible, thought Vera.

As soon as the lights went down in the movie theater, Ned reached out for Vera's hand. She moved her hand just in time. Then Ned tried to put his arm around her shoulder.

"Not here. Not now," she said. "Wait until we're alone." Ned moved his hand back, feeling frustrated, but excited. Phyllis and Bobby sat three rows behind them and giggled in unison every time Vera put Ned's hands back where they belonged.

At the end of the movie, Ned asked Vera, "Where would you like to go now?", thinking that she would mention any one of a half dozen places they could go for a snack.

"Honey, you have to take me home," Vera said. "Seems like I just started my monthly, right here in this theater, and I've got to go take care of it." She held his hand so he would believe what she was about to say or to be too excited to even think about it. "I can't fully enjoy you with this going on."

Ned shuddered at the thought of blood dripping down her legs. "Of course you can't" he said. He picked up his pace to get her to the car. "I'll get you home as soon as possible."

Vera knew that Ned would be disgusted and anxious to get rid of her. Men wanted to get between your legs, but they didn't want to think about what happened on up in there.

"Thanks for being so understanding," Vera said. She batted her eyelashes and added, Once this is over, it'll be safe to . . . well, you know.

It's something I've wanted for a long time." She dug her fingers into the palm of her hand to keep from laughing out loud.

When they got to the car, Ned said, "Let me get a cloth from the trunk to put on the seat so you don't get blood on it."

"Don't bother, sugar," Vera said. "I plugged enough toilet tissue in my underwear to make it to Welsh Road."

Ned ignored every speed limit as he drove Vera home. He drove past Vera's house looking for a parking space.

"Don't bother to park, honey," Vera said. "I can feel that I don't have time to walk down the street without making a mess. Just let me off in front of the door."

Ned backed up and stopped the car. Just as he leaned over and pursed his lips to kiss her, Vera popped open the car door and said, "Gotta run, sugar. I can feel it working its way down my leg."

With that, she hopped out of the car, slammed the door, and ran up the steps to the house.

Inside, she closed the door, leaned her back up against it and burst out laughing, her mind fixed on the picture of Ned Daniels with his lips poked out.

The next morning, Bobby walked into the kitchen where Vera was fixing herself an omelet for breakfast.

"I sure hope you and Phyllis enjoyed that movie last night because Ned liked to make me sick, always trying to get his arm around my shoulder or hold my hand. His hands are so soft, they feel like a woman's," she said. "You can tell that punk never does any real work."

"Show me again how he was looking for a kiss," Bobby said. He chuckled as he poured a cup of coffee. Vera poked out her lips, opened and closed them like a goldfish sucking food off the top of the water, and howled.

After they both had a good laugh, Vera said, "Now seriously, little brother. I have to speed up this plan. I thought I could stand Ned for a couple of dates, but now I know that I can't. I've got to get rid of that jerk." She flipped the omelet and started to think.

After breakfast, Vera headed down Welsh Road. The porches were mostly deserted now as people went about their Saturday morning chores. She passed half a dozen kids walking down the street. She greeted and thanked each one for helping out last night. At the end of the street, she turned left onto Spring Avenue. She waved to the girls in Hazel's House of Beauty. At Dent's barber shop, Vera slowed down and looked in. Mr. Dent, the barber, nicked the customer he was shaving as he watched Vera walk by and wished he was 20- no 30-years younger. Vera crossed the street, waved to the kids working the vegetable stand at Goldstein's Fish Market, and turned onto Walnut Street in the direction of the Hotel Washington.

Vera's grandparents, Alfred and Ramona Washington, owned the Hotel Washington. The Washington's called it a hotel because that sounded more respectable than boarding house. Alfred bought the three-story wooden house when he moved to Ardmore some 20 years before. The house was too big for just he and Ramona and their three daughters, so Ramona got the idea to take in boarders. Once she saw all the men who came to town to work at the Autocar plant and who needed a place to stay.

The Hotel Washington quickly became known as a place where a man could get a clean room, a good home-cooked breakfast and dinner, and a peaceful night's rest because Alfred and Ramona didn't allow any carrying on in their house. The men raved about Ramona's cooking to their friends who started coming by asking for her special homemade ice cream or that spicy sausage she made with pork that she bought after driving almost 20 miles to Weaver's Farm in King of Prussia. "That pork around here doesn't quite taste the same," Ramona always said. Alfred built a special window in front of the hotel to sell ice cream in the summer and sausage and home cooked meals year round.

"Hi, Delila," Vera said as she walked up the hotel steps, past the window where a line of customers already lined up to purchase ice cream. Delila stopped scooping strawberry ice cream into a half-gallon cardboard container and looked up.

"Hey, Vera. Whatcha know, girl?" she said.

"Nothing you don't know, girl," said Vera. "We need to talk. I'm coming around back."

She grabbed the brass handle, opened one of the huge green double doors, and entered the hotel.

"Hi, Grandpa," said Vera, as she peeked into the hotel office on her left side. Alfred Washington sat behind a mahogany desk that stretched from one end of the wall to the other, leaving only about a foot for him to squeeze his 250 lb. frame through to get by.

"Hey, baby," said Alfred. "Come on in here and give me some sugar."

Vera walked in and kissed her grandfather on the cheek.

"You come here to see Delila? She's working on the ice cream," he said.

"I know," said Vera. "I saw her on the way in."

"Good," said Alfred. "Now don't you two girls go getting in any trouble."

"I won't, Grandpa," said Vera. At least not until I get it all planned out right, she thought.

Delila Washington was Vera's aunt, although she was only a year younger than Vera. She was one of those babies born at the change of life, an unexpected bundle of joy for the Washingtons. When Delila was born, her sisters were grown. Emma was 18, and Alfreda was 20. Emma had her own babies—Vera and Bobby—to take of when Ramona gave birth to Delila.

Ramona worked like three men keeping the hotel going. She didn't have time to slow down and change her life for a change-of-life baby. She asked Emma to take care of Delila while she worked at the hotel. Even though Emma already had her hands full with two babies in diapers, she couldn't turn down her mother—and her sister.

For the first few years of Delila's life, Emma usually carried one of her babies in one arm and Delila in another. She lined up Delila in a little high chair right next to her own children and spooned cereal into Delila's mouth the same as she did for the others on the assembly line. Delila and Vera grew up like sisters, not like aunt and niece. When Delila became old enough to choose where she wanted to be, she spent as much time at the Marshall house as any of the Marshall children.

Vera walked into the back of the ice cream booth, behind Delila.

"What's going on Vera," said Delila, turning around to scoop out a dish of pistachio ice cream.

"I've got to speed up this thing with Ned," Vera said. "He's getting on my last nerve. I can't keep up this game we've all been playing to keep Bobby and Phyllis together. We've all spent too much damn time trying to satisfy one worthless punk. It's time to bring this thing to a close."

"Didn't enjoy your date with him, huh?" Delila asked, laughing and knowing full well that Vera didn't.

"Now, you know girl. That was our first date and our last," Vera said, pulling up a chair close to Delila. "Here I got that fine Billy Patterson ready to come running when I snap my fingers, and I'm wasting my time with Ned. Oh, no."

"It's time to work that punk so he leaves me alone and lets Bobby and Phyllis go about their business," Vera said.

"Lord, chile. You always got something going," Delila said, admiring her niece's spunk.

"If I don't, how am I going to get anywhere?" Vera asked.

"Now here's the plan," she said, whispering in Delila's ear so that none of the customers who were looking dead in her face could hear what was going on.

CHAPTER 10

Every Wednesday night, Alfred and Ramona Washington went to Bible Study at Bethel AME Church across the street from the hotel. Ramona helped found the church and engineered its move across the street from her home so she wouldn't have to go too far to get to services or serve the Lord on any of her many church boards or committees. Bible Study started promptly at 7 p.m., giving everyone time to get home from work, eat dinner, shower and shave, and head on over. People dressed for Bible Study the same as they did for church.

Roughly 20 people sat in a circle in the church basement reading and discussing Bible passages under Rev. Carson's trusty hand until 9 p.m. Then they'd have punch and cookies and cake until around 9:30. Ramona and Alfred helped clean up and arrived back home at around 10:00. Their Wednesday evening routine never varied.

Ramona and Alfred only made Delila go to Bible Study in the summer. During the school year, they allowed her to stay home and finish her homework. Ramona and Alfred made sure that all the boarders ate and their dishes were washed by 6:45. They didn't worry about leaving Delila alone in the hotel on Wednesday evenings because, after all, she was 17 and almost grown and, if anything happened, she could just walk across the street to get them.

Precisely at 6:55, Alfred and Ramona headed for the front door. Delila sat in the office doing homework at Alfred's massive desk.

"We're going now, Delila," said Ramona. "Take care of everything and remember, if you need us, we're right across the street." She repeated the same words every Wednesday.

"Yes, Mom," said Delila. "I know. I'll see you when you get back. Everything will be fine."

The door closed behind them, and Delila waited. At 7:15, Vera appeared at the doorway carrying a brown paper bag.

"They're gone, aren't they?" Vera asked.

"Of course," said Delila. "You can go up. Use Room 3."

Room 3 was about the smallest room in the hotel. It was on the second floor, next to the fire escape that ran down the back wall. Vera opened the door and placed the bag down on the small bedside table. She pulled out three red candles she had taken from Emma's dining room mahogany sideboard, candles usually reserved for holiday dinners or power failures. She placed two candles on that table and one on the dresser across the room and lit them.

Vera reached inside the bag and pulled out a long red satin nightgown. It had spaghetti straps, a slit to the thigh on the left side, and a heart-shaped neckline. She bought it one size too small so that every inch of the satin pressed against her skin. She brushed her long hair and fluffed it out. She reached in the bag and pulled out the crystal earrings Jimmy gave her after a particularly good night.

She rustled around in the bag for the perfume she used on special occasions—Mitsuoko by Guerlain, just one of her signature scents, all by Monsieur Guerlain. When Mrs. Harrison, that arbiter of 400 taste and style whose husband owned Harrison's Department Store, brought the scent to Harrison's, *The Elevator* quoted her as saying that Mitsuoko was "a refreshing change from the scent that so many fine women wore." She didn't mention the scent by name, but anyone who read the article knew that Mrs. Harrison was referring to Chanel No. 5. All the women in the 400 wore that. Vera usually copied those women, but when she read about the history of Mitsuoko, she broke ranks.

It is said that Mitsuoko was named for a Japanese girl who fell in love with a British naval officer during the Russo-Japanese War. The lovers separated, but whenever the officer's heart turned east or whenever he came upon a spicy Oriental scent, he thought of her.

Vera wished to be like Mitsuoko, someone who stirred a man's heart, gripped his senses, and hovered in the air of his thoughts. And even though she had none of those feelings for Ned, a seduction was a seduction, and she wasn't going to change her style for him.

So she put Mitsuoko behind her ears, between her breasts, on her wrists and in the bend of her elbow. She slipped her feet into red patent leather mules with ostrich feathers on the front strap. The color of the mules complemented the red polish on her toenails. She looked in the mirror, approved of what she saw, sat in the chair next to the table, turned off the light and waited.

At 7:30, Ned walked up the steps to the hotel. He did just what Vera told him and turned to the left to the office. Delila noticed him coming in but pretended to be engrossed in her homework.

"Excuse me," he stammered.

"Oh, it's you," said Delila with a sigh, trying to make it seem like the mere sight of Ned bored her. "She's in Room 3. Up the stairs. Last room on the right."

Ned didn't even bother to say thank you. He turned on his heels and headed up the stairs.

Five minutes later, Bobby, his brother Stevie, and cousins Paul and Charlie walked into the office.

"They're both upstairs," said Delila. "Go wait out on the front porch and wait."

The door to Room 3 was slightly open. Ned knocked lightly on it anyway, and Vera called out, "Come in."

When his eyes adjusted to the candlelight, he saw Vera sitting in the side chair, the split giving him a view of her legs from feet to upper thigh. "God, you look beautiful."

"All for you, baby," she purred. "All for you."

Ned rushed over to the table and extended his hands to pull Vera out of the chair and next to him.

"Slow down, honey," Vera said, pushing his hands away. "Take a good look first." She smoothed her hands down her body outlining every curve from her breasts to her hips.

"There's no need to rush," she said. She puckered her lips like she wanted to kiss him. "We have all night."

Ned had no choice but to stand there and look. Vera turned around with the flourish that impressed everyone in the modeling club.

She pointed to the bulge in Ned's pants and said, "I can see that you like what you see." She smiled and added, "I think I'm going to like it, too," knowing full well that the thought of Ned getting between her legs or anyone else's made her sick.

She walked over to Ned and unbuttoned the top button on his shirt. He instinctively reached out for her.

"I said don't rush it," she said, stepping back. "Let me take my time seeing what you've got, because time is what we've got plenty of."

"I'm about ready to explode," Ned stammered. "I don't know if I can wait."

"Well, you have to wait, sugar. What I've got planned for the evening can't be rushed, and believe me, it's well worth waiting for, so just hold it in. We're not even halfway to the starting gate."

Vera finished unbuttoning Ned's shirt, being careful not to touch any of the flesh that so repulsed her. She peeled it off him and unbuttoned the top button on his pants. If he comes all over me now, I'll get grandfather's gun and shoot him, she thought.

"Hold it in there, Ned," said Vera, as she unzipped his zipper. Thank God he's wearing underpants, she thought.

"You're driving me crazy, Vera," Ned said.

"What I see is driving me crazy, too," she said, but as far as she could tell, what he had looked too small to drive her anywhere.

His pants fell to the floor.

"Step out of your pants, honey," Vera said. She took a few steps back, pretending to admire him. His body was not what you would call taut. On a younger boy, you'd call it baby fat. His skin color looked like the runny baby crap that Vera had washed out of hundreds of dirty diapers. She couldn't wait to be finished with him.

Ned reached to pull his underpants down.

"No, not yet," said Vera, raising her voice slightly. She didn't want to see him fully naked. At least not yet.

She said, "I don't want to see all of your goodness just yet. I want to see it when we're in bed, where I can look *and* touch. I'm not ready for you yet, honey. I like to build up to it, if you know what I mean."

"I know what you mean," Ned said, knowing full well that he didn't know what she meant since he'd never made love to a woman before, although he had an orgasm hundreds of times.

But Ned was tired of waiting. It was time to be a man. He walked over to Vera, arms stretched out, ready to take her. Vera let his palms touch her back, and then she pushed him away. Ned pulled her in the direction of the bed.

"Come on, Vera," he said. "I'm ready."

She held out her hand to stop him. "No you're not, not yet," she said. "I don't make love with a man without washing him off first. No telling where he's been. No offense. I like you and all, but you're a man just like any other."

Ned looked at her like he didn't believe what she was saying. Not that he knew any better about what happened before people had sex.

Vera stifled her revulsion and put her hands on Ned's chest. "Some men say the way I wash them off feels almost as good as the way I make love to them . . . . Almost. The way the warm water feels sliding against their skin, the way my hands feel all smooth and slippery and warm as I use my fingers to clean off every inch of your manhood, getting underneath every fold of skin, applying just the right amount of pressure. Then I dry you off with a soft cloth and get you wet again. That's what you want, isn't it, Ned?"

He could barely speak.

"Yes, that's what I want," he finally said.

"Then take this," she said, reaching for the pitcher on the night table, "and go across the hall and get me some warm water. Not cold, or lukewarm, but warm. Let it run until it gets really warm."

Back in his right mind, Ned said, "I can't go out in the hall like this—in my underwear."

Vera said, "Nobody's going to see you. I told you nobody was here. All the boarders are at the Wednesday night poker game at the American Legion, and my grandparents are at Bible Study. Delila's the only one here, and she stays downstairs until her parents get home. Besides, the hallway's dark."

Ned didn't move.

"Well here," said Vera, reaching for the towel next to the washbowl. "Put this around your waist. Nothing unusual around here about a man with a towel around his waist going to the bathroom."

Ned thought about that for about a minute, put the towel around his waist and headed towards the door.

Vera grabbed his arm. "Wait a minute," she said. She reached under the towel and pulled at Ned's underpants with both hands, bent down and slid them down to the floor. He stepped out of them. Then Vera stood up and put her hands on his hips. "I want you to be ready when you come back," she said.

Ned smiled and walked out of the door. As soon as he got on the other side of the door, Vera locked it from the inside. She blew out the candles and threw them and all her other things into the paper bag.

She lifted up the window, stepped out onto the fire escape and walked down. On her way down, she knocked on the office window where Delila waited.

"Go, girl," Vera said.

Delila jumped up, grabbed Ramona's make-enough-stew-to-feed-the-whole-hotel pot with its heavy ladle and ran to the stairway leading to the second floor. Delila hit the pot like a drum and yelled, "Fire. Fire. Fire. Get out of the hotel."

Ned heard the pots clanging. By the third time Delila yelled fire, he understood what was happening. He ran out in the hall, pitcher in hand, leaving the water still running down the drain.

Further down the hall, the doors to rooms 1 and 2 flew open. The men who boarded there ran out into the hall. They paused and looked at the half-naked Ned who stood at the end of the hall, frozen with fear.

"Fire," Delila yelled, clanging the pot even faster. "Come on Ned," she said. "Get out of here." She ran down the stairs.

Forgetting Vera who, as far as he knew, waited naked inside Room 3 for him, Ned ran down the stairs as fast as he could and pushed open the double doors. Bobby and the other boys saw Ned push through the double doors, and they sprang into action.

Bobby, waiting right behind the door, pulled on Ned's towel as hard as he could. Bobby held the towel up like a jockey holding his trophy at the end of the race. Ned yelped and jumped up in the air. He tried to cover his now flagging manhood with his hands. By this time, the two boarders, and Stevie, Charlie and Paul stood on the sidewalk watching Ned jump around. The clanging pot and loud voices made the street come alive. People on both sides of the street opened their windows and doors, ran out on their porches, and looked out at the crowd gathered in front of the hotel.

Paul ran up to Ned and said, "What are you doing around here with no clothes on? Don't you know that this is a respectable hotel?"

Stevie and Charlie ran over and grabbed Ned's arms, stopping him from using them to cover up between his legs.

"What should we do?" Paul called out to no one in particular, but to everyone who was looking at Ned and pointing and wondering where the fire was. "Should we call the police and have him arrested for indecent exposure? Or should we call his parents and have them come bring him some clothes?"

Ned's face turned red and Stevie's and Charlie's hands dripped with moisture from all of Ned's sweating. Then he started breathing hard and getting limp. They instinctively tightened their grip on his arms, thinking that he was about to fall out.

Instead, Ned cried out, "Oh, my God. Get your hands off of me. Can't you see that I'm naked?"

Everybody on the street convulsed with laughter.

"We can see that mighty good," Paul said, as calmly as he could.

"Let me go," Ned yelled. His embarrassment turned to anger, which gave him back his strength. He tried to wrest his arms free from Stevie's and Charlie's strong grip.

"Tell you what, Ned," Paul said as he stepped in front of Ned to shield his body from the eyes of the growing crowd. "We'll let you go, but on one condition."

"Anything," Ned hollered. "Just let me out of here."

Paul put his face right in front of Ned's and said, "We'll keep our mouths shut about how you were found standing naked in the hallway of the Hotel Washington and out here on Walnut Avenue if you leave Bobby and Phyllis alone."

Paul grabbed Ned's arm for effect. "And stay away from Vera. Do you think that she'd really be interested in your punk ass. And if you ever think about saying anything to your parents about Bobby and Phyllis, we'll be right up there telling them about this little incident tonight. And with all these people around," he said, waving his other arm at the crowd, "they'll believe us. Especially if you look right over there at the corner."

He pointed past the crowd to the right. "There's old Mrs. Greene, the notary, watching the whole thing. You won't be able to explain this away, Daniels. And, I'm sure your momma and daddy wouldn't want their holy family name mixed up in anything like this."

"Do I make myself clear?" Paul asked. He said right into Ned's ear, "Stay away from Bobby and Phyllis and Vera."

"Perfectly clear," said Ned, indignant as ever since he realized that he was set up. "Now will you let me go?"

"Certainly," said Paul. He let go of Ned's arm.

"And here's your towel," said Bobby. He stepped out from behind the door and handed the towel to Ned. Ned snatched the towel out of Bobby's hand and tied it around his waist.

"What about my clothes?", Ned said.

"Evidence," said Bobby, and he smiled. "Now get out of here."

Ned ran down the steps and all the way to his car. He sped off down Walnut Avenue so fast his tires squealed. Vera stepped around onto the porch from behind the other door, gave Bobby the thumbs up sign, and burst out into hysterical laughter with the rest of her family and friends.

CHAPTER 11

Every day that God sent until the end of the school year, Bobby and Phyllis met after almost every class and walked hand-in-hand until the next class. They spoke to Ned every time they walked by him although he never spoke back.

Ned usually scurried from class to class, looking straight ahead with his chin up in the air, dodging the laughter, snickers and whispers of any of the kids who saw him naked that Wednesday, or who heard about it, which was almost everybody. Ned with his nose in the air was nothing unusual, but the other kids knew he couldn't act like he was better than them when half of Ardmore saw him standing naked on Walnut Avenue.

Ned didn't try to see or talk to Vera, but he didn't ignore her. Every time he saw her, he seethed with a mixture of anger, embarrassment and desire. She got the best of him, that's true; but she of all people would never be better than him. After all, he was going to enter Howard University in Washington, DC like his mother and father before him to take his place among the talented tenth. And she'd never be in that esteemed group, of that he was sure. So whenever he saw or passed by Vera, he looked her straight in the eye, frowned, and never broke the gaze first. As far as Ned was concerned, there was no need to hide from Vera.

With Ned off her back, Vera spent her free time enjoying Billy Patterson and counting the days until graduation. Vera knew that she put Ned in his place, so that when Ned gave Vera the evil eye, she just rolled her eyes and kept on going. She truly had better things to do than worry about what Ned was going to do to her—or die trying to do it.

"What are you going to do when you graduate," Emma asked Vera one night as they sat alone in the dining room sharing the one piece of chocolate cake that the other kids didn't devour at dinner.

Vera put down her fork and opened her eyes wide so that Emma could see that she was serious. "What I've told you a hundred times, Mom, but what you refuse to accept. I'm going to go live with Aunt Alfreda," she said.

Emma shook her head. Again. "I wish you wouldn't do that Vera," she said. "Alfreda has her wild ways, and Lord knows, you don't need to get any wilder."

"I'm eighteen, Mom. I'm grown," said Vera. "I can take care of myself, believe me."

"I believe you, Vera," said Emma, "but there's things out there that you still don't know. Alfreda's not the one to teach them to you."

Aunt Alfreda can't teach me anything that I don't already know, Vera thought with all the confidence of an eighteen-year-old. Vera figured that she didn't grown up in the country like Emma, and she was sure that the world "out there" held no surprises that weren't pleasant ones.

"I can't stay in this little town any longer, Mom," said Vera. "It's not going anywhere, and I am. We don't meet the right type of people here. We don't travel in the right type of circles."

Emma dropped the fork on the plate and reared her head back. "What do you mean, 'right type of people?' People like those high siddidy Daniels that nobody can stand. Except for that nice girl, Phyllis."

"Not like them, Mom," Vera said, "but people who are *really* doing something. If the Daniels's were really doing something, they'd live in town where the rest of the 400 lives. You know, in Mt. Airy or Overbrook."

"You and that 400," Emma said. "I hope you get in it because I sure am tired of hearing about it. Maybe if you get in it, you'll see that it's not all it's cracked up to be. Lots of things look better from a distance, you know. You get up close and you can see all the cracks and chips, how it's all patched together." But headstrong as you are, you're going to have to see it for yourself, thought Emma, as she looked at her beautiful and independent first-born.

Emma shook her head. "I want the best for you Vera, but going in town with Alfreda and chasing after the 400 is not the way."

"Well, I'd rather see it for myself," said Vera. She touched Emma's arm lightly. "You have to trust me, Mom. Besides, Aunt Alfreda's the only one in the family who understands why I have to leave Ardmore. I'm just like her in that way. So what if Aunt Alfreda drinks and hangs out in bars? That's part of her job, and she's making good money doing it," said Vera.

Emma couldn't deny that.

"Still, I don't want you running with that crowd of Alfreda's," Emma said. "Drinking, smoking, partying, running with men and Lord knows what else."

Vera knew what else and so did Emma, except she was too embarrassed to say it. Vera thought that after having ten children, Emma shouldn't be embarrassed to talk about sex beyond the typical "keep your skirt down, your legs closed and your feet on the floor."

"I can run with folks like that here or in town. What's the difference?" Vera asked.

"They're a lot rougher in town," Emma said. "Alfreda can't watch you every minute."

"I don't need her to watch me, Mom," Vera said. "I can watch myself." She patted Emma's arm again. "You'll see. I'll be fine," she said.

"Well, God knows I can't stop you, Vera," Emma said. She leaned back in her chair and set her fork down on the table in defeat. "Just don't try to keep up with Alfreda. You'll never make it."

"I've got my own path to follow," Vera said, "and Aunt Alfreda can't show me the way."

I hope not, thought Emma, because Alfreda was too fast for her own good. Her drinking, pipe smoking, and carousing got her thrown out of the house as soon as she graduated from Ardmore High School. Alfred wanted to put her out sooner for disobeying his rules and running with men, but Ramona intervened. Just let the child finish high school, Ramona said. We've come this far, and she'd be the first one in the family to graduate from high school. Let her at least do that. I can't stop what you do after that, Ramona rightly admitted. Alfreda graduated one night, and Alfred made her pack her bags the next day.

Emma chuckled as she recalled how Alfreda stumbled around, throwing clothes in a suitcase, because she stayed out all night celebrating and had a massive hangover that morning. Ramona and Emma went downstairs and pleaded with Alfred to let Alfreda sleep it off before he put her out. You can't have her out there hung over and sick and stumbling all over Ardmore, they told Alfred. Then *you* look bad. Alfreda got her day of rest.

"I can't stop him anymore, child," Ramona said to Alfreda the next morning between tears as she helped Alfreda get her clothes in the suitcases. "Mend your ways, child, and then come on back home," she told Alfreda as she walked her to the door.

"Mrs. Hunter has a room waiting for you. Respect her rules and you won't have any trouble out of her," said Ramona. She hoped that Alfreda wouldn't embarrass her, since she had assured Mrs. Hunter, who she met at the Eastern District Conference of African Methodist Episcopal Mothers of the Church, Mrs. Hunter being the mother of Emmanuel AME in West Philadelphia and Ramona being the mother of Bethel AME-Ardmore, that Alfreda was raised in a Christian home. That she was a trifle prone to backsliding was beside the point, thought Ramona. Raise a child in the way he shall go, and she shall never depart, was the scripture. And Ramona held God to his word, even when it came to Alfreda.

"Let me hear from you, now," Rhoda said as she helped Alfreda get her bags on the Number 7 Streetcar to Philadelphia.

Alfreda's Christian training lasted one week before she broke Mrs. Hunter's rules forbidding drinking and entertaining men in her room. Mrs. Hunter called Ramona in shock, and all Ramona did was apologize and ask Mrs. Hunter to join her in prayer for Alfreda's redemption.

Mrs. Hunter simply said, "I'll pray with you, sister. But I still have to put her out."

Between all the drinking and partying she did that week at Mrs. Hunter's, Alfreda still managed to find a job as a typist at a small colored insurance company in West Philadelphia. The owners of the company thought that Alfreda's diploma from Ardmore High School on the Main Line meant that she was smarter and better prepared than the colored kids who usually presented themselves for jobs with diplomas from Philadelphia high schools. Alfreda knew there was no truth to that, but she let them think it anyway. If some colored folks thought that the white man's grass was greener, she wasn't going to be the one to tell them any different.

Alfreda earned enough money to easily pay the rent on a small one-room apartment. After about a year, she had saved enough money to buy a three-floor brick twin home in West Philadelphia. The house had a massive bedroom, living room, dining room, and a foyer that was as big as the one room she had at Mrs. Hunter's. She didn't listen to much that her father said, but when he said, own your own home and no man can own you, she believed him. No matter how late or rowdy the evening, Alfreda always had enough sense to know that, in the morning, she'd better make it to the job that kept her living in the style to which she rapidly grew accustomed.

Every six months or so, Alfreda had someone deliver a note to Ramona asking her to meet her for lunch. Ramona would take the streetcar into West Philadelphia and meet Alfreda at whatever local colored restaurant she choose. Ramona was proud that Alfreda could take care of herself well enough to eat at restaurants because she could count on one hand the number of times that she had. Even though she doubted Alfreda's methods, Ramona never really doubted that Alfreda would be fine. Alfreda was wild, but she wasn't stupid, and her stubborn streak would keep her from failing.

"How's Daddy? How's Emma and Delila?" Alfreda always asked.

And Ramona always answered, "They're fine, but you can come out to the house and see for yourself."

"Not yet," Alfreda always answered back. "Not yet."

While Alfreda was away from Ardmore, all sorts of rumors drifted back about what and how she was doing. Living in a beaten up one-room shack was one. Standing on the corner selling herself was another. Sitting in the bar spending all her money on liquor was a third, which, on some nights, was not far from the truth.

Emma missed Alfreda. Even though they fought too much over what was right and what was wrong during Alfreda's last year at home, Alfreda still was her sister, and she remembered the good times when they got along as sisters should. But Alfreda started calling Emma names like Goody Two Shoes and Little Miss Perfect because she led the upstanding Christian life that Alfred and Ramona so carefully planned for them.

One Sunday, five years after Alfreda left home, the congregants of Bethel A.M.E. stood on Walnut Avenue for a few minutes of fellowship before they walked home to sit on their porches or go directly inside to get dinner on the table. A boat-sized black Cadillac with dark windows appeared at the end of Walnut Avenue. Heads turned to watch it sail down the street and turn left onto Spring Avenue.

As the car turned the corner, Alfred said to Ramona, "It's a shame those white folks made that driver work on the Lord's Day."

Ramona shook her head and said, "They think they have their heaven right here on earth, so they ain't studying about how to get in there. But, you know. God don't like ugly."

Alfred, Ramona, Emma and Delila walked across the street toward the hotel as the car came around again. This time, as the car got up to different groups of people walking or standing on the sidewalk, it stopped, like the driver was looking for directions. One-by-one, as people looked in the driver's window, their eyes got wide and their mouths' flew open. Once the initial shock of recognition passed, they smiled and waved.

Finally, the Caddy pulled into an empty space in front of the hotel. Alfred looked at the car so hard that he walked right into Ramona who already had stopped dead in her tracks.

"Hi, you all," shouted Alfreda as she put the car in park and opened the door.

"Alfreda?" said Alfred, knowing full well that was his daughter.

"In the flesh, Daddy," said Alfreda, running her hand along the rim of the car door. "Do you like it?"

Emma and Delila squealed, ran over to Alfreda and hugged her.

"Welcome back," said Emma. She stepped back and took a good look at Alfreda. "It sure is good to see you. You look great."

"Is this your car,?" asked Delila, running her hand up and down the chrome trim Alfreda polished to a bright shine before she left home.

"Sure is, little sister," Alfreda said, with a self-satisfied grin. "Sure is."

Alfred finally closed his mouth and walked over with Ramona.

"You sure know how to make an entrance, missy," said Ramona. "Now let's get down to business. Do you own this car?"

"Hook, line and sinker," said Alfreda, running her hand around the brim of her black fedora.

"I see that you're doing all right in the world," said Alfred. Certain that God would not reward a wayward child, he said, "You must have changed your ways."

"I've only changed the way I work, Daddy," said Alfreda, proud of herself. "I learned to work smarter, not harder," she said as she tapped the side of her head with her finger. I'm not typing anymore. I'm selling insurance now, and to the folks who really need it. Who wants insurance more than folks who think they're going to die? I sell insurance in every taproom, pool hall and beer garden in Philadelphia, to every crook, drunk and low-life who wants it. They know they're doing wrong, and I tell them that if they have to pay for their mistakes, at least let someone else use the cash."

She laughed, but Alfred and Ramona looked at her like they were puzzled. Selling insurance in beer gardens? Ramona thought, "what good is it if a man gains the whole world and loses his soul."

Before Ramona could even say what she was thinking, Alfreda said, "Those jokers have women and kids all over town, but even the worst of them can find somebody they'd like to take care of with a little money when they die. They aren't all bad, Momma, although I bet you think most of them will go straight to hell."

Ramona cracked a smile. Alfreda found a way to make money doing something legal with that crowd she ran with. The girl had spunk.

"You're selling insurance?" asked Alfred, incredulously.

"Top salesman . . . excuse me, saleswoman, with the company," said Ramona.

Alfred puffed out his chest like he took credit for Alfreda's success. "Well, God has answered my prayers," said Alfred. "You've changed your ways. You're down there in town doing respectable work." He put his arm around Alfreda's shoulders. "Come inside, honey, and join us for dinner." He led her up the steps to the hotel, opened the door for her, and led her inside.

The prodigal daughter returned.

Vera graduated on Wednesday and, on Saturday, Emma and John loaded Vera's two trunks and four suitcases full of clothes into John's seven year old Ford truck. The other Marshall children stood on the steps and on the sidewalk waiting for their big sister to leave them. The youngest ones were excited at the prospect of Vera moving so far away, and the older ones were sad. They knew they would miss her; that like Alfreda, once she left, she wasn't coming back. Vera gave each one a big hug goodbye.

As she put her arms around Bobby, he held her tight. "Take care of yourself, Vera. Don't do anything crazy down there."

"You know me, little brother," she whispered in his ear.

"I know, I know," Bobby said as he extended his arms and took a good look at Vera. "Crazy isn't your style . . . bold is."

"Got it," said Vera. She hugged him again.

"You take care of Phyllis," she said. "She's a nice girl, and now that brother of hers is out of the picture, it'll be better than ever for you two."

"I hope so," Bobby said.

It took half an hour for Vera to make it down the line. When she finished with her brothers and sisters, she started on the cousins and friends who had lined up for the big event.

Some of her sisters and cousins started to cry. Vera tried to assure them, although she was fighting back the tears in her own eyes. "I'm only going to Philly, you all. It's not like I won't be back home or the street car won't run you in town anymore."

"Once you leave here, you won't be back," said Valerie, wiping a tear off her cheek.

"Not back to stay, Valerie, but surely to visit," said Vera. She put her hands on her hips, then waved her hands from one end of the group to the other. "Y'all know that I have to leave to get where I'm going. But rest assured of one thing," she said, shaking a finger at them, "when I get there, I'm a bring all y'all with me."

She adjusted her pocketbook and said, "Now, let me get on in this truck and be gone." She turned to John and said, "I'm ready, Pop."

John opened the back passenger door for Vera and then the front door for Emma. He closed the doors behind them and walked over to his side of the car with his head down, trying to keep anyone from seeing the tears welling up in his eyes. His first born, his baby girl was leaving home. No matter if she is grown or has thought that she was for years, she's his first. Now, here he was taking her into town to live with a wild woman. God help her, thought John, as he wiped his cheek with his handkerchief. He also quickly wiped his brow so that anybody who looked would think that he was only wiping the sweat off his face on that hot June day.

Vera stuck her head out the window and yelled, "Bye, everybody. Take care of yourselves" as the old Ford slowly rolled down Welsh Road.

Chapter 12

West Philadelphia 1955 bustled with middle class, striving colored folks. Accomplished striver Alfreda Washington bought herself a three-story brick rowhouse on a relatively quiet tree-lined street and converted the third floor into an apartment. The rent she received from that apartment just about paid for her mortgage, so she could use her money for better things. Like the imported hand-carved pipes that she puffed on constantly, filling the air around her with the sweet smell of burning tobacco. Like the expensive men's hats that she bought once a month and wore every day, her only concession to vanity.

Alfreda lifted up her right hand, placed the pipe in her mouth and took a few puffs. She lifted up her left hand, put the mug to her lips and took a few sips of coffee—black, just about the color of her skin. She leaned her head back on the chair and pushed her thick, black, horn-rimmed glasses up on her head. The two drugs started clearing her head of Saturday night's excesses and working through the rest of her body in time, she hoped, to give her the strength to change out of her bathrobe, slippers and nightgown before Emma and John arrived with Vera. Normally, she dressed as she pleased in her own damned house, but even she had some modesty left when it came to her family.

Not more than an hour ago, she told her overnight guests to get their asses out by noon because her niece was coming to stay with her. She put her crowd on notice that things would be different when Vera came—at least for a while.

Alfreda heard the truck pull into the driveway and snuffed out the pipe. She ran upstairs, threw on a blouse and some pants and ran a comb through her hair. By the time John rang the doorbell, she looked perfectly respectable.

"I'm coming, I'm coming," she said as she ran downstairs and opened the door.

John stood there alone, a black leather steamer trunk leaning against his leg.

"Let me help you with that, John," Alfreda said, reaching for the trunk, instead of him. Alfreda might have stood about 5'4", but she was broad and stocky and had exceeding strength.

"Aw, bush, woman," he said. "I can get this in here by myself. Just tell me where Vera's room is and I'll take it there."

"Second floor, last room on the right," said Alfreda as she brushed past him, dismissing him, looking for Emma and Vera.

John lugged the trunk up the steps. It slid easily on the carpeted steps once he got the right angle.

Vera ran over to Alfreda with open arms and a big smile. "Hi, Aunt Alfreda," she said. "I'm so glad to see you."

"I'm glad to have you here, baby," said Alfreda as she hugged her tightly. "Make yourself at home."

Emma brought up the rear. She always was slow, thought Alfreda. Always complaining about her bad legs and bad feet. Nothing that losing 50 pounds wouldn't cure. Naturally big bones combined with the weight leftover from 10 children sure have taken their toll.

"Do you need any help, Emma?" Alfreda asked, hoping that she'd say no.

"No. My leg's just cramping a little bit after being squished up in that truck. Let me just rub it a bit and bring it back to life," Emma said, reaching down and massaging her left leg.

She massaged the leg and shook out the cramp. Then she started down the walkway with steps that could only be called baby. To what seemed to Alfreda like five minutes later, Emma reached the door.

"Come on in. Let me get you something to drink," said Alfreda.

"Nothing too strong, now," said Emma. "Iced tea or lemonade would be just fine."

Iced tea or lemonade, thought Alfreda. Now she ought to know that I don't keep any of that stuff in my house.

"How about a nice cool glass of water," said Alfreda.

"That would do just fine," said Emma as she fanned herself with her hat.

As she looked around Alfreda's house, Emma had to admit that she was impressed. The house that her sister had brought for herself only was bigger than the one she was lived in with 10 children, now 9, and a husband. Nice furniture, too. The living room couch and loveseat were upholstered in a maroon brocade pattern, and they rested on top of an Oriental rug with the most beautiful burgundies, blues, and greens that Emma had ever seen.

Two mahogany coffee tables graced either side of the couch. Matching crystal lamps with a fringed lampshade sat on each table. Alfreda sure did have good taste in furniture. Emma sat on the couch.

Alfreda carried in the water in a pitcher on a tray with four glasses. She figured that John and Vera would want some water after carrying Vera's things upstairs. She sat on the black leather club chair across from the couch.

Emma took a long sip of water and looked directly at Alfreda. "Take good care of my baby, Alfreda," she said.

"Vera can take care of herself," said Alfreda. "You know that."

"No, I don't know that, Alfreda," Emma said, putting her glass down on the coaster Alfreda laid out on the table, "and she doesn't know what's out there."

"She knows," Alfreda said, "and what she doesn't know, she'll soon find out. You can't keep her from the world."

But I can try, thought Emma.

"I know she'll learn, but I want her to learn on her own. I don't want you or your friends teaching her things she doesn't need to know now or later," Emma said.

"I'm not going to drag Vera anywhere, but I'm not going to babysit her either. When she starts working and has her own money, she can go and do pretty much anything she wants. I'm not going to open doors for her, but I'm not going to stop her from going in them either," Alfreda said.

She leaned closer to Emma and said, "Don't worry. "I told all my friends that things are going to be different around here for a while since my little niece was coming," Alfreda said.

"I'm counting on you, Alfreda," Emma said.

"Now you ought to know not to count on me," Alfreda said. She laughed and walked back to the club chair. She sat down and leaned back. "Count on Vera and count on yourself. If you raised her right, you don't have anything to worry about," she said, turning to the side and putting her feet up on the mahogany coffee table.

Vera bounced into the room and waved her hand in the air with a flourish. "That's it. That's the last of the suitcases. I'm officially moved in." She grabbed a glass of water and sat on the loveseat, all smiles.

John came down the stairs and wiped the sweat off his face.

"Have a glass of water," said Alfreda, handing it to John.

Since everybody had a glass, Alfreda said, "Although this ain't alcohol, I'd like to drink a toast to Vera's new life." She raised her glass and looked at Vera. "I hope you get everything you want, baby."

"Here, here," Vera said.

"God help you," said Emma.

"Here's to my little girl," said John.

Since they'd never been in her house before, Alfreda showed off a bit and took John and Emma on a tour of the house. Ramona's home training ever in her mind, Alfreda served the trio cake and her black coffee that was strong enough to wake the dead, which is what Alfreda was after a Saturday night.

"Come on, John," said Emma. "I've got to get home and check on dinner." She brushed the crumbs off her dress, stood up and held her arms out to Vera. Vera practically ran into them.

"Take care of yourself, baby," Emma said. "Call me if you need anything, hear?"

Vera said, "I'll be fine, Mom. Don't worry about me."

John put his cap on his head while Vera and Emma hugged and waited his turn. Vera ran over to him, and he wrapped his arms around her.

"Best of luck to you, honey," John said. "Let me know how you're doing. And remember, just because you leave home doesn't mean that you can't come back."

"I know, Pop. But I'm here now. And you always told me, if you keep looking back, you'll never get where you're going because you'll never see the path," Vera said.

John lightly tapped Vera on the head with his knuckles. "I'm glad to see that some of what your old Pop told you has sunken in."

More than you'll ever know, thought Vera. My eyes are stuck on straight ahead and don't look back.

Emma hugged Alfreda, and John shook her hand. Alfreda and Vera stood out on the steps and watched as John let Emma in and then drove the old truck down the street. When the truck's rear gate disappeared in a jumble of streetcars and sedans, Vera jumped up in the air and said, "Hallelujah."

At 6 a.m., the alarm clock John gave Vera as a graduation present went off. Vera hopped out of bed and hurried to the bathroom that Alfreda said was all hers. Nobody to share it with, nobody to tell her to hurry up and get out. She couldn't believe the extravagance of having a bathroom all to herself. Even though she could have taken her time washing off, she didn't. She rushed it because she wanted to get the morning paper as soon as she could. When she came downstairs at 6:45, Alfreda was still sleeping. She told Vera that most days she didn't get up until 10 or 11 and didn't get to the office until 12 or 1. That left her plenty of time during the day to do whatever paperwork she had to do before heading out to the bars and beer gardens to see her old customers and to get new ones. She usually stayed out until 11 or 12 at night.

Vera remembered where the coffee was and fixed herself a fresh pot. After eating some toast, she took the key off the table and headed down to the corner store. Vera marveled at how these three story, red, stone twin houses on the street were a lot bigger than the ones in Ardmore. She walked on smooth slate sidewalks under leafy trees giving lots of shade. When Vera got to the corner, she felt a part of all the activity going on around her. At least twelve people stood right at the intersection waiting for the streetcar. Every few seconds, people walked out of the corner store with newspapers, cups of coffee and what looked like hot, sweet rolls.

Time to make her entrance, Vera walked over to the door with faded red lettering that spelled out "Arthur's Stop 'N Shop." Vera raised her head and walked boldly into the corner store, saying good morning to people as she walked pass them. You never know, they might be her neighbors.

She walked over to the cashier and said, "Good morning. I'd like to buy an *Elevator*."

A petite woman who could barely look over the top of the cash register reached into the glass case, took out a newspaper and handed it to Vera. "That will be 5 cents, honey."

Vera knew that. She already had the coin in her hand, and she gave it to her.

Vera then said, "I'd like to introduce myself. I just moved down the street yesterday, and I suspect you'll see me in here a lot. My name is Vera Marshall."

"Why, hello, Vera Marshall," said the woman. "My name is Arthurine Forman. Welcome to my store."

"Arthurine," repeated Vera. "Arthur for short?"

"That's right," said Arthurine. "Doesn't hurt for people to think that a man runs this place. Keeps the riff-raff in line, you know?"

"I can't believe you'd have too much trouble around here. My aunt says this is a nice neighborhood," said Vera.

"Who's your aunt?" Della asked.

"Alfreda Washington," Vera said.

"Alfreda's your aunt? I never heard her talk of any family," Arthurine said.

"Some things don't need talking about," said Vera.

Ain't that the truth, thought Arthurine.

"Well, Alfreda's one of my best customers," Arthurine said. "Did she send you down here?"

"No," said Vera. "I just came in to get the paper. I'm looking for a job. Just graduated from high school last week."

"Do tell!" said Arthurine. "You're younger than you look, honey, and I mean that as a compliment." Other customers now stood behind Vera, giving Arthurine evil looks, waving money and merchandise in the air, trying to get attention.

"Congratulations. Let me take these other customers," she said to Vera, looking past her. "You tell Alfreda hello, you hear?"

"I'll do just that," she said as she ignored the evil eyes and walked out the door.

Vera walked back home, poured herself another cup of coffee and turned immediately to the classified section. It didn't make any sense looking in the daily papers for a job, even though they had about ten times as many listings as the *Elevator*. At least any company that advertised in the *Elevator* knew that the folks who showed up looking for jobs would be colored.

Vera started down the list. It was depressing. Most of the ads for women were for maids and cooks and housekeeping, both in Philadelphia and out on the Main Line. She quickly jumped over those ads to the small section for typists and receptionists. A few colored businesses and professionals needed girls to type 65 words a minute. One ad caught her eye.

"Models wanted. Experience necessary. Harrison's Department Store, 52nd and Market Streets."

"That's the job for me," Vera said. She put the paper down, finished her coffee and went upstairs to get dressed.

The dress had to be something outstanding, but not too revealing, showing just enough to let them know she had more. She selected a navy blue linen dress with a scoop neck that stopped right at her collarbone. White point d'Alencon lace graced the cuffs. She selected a pair of matching white lace gloves. She reached up to the top shelf in her closet and picked out a white straw hat with a navy blue ribbon around the rim. She brushed her hair and twisted it into a french roll. She pulled the pearl earrings out of her jewelry box and clipped them on. She was ready.

Alfreda was fixing breakfast in the kitchen when Vera came downstairs.

"You sure look pretty Vera," she said. "You going to look for a job?"

"Sure am," said Vera. "Harrison's Department Store is looking for models. $2 an hour."

"That's good money for someone just starting out," Alfreda said. "Good luck."

Vera said thank you and started for the door. "Oh, I met Arthurine this morning. She told me to tell you hello."

Here we go, thought Alfreda.

"Is that all she said?" Alfreda asked.

"That's all," Vera said.

Thank God, thought Alfreda. "Arthurine's good people," she said.

CHAPTER 13

Vera walked back down to Arthurine's to catch the streetcar. She took her place among the crowd waiting for the Philadelphia Transportation Company (PTC) Walnut Street, Number 3 Trolley to 52nd Street. An assortment of men in overalls, uniforms with utility company logos and hospital names, a few men in suits and hats, and women in the white maid uniforms of private service, the pink and white uniforms of the hotel maids, and other women dressed like Vera in conservative dresses, hats and white gloves. A few people talked quietly among themselves, but it seemed like most of the others were engaged in animated conversation, laughing, talking loud, and throwing much hands on hips. Giving each other strength for the day and one last chance to be themselves before they had to spend the next eight hours holding it all in.

Vera approached one of the men in a suit. "Excuse me, sir," she said, tilting her head to the side, smiling and batting her long eyelashes. "How much is the fare?"

She honestly didn't know. Vera had been around the city plenty, but she never had to ride public transportation. She always had a ride. Give her a few weeks and she'd have a ride again.

Vera had the 20 cents fare ready when the trolley arrived. She dropped her money into the fare box and moved to the back with the rest of the women who got on first so there'd be room for the men who politely practiced ladies' first. Vera found a seat about half way back next to an elderly lady with a white shirt, black skirt, black flat shoes and her hair pulled back into a bun.

Vera nodded hello, but then ignored the woman and looked out of the window. Whenever she felt the least bit nervous about interviewing for a job she so desperately wanted, she looked around at the other women on the streetcar. Objectively speaking, none of them looked better than her. Some may have been prettier in the face, but only slightly, and they didn't accentuate what they had like Vera did. She knew how to make the best of what God gave her, and what he gave her was pretty good. Why wouldn't a woman want to buy a dress if she thought she could look like Vera—at least a little.

Harrison's was the only colored department store in Philadelphia. The other department stores like John Wanamaker's, Strawbridges & Clothiers, and Gimbel's weren't officially segregated, but colored people weren't welcome there like white. The colored folks cooked the food that the stores served in their elegant dining rooms with fine crystal and silver, but they weren't truly welcome to eat there. Colored people worked as seamstresses and in alterations making dresses and gowns fit perfectly, but they had better think twice about trying them on themselves. Colored people worked as trimmers to decorate the ladies' hats that they dare not put on their hair, hot-combed straight and full of greasy pressing oil and Dixie Peach pomade so that it wouldn't turn back.

But at Harrison's, colored people could shop just like anyone else. Customers entered through a glass front door with the lettering, "Harrison's Department Store—Fine Merchandise for Fine People". The women's department was directly on the left, and the men's department was directly on the right. The beauty salon was situated behind the women's department, and the children's department was to the right of that. The women's cosmetics counter stood almost directly in front of the main door. It held the most extensive selection of hair pomades, hot combs and straightening products in the city. The counter always was crowded with women bewitched by the possibility of transforming their regular, nappy, stiff colored hair into silky wavy hair that moved or at least let a comb slide through it without breaking.

The second floor housed a furniture department that promised fine furniture to those with good credit and for those without, forever layaway with $1 down and $1 a week. The appliance department offered the latest gadgets to those who could pay for them or thought they could. Harrison's Silver Dining Room seated 50 and imitated one of the dining rooms at Wanamaker's with gold paint on the walls and gold tablecloths. Harrison's dining room served the kind of food that you could never find downtown but that always kept it full of customers—greens, corn bread, black eyed peas, fried chicken, smothered chicken and spare ribs.

The Grand Hall was next to the restaurant. The hall was divided by a runway down the center surrounded by either chairs or tables, depending on whether one of the many colored clubs or churches rented the hall for a luncheon, meeting or fashion show. At least once a day, and more often by special request of its best customers, the women's department held a fashion show of its finest merchandise. Colored women from the 400 looked forward to coming down and seeing the latest fashions before they hit the sales floor. And, if a good customer couldn't find that exact gown or dress or other garment that she wanted among the clothes immediately on hand, Harrison's arranged a special showing to see whether anything they could find would meet their customer's requirements. Men and women attended the shows. The women for themselves; the men for their wives or mistresses.

The personnel and credit office was next door to the showroom. Lines for both purposes spilled out into the hallway. Most people needed credit, and a lot more needed a job. Harrison's offered good steady work with decent pay in a comfortable environment—something that was hard for colored folks to come by. Vera couldn't tell whether some of the women in line were there for the modeling job or for sales jobs, but she didn't worry. Lack of confidence was not one of her problems.

Vera strode up to the receptionist's desk and said, "Good Morning. I'm Vera Marshall. I'm here to apply for the modeling job."

"Good morning, Miss Marshall," said the woman behind the desk. "Welcome to Harrison's." Everyone in the store was instructed to be polite. Good customers were worth working for.

The woman picked up a clipboard with some papers attached and handed them to Vera. "Please fill out this application. When you return it to me, I'll have someone interview you."

Vera took the clipboard and sat down next to two other women filling out the same application. When she reached the section asking about previous experience, she didn't want to lie, so she fudged the truth just a bit. "Modeled for Janet Devereaux, owner of the Main Line Modeling School, September and October 1954." Anything more would get her into trouble, she reasoned, and anything less wouldn't get her the job.

She handed the application back to the receptionist and took her seat with the other girls, who were called one by one ahead of her. Each interview took about 15 minutes, and 45 minutes later, the receptionist called out, "You may go in Miss Marshall" after her intercom rang with her instructions.

Vera opened the door to the office of opportunity. The name tag on the desk in front of her said "Mrs. Harrison." Vera tensed, but only ever so slightly, and not so that Mrs. Harrison would notice. Here she was meeting everything she wanted to be: a woman with money, beauty, a successful husband, a business, and membership in the 400.

Vera smiled, thrust out her gloved hand, and said, "Good morning. I'm Vera Marshall and I'd like the honor of being one of your models."

Catherine Harrison smiled and then laughed, "Honor? Miss Marshall," she said. "What a marvelous way of putting it."

"Why it is an honor," Vera said, meaning it. "Not every girl can have the opportunity to model for the largest colored department store in Philadelphia."

"That's exactly true," said Catherine. "Many girls apply for these positions, but few are chosen."

"Have a seat, Miss Marshall," she said, motioning to the imitation Louis XIV arm chair directly across from her desk. "I've looked over your application, and I must say I'm impressed. We don't get many girls here from the Main Line. I see you just graduated from Ardmore High School. That's quite an accomplishment."

"Thank you," said Vera. She thought that an Ardmore High School diploma wasn't so much an accomplishment, but a bridge to get to the other side.

"And you have experience with the Devereaux Modeling Agency. Tell me about that," Mrs. Harrison said.

"Well," said Vera, shifting on the white jacquard upholstered seat. "I modeled three times at the request of Mrs. Devereaux, the owner of the agency." That wasn't exactly a lie, she thought.

"I find it hard to believe that a white agency would use a colored model. Where did you model?" Mrs. Harrison asked.

"In private showings of dresses for selected groups of young women," Vera said. That was the truth. The high school modeling club was private, and the members were young women.

"Not unlike what we do here," said Mrs. Harrison. She leaned back and nodded her head as if she was satisfied with Vera's experience.

"Exactly," said Vera.

"Let me see an example of what you can do," Mrs. Harrison said. She waved her hands in the air as if she was conjuring up a fashion show. "Model for me now, describing your dress as you do."

Vera stood up, walked to the door, and began.

"Our next model is Miss Vera Marshall. Miss Marshall is wearing a navy blue cotton dress with empire sleeves accented by a thin veil of alencon lace at the sleeves and the neckline." As Vera continued modeling and describing her dress, shoes, purse and hat, Mrs. Harrison peered over her bifocals and studied Vera's every turn, twist and flourish. She was impressed with her figure, her apparently effortless carriage, and her flair for putting together an outfit that highlighted her best features and looked absolutely smashing.

When Vera finished with her hands on her hips, her fingers appearing to caress the top of her hip bones, Mrs. Harrison started clapping.

"Bravo, Miss Marshall. I like your style," she said.

Vera smiled and said, genuinely, "Thank you so much." Then she sat down and waited.

Mrs. Harrison took off her glasses and twirled them by the arm. "I'd like to give you a chance, Miss Marshall," said Mrs. Harrison. "We start you off on a probationary period for 30 days to see how you handle the job and how our customers react to you. During that period, you'll do a mix of the retail floor modeling and private showings. You are expected to always look your best, of course. From now on, the beauticians in our salon will style your hair every day and manicure your nails as needed," she said.

Vera's eyes opened wide. She added up in her head the cost of daily hairdressing services and regular manicures and realized that she'd only bring home enough money for car fare.

Mrs. Harrison looked at Vera and smiled. Poor dear simple girl, she thought. "All of these services are at our expense, of course."

The size of Vera's eyes went back to normal. Her mind raced with all the different ways that she would wear her hair now that she had a hairdresser at her beck-and-call.

"You should at all times wear clothes purchased from this store because you are a reflection of Harrison's best 24 hours a day. Most of our employees have a 20% discount on clothes, but yours will be 40% because we want you to showcase our fashions at all times."

Vera bit her tongue to keep from jumping up, clapping her hands, and kissing Mrs. Harrison like she knew her. This job was even better than she imagined. Someone actually encouraged her to buy fine clothes instead of criticizing her. And she could buy the clothes at a discount.

Mrs. Harrison continued, "At the end of the 30 day period, we will speak again about your future with Harrison's. Report here the day after tomorrow at 9 a.m." She put her glasses on, stood up and held out her hand to Vera. "Good luck, Miss Marshall. I hope you have a bright future here at Harrison's." She had no doubt that Vera would, and neither did Vera.

On the escalator down to the first floor, Vera looked like somebody who should be in Haverford—the state mental hospital located on the Main Line—laughing to herself, shaking her head out of disbelief, and smiling, seemingly at nothing or no one in particular. She stopped at the cosmetics counter and bought a new lipstick—Fire Engine Red by Max Factor—to celebrate. She asked the lady behind the counter for a tissue and wiped off the old lipstick. Then she put on two coats of the new, pressed her lips together, and walked out of Harrison's different than when she came in.

CHAPTER 14

Alfreda's car was parked in the driveway when Vera returned. Vera walked into the house shouting, "Aunt Alfreda! I got the job!" Alfreda sat in the kitchen, feet propped up on the table, with a plate of half-eaten fried fish, collard greens and rice in front of her when she heard Vera's yelling.

"Is all that yelling about that job at Harrison's," Alfreda said, truly more interested right now in stopping the yelling rather than hearing about the job. She wasn't used to all that commotion in her house, at least until the weekend. "Come on in here where I can hear you without all that yelling," she said.

"Yes, I'm talking about the job at Harrison's," Vera said, still yelling from the living room. She heard Alfreda, but damned if she didn't have something to yell about, at least once in her life, and she was going to yell no matter whose house it was.

Vera carefully took the hat pin out of her hat and laid it on the couch. One thing she liked about Alfreda's house was that she didn't have to worry about some kids sitting on her things, or getting peanut butter on them, or using them as makeshift footballs. She could leave her things where she pleased without fear that they'd be in no shape for her to want them when she got ready to use them again.

She reached down and eased off her shoes one by one and laid them on the floor in front of the couch. Then wiggling her toes like an excited baby does when somebody is tickling her feet, Vera walked into the kitchen to see Alfreda.

"You got a job, girl?" Alfreda asked again.

"Absolutely," Vera said as she launched into a description of her duties and the perks that went along with it.

"That's cause for celebration," Alfreda said twisting her feet around off the linoleum chair and letting them plop on the ground. "You got your own job. Your own money. I'd say you're really grown now." Alfreda walked over to Vera and hugged her. Then she walked toward the cupboard. Alfreda hid some of her liquor in honor of Emma and John coming to the house; she wasn't sure if Emma would get a notion to snoop around. The spices, flour, sugar and other baking items that Alfreda rarely had use for were right in front of her face when she opened up the cupboard. No casual snoop could see around the tall, fat sugar and flour sacks, and anybody trying to be slick would risk detection by moving the stuff out of the way.

"Let me get this right here," Alfreda said. She took down the flour and sugar, reached in the back of the cupboard and pulled out a bottle of gin.

"I know Emma doesn't let you drink, but there's no harm in a little taste to celebrate your new job," Alfreda said. She pulled two glasses down from the other cabinet. "I'll cut yours with lots of juice if you want."

"I've drank liquor before," Vera said, figuring that she could tell Alfreda what she couldn't tell her mother. "Not much, but I've had a taste."

"Well, then," Alfreda said. "A little taste more won't hurt you."

Alfreda put three ice cubes in the glass, a finger full of gin, filled the rest of it with orange juice and handed it to Vera. For herself, Alfreda just poured the liquor into the glass and held it up.

"Here's to your new job and your new life. May you have everything you want," Alfreda said.

"And then some," added Vera, raising her glass and touching Alfreda's.

Alfreda tilted her head back and let the gin slide down her throat. She closed her eyes, pursed her lips, and then smiled. Alfreda looked as satisfied with that drink as Vera did with a good lover.

Alfreda snapped her head forward, shook it to clear it, and said, "Whoo. That's good."

Vera could hardly taste the liquor in her glass, but the cool drink sure tasted good.

"When do you start?" Alfreda asked, between gulps.

"Day after tomorrow," Vera said. "9 a.m."

"So you have tomorrow off?" Alfreda asked.

"Sure do," said Vera. "One day to get myself together. I'm going to go get my hair and nails done."

Alfreda put down the glass. "Well, if you want to, you can go out with me tonight. I have to visit some customers at some joints on Lancaster Avenue." She shook a bony finger at Vera and said, "It'd be good for you to come along. I want those niggers to know that you're my niece. That way, if they see you on the street around here, they won't give you any shit."

The moment I've been waiting for, thought Vera. "What time should I be ready," she said.

"Be ready at 9," Alfreda said. "I've got to catch those niggers before they drink too much and run out of money. Or sense. Or both."

By 8:30, Vera walked into the front room, ready to go. The clothes she had on that evening couldn't have been more different from what she wore that morning. She filled out every nook and cranny of a red silk jaquard sheath with one inch wide straps and a two inch wide bow at each shoulder. She wore silk because it felt about as smooth as her skin, and some lucky man that evening would realize that.

When she heard the sound of a key turning in the door, Vera stood up to get her pocketbook. Alfreda opened the door, glanced at Vera and said, "Whoa, girl. We're just going to some bars, not to a cabaret. No need for you to wear your finest where we're going."

Vera was incredulous. "This isn't my finest, Aunt Alfreda," said Vera. She ran her hand down the right side of her dress, starting from her breasts to her hem. "This is a date dress. I have real gowns for cabarets."

"Good Lord, girl. Now I see what Emma meant," Alfreda said. As she emptied out her briefcase, she said, "Listen, Vera. I don't have time to be keeping these men off of you." She continued fussing. These young girls are always asking for trouble, she thought. These men don't know how to control themselves. Give them a few drinks, and they lose what little sense they do have. "I've got to collect my money and hook me some new customers. You're going to have to keep those niggers in line yourself, but by the looks of that dress, it seems like you have plenty of experience doing that."

"I can take care of myself, Aunt Alfreda," Vera said. "I'm only trying to attract the right type of man. Anything else, I get rid of."

"Good," Alfreda said as she picked up her briefcase and walked to the door. "You got your work cut out for you."

At 9:10, Alfreda stopped her Cadillac Fleetwood in front of a red brick storefront on Lancaster Avenue with two large picture windows that you couldn't see inside of. On top of the building, a flashing red neon sign in letters a foot high spelled out "Velvet Slim's" and underneath in letters half that size, "Home of the Slim Goodie."

Alfreda put the car in park and said, "Get ready, Vera. It's show time."

A tall husky man in a red jacket hurried around to the front of Alfreda's car and opened her door.

"Good evening, Miss Washington," the man said.

"How ya doing, Tony," Alfreda said. "Is the joint jumping?"

"Just percolating," Tony said. "You know it won't explode until later." He grabbed the top of Alfreda's arm and practically pulled her out of the car, not because he was trying to, but because he had so much strength in one hand, what seemed like an assist to him felt like a tug to everyone else. He looked over at Vera and he said, "I see you have company."

"This is my niece, Vera Marshall," said Alfreda as she stuck her head back in the car so Tony, who leaned over the driver's seat looking at Vera, could hear the introduction. "Just graduated from high school and got a job today, first time out."

Vera held out her hand, slightly angled, as if she expected it to be kissed. It wasn't. Tony shook her hand as he would anyone he just met, and said, "Pleased to meet you."

Vera took her hand back and said, "Likewise."

"Stay right there, Miss Marshall," Tony said, extracting the top half of his body from the car. "I'll be right over to open your door."

"I had no intentions of leaving," Vera said, smiling.

Tony followed Alfreda to the sidewalk and opened Vera's door. He put out his hand, touched Vera's arm, and let his hand rest there long enough for Vera to know that he wasn't just doing his job. "That sure is a beautiful dress you have on, Miss Marshall," he said. "Bright red, just like a siren . . . or is it a stop sign."

Vera raised her eyebrows. "That depends on who's looking," she said.

Damn her, thought Alfreda. It's starting already. "Come on, come on," Alfreda said. "Enough of the chitchat. Let's get inside."

Tony didn't take his eyes off Vera, which took some doing, since he stood in front of her and had to walk backwards to reach the door. He made it without stumbling, though, and he reached behind him and opened the heavy wooden doors. "Have a good evening," he said, looking right at Vera. "I'll be right here when you leave."

"Well then I'll see you later," Vera said.

Velvet Slim did a lot of things to excess, but lighting the inside of his club was not one of them. It took Vera a few minutes to get accustomed to the dim lighting.

She looked like Velvet Slim's decor—red on black. Red vinyl covered the tables. Red leather covered the chairs. The surface of the bar that stretched across the left wall was red, marked by the occasional black spot where a drunk or a player in the heat of action left a cigarette burning too long. Each of the 20 or so tables for two was topped by a small lamp with a red and gold lampshade.

Alfreda walked in like she owned the place. Everybody recognized her, and people shouted greetings from all over the club.

Alfreda said to the maitre d', who stood behind a small podium that separated the tables from the bar area, "Frank, I'll have a table tonight. This here's my niece, Vera. We're celebrating tonight. She just got a job."

"Another working girl," said Frank. "Congratulations." Frank adjusted the red carnation in his black suit and led Alfreda and Vera down three steps to a table in the center. The bartender caught sight of Vera in her red dress as he finished wiping down the counter and said, "Lord have mercy. Check that out." The boys at the bar turned around and put their drinks down. They watched Vera strut her stuff until she sat down at her table. So did every other man . . . and woman . . . in the club. The women looked only long enough to size up Vera as a threat and do something to get their men to turn back and look at them.

"Send over a bottle of good champagne," Alfreda said to Frank. "You know I don't normally drink that stuff, so just send me over something that Velvet himself would drink." Then she thought a few seconds and said, "Better yet, make it something that Mrs. Velvet would drink."

Frank didn't bother to ask Vera's age although he assumed that she was under 21 just having graduated from high school. But he figured that anybody with a body like that was old enough to handle whatever she would find in a bar.

As Alfreda and Vera waited for the champagne, news of Vera's arrival traveled to the private poker game in the back room. Someone whispered into Velvet's ear to go out front and see what Alfreda Washington was trying to pass off as her niece. As bad as Alfreda looked and as good as Vera looked, it was hard to believe that they came from the same family. Velvet knew that this girl must be something special because his men knew not to disturb his game except for an emergency, like the cops or a fight or someone trying to steal his money, which didn't happen very often. Velvet was tall and smooth and as fine as Vera's favorite singer, Arthur Prysock, but he could fight like Joe Lewis and cut like a butcher.

Velvet threw down his hand. "Straight flush. Game's over fellas. Next one in 15 minutes." Velvet scooped his hands around the tables, collecting his winnings from the group of lawyers who were smart enough to get the most guilty criminal out of jail, but too dumb to quit while they were ahead. They all owed Velvet money from games that they just had to play. And Velvet never turned away a chance to make money, even if sometimes it was only in the book of gambling debts that he meticulously kept in his office.

Velvet handed the money to an employee who knew that Velvet knew exactly how much was in that pile and would count it on his return. Then Velvet stood up and parted the red curtain that separated the back room from the front.

Nobody had to point out Vera to him. His eyes scanned the room in less than 30 seconds, taking in every detail—a necessary survival skill in a world of gangsters and lowlifes. Vera was holding a champagne glass to her lips when he saw her. Red lips just touched the rim, head tilted slightly back. He immediately wished that she was holding a part of him instead of that champagne glass.

Velvet straightened his tie, smoothed down his wavy, conked hair, walked over to the table and said, "Good evening Alfreda. How are you doing tonight?"

"Fine," said Alfreda, pausing because she knew Velvet didn't come over to the table to see her. Velvet looked directly into Vera's eyes and said to Alfreda, "I hear this young lady's your niece."

"You hear right, Velvet. I knew you'd be out here soon. This here is Vera Marshall, my niece who just came to live with me. Vera, this is Velvet Johnson, the proprietor of this esteemed establishment," she said as she waved her hand around the room.

Vera held out her hand again like she expected it to be kissed, and Velvet didn't disappoint. He took Vera's hand in his, lowered his head and placed his lips on it as gentle as a butterfly landing on a flower. "Pleased to meet you Miss Marshall."

"Good God," groaned Alfreda. "You're really turning on the charm."

"I have good reason to, Alfreda," said Velvet, smiling at Vera.

"Thank you, Mr. Johnson. It's a pleasure to meet you, too," Vera said, not pulling her hand away like a lady would.

"Call me Velvet," he said.

"And call me Vera," she said.

Alfreda sucked her teeth. "It's your own damn club, Velvet, so you might as well have a seat instead of standing there gawking at Vera," she said.

Velvet started to pull over another chair.

"Don't bother," said Alfreda, standing up. "Take this one." She picked up her briefcase and said, "I can see you'll be well occupied for a little while, Vera. At least with Velvet here, I know none of these other niggers will bother you. I'm going to go make my rounds," She drained her champagne glass and walked away.

Velvet pulled the chair closer to Vera. "Your aunt sure is some character. But she's good people. Tough and hardworking. I like that."

Vera let Velvet go on talking as she took in every detail of this man who was a living legend. Every colored person in the Philadelphia area knew of Velvet Slim's. His club was a cut above those North Philadelphia jazz joints. Most people attributed that to Velvet being a cut above most men—taller than most and finer than most with the wavy hair, dark skin, and make-you-wet-in-your-panties voice like Arthur Prysock. Everything at Velvet's was first class because he knew he had to do something different to draw the folks away from North Philly.

Many a head got bent after drinking one two many Slim Goodies, a volatile combination of gin, vodka, tequila, lemon juice and rum that Velvet concocted that always was served in a tall, slim, frosted glass. It went down smooth and hit hard. Customers thought it was a mix of the dark liquors—bourbon, scotch, whiskey—because Velvet added a few drops of dark food coloring. Many tried but none could ever duplicate the drink. Imbibers all over Philly tried to duplicate the Slim Goodie but couldn't. Only Velvet knew the precise measurements. He mixed a big batch every evening before the bar opened and left it for the bartender. Besides the card games that went on from opening to way past closing in the back room, Velvet made his money off the Slim Goodie.

Velvet wasn't a gangster, but he consorted with them and knew how to keep them in line—hire a few for security and don't take any shit yourself. Velvet could shoot and cut if he had to, but he rarely had to. Anyone who had seen or heard about any of his victims knew that Velvet was not a man to be messed with.

Vera liked that.

Vera told Velvet about her job. He poured her another glass of champagne and toasted her. One of his employees approached the table, whispered in Velvet's ear, and he stood up. He took Vera's hand and said, "Excuse me, Vera. I hate to leave you, but I have some important business to take care of." No woman, not even one as fine as Vera, was worth missing a card game for, especially when his luck was running good.

He leaned down and put his arm around the back of her chair, his hand lightly touching the skin on her back. He put his face so close to Vera's that she could feel the heat of his breath and smell every drop of his cologne.

His lips weren't an inch from her ear when he said, "I'm sure I'll see you again, Vera. In fact, you can count on it."

He walked away. She poured herself another glass of champagne and took a few sips to cool down.

CHAPTER 15

A sliver of morning sun shined into the bathroom where Vera knelt in front of the toilet like she was praying to the God of the Young and Dumb to cure her hangover.

Alfreda yelled to Vera through the closed door, "You have to learn to handle your liquor better than that."

Vera called out weakly, "I never drank that much before."

That I could tell, thought Alfreda.

She leaned against the door so that she didn't have to yell for Vera to hear her, knowing that a loud voice is the last thing a hungover drunk wants to hear. In her wise old aunt voice, Alfreda said, "the secret to drinking is putting some food in your stomach before you leave home. Don't go out drinking thinking that you'll eat when you get there because it seems like there's always time for drinking but never enough time for eating. Give that liquor something to rest on so it doesn't start eating up the inside of your stomach, and you'll be fine."

Vera let Alfreda's words sink in slowly because that was the only speed working that morning, except when she vomited. That came fast and furious.

"I'll keep that in mind next time," Vera said. "But bad as I feel there may not be a next time."

Alfreda chuckled. "There'll be a next time, believe me. Much as you liked being in that club, there'll be a next time."

She leaned up off the door and said, "I'm going to haul my colored ass to work now. Call me if you need anything. Otherwise, get some rest. You'll need it for tomorrow."

Vera pulled herself up, straightened out her bathrobe, teetered to the door and opened it. "I sure do need the sleep. It seems like every time I put my head down and closed my eyes last night my head started swimming so I just propped the pillows up behind me and sat straight up, staring ahead. I don't know when I finally went off to sleep, but it didn't last long before I felt the light on my eyes and had to wake up. Now, I'm going right back up there, pull those shades and get back in bed," Vera said.

"Always worked for me," Alfreda said, as she went to her room to get dressed.

It was five o'clock that evening before Vera woke up. The churning in her stomach had subsided, and she could stand up straight without thinking that she was tipping over. What kind of model would she make if she couldn't walk straight, she thought.

Vera spent the rest of the evening getting herself ready for work. She selected another conservative dress from her collection, starched and ironed it, and picked out another pair of lace gloves and ironed those. She polished her shoes and buffed them until she could clearly see her reflection. She spent close to an hour placing pincurls in her hair so that it would be curved, curly and bouncy when she let it out in the morning. Then she carefully laid out her emery board, orange stick, cotton balls, buffer and nail polish and went to work on her toenails. She didn't know whether she'd be asked to model swim wear or other clothing that would require a peek at her bare feet, so she had to have them looking good.

When the toenails showed a perfect red, she went to work on the fingernails, buffing and polishing until they looked wet and hard. She took the blue ice eye pack out of the freezer and strapped it across her head. She laid down for 30 minutes feeling the cool plastic against her eyes, waiting for it to do its job and rid her eyes of all traces of puffiness and last night's excesses. It worked.

By 9 p.m. when Alfreda came home to get ready for her night rounds, Vera was in bed asleep, hair tied up in a silk scarf, black satin mask over her eyes.

The streetcar stopped right in front of Harrison's. Vera got off with about ten other people and walked through a small alleyway to the employee entrance in the back. My dreams are one step closer to coming true, she thought. All of the other people waiting in line to punch in mostly had on the blue and white striped dresses or white shirts with blue and white striped ties and navy blue pants that every Harrison's employee, except the models, was required to wear. The models could wear anything they wanted to work; they just had to look the part. And Vera did, judging by the looks she got from the other people standing in line.

"You must be a model," said one woman as she shuffled towards the time clock. "Never seen you before, though. Are you new?"

"This is my first day," Vera said proudly. "My name is Vera Marshall." She stuck out her hand, the woman stuck out hers, and they shook hands.

"Well, good luck to you, Miss Marshall," the lady said. "I'm proud of you model girls. You all look as good as any of those white models you see in the fashion magazines. I like to see our people get ahead, especially you young women. More power to you, I always say." She picked up a punch card and stuck it in the slot on the time card machine and said, "See you around."

Vera smiled, picked up her card, and punched it in. She walked to the middle of the store and rode the escalator to the top floor. She walked down a long hallway dotted by settees with pink brocade upholstery gathered with matching buttons every few inches and gold trim around the edges. One settee was placed outside of each of four private showing rooms named after a place the clients wanted to be— Park Avenue Suite, Salon de Paris, Beverly Hills Cabana, and Rittenhouse Square, an area in Philadelphia that was surrounded on four sides by some of the city's most expensive townhouses and apartments. The names were different, but the insides were the same. Bubblegum pink walls. A gold and crystal chandelier in the middle of the ceiling. Six high back chairs with pink and gold striped fabric, three chairs in the front row and three in the back.

Vera opened the door marked private at the end of the hall. She walked up to the French provincial desk, white with gold leaf. The receptionist looked at Vera and said, "You must be Vera. I'm Charlene. I run the modeling salon," she said. She stood up and thrust out her hand, "I'm glad to meet you. And you're every bit as beautiful as Mrs. Harrison described."

"Thanks ever so," Vera said, just like Marilyn Monroe.

"Let me show you around," Charlene said.

She led Vera down a pink and white hallway past five dressing rooms with wooden doors and names painted on in cursive writing and gold paint. Vera noticed a few of the names: Miss Johnson, Miss Washington. At the end of the hallway, Charlene said, "This will be yours."

It read, "Miss Marshall."

Vera just wanted to stop and stare at her name on that beautiful pink door, but Charlene opened it and showed Vera inside. There was a vanity that looked like a smaller replica of the desk out front with the white and gold leaf, a brass vanity chair with a white and pink faux leather upholstered seat, a clothing rack, three full length mirrors so the outfits could be seen from any angle, and a white overstuffed loveseat.

Charlene explained, "On top of the vanity, as you can see, is a selection of fine perfumes and body lotions. We want you to smell good and look good as you model our clothes, and these are the only approved fragrances and lotions you can use. Chanel. Balenciaga and Guerlain, which I notice you're already wearing. They smell good on almost everyone."

Opening the top right hand vanity drawer, Charlene continued, "You have a comb and brush set if your hair needs any minor repairs or last minute touch ups that do not require a trip to the beauty salon. Otherwise, the operators in the beauty salon are instructed to give the models priority for any of their styling needs. The success of our modeling operation leads to the overall success of our store and everyone is invested in your looking good."

"This drawer," she said, opening the one at bottom right, "has an assortment of hosiery—Mrs. Harrison noted what shade she thought would work for you—and a half slip. You'll be measured for bra size and given a collection of bras in white, black, tan, and brown, and slips to match. You may purchase your own underpants, using your discount, of course."

"Any questions?" Charlene asked.

"None so far," Vera said.

"Good, let's go to the showroom," Charlene said, turning around and heading down another hallway.

The showroom was 20' x 20', each wall lined with dresses, coats, shoes, hats, gloves, bathing suits, shirts, blouses, skirts, and gowns. The middle of the room held four round platforms that looked like the kind the circus performers tried to get the animals to jump up on.

"This is where the clothing that you will model is selected. Usually, I select what's right for you to model. We'll sometimes ask you to get on one of these platforms and hold the garment in front of you or put it on in your dressing room and come back, so that we can see how the garment will look. This is usually only until we work with you long enough to know what looks best on you, although looking at you, it seems like everything will look good on you," Charlene said.

She continued, "I have two dressers who assist me in making sure that your outfit is just right. They help select the accessories, make sure the buttons are properly buttoned, seams straight, that sort of thing. You'll meet them later."

"Today, you'll be doing in-store modeling," Charlene said. "As I'm sure Mrs. Harrison explained, that's when you function as a traveling mannequin. You'll be walking around the store modeling dresses with a card in front of you that has the name of the designer and the price of the dress. We like our customers to know how much these dresses cost, unlike some of the stores downtown which only tell you the name of the designer. The customers that can afford it will buy it, and the ones who can't afford it will work for the day when they can. You'd be surprised at how many customers we have who said they saw the dress while they were walking in the store and saved up for weeks until they had the precise amount. Here at Harrison's we want to let our people know that nothing is out of their reach if they are willing to work hard to get it."

Charlene then asked Vera to stand on one of the platforms. She walked around her slowly, checking her out with eyes as intent as any man's. Vera got a bit uncomfortable when Charlene started feeling her body, but Charlene explained that she was just trying to get a real working sense of Vera's proportions. Charlene called in someone from lingerie was to measure Vera's chest, waist and buttocks. She appeared a few minutes later with the most gorgeous collection of lingerie that Vera had ever seen, and Vera always thought that she bought herself nice drawers. Charlene explained that they wanted the models to feel pampered, sexy and at their absolute best in their clothes because that shows through as they model them.

"You'll be wearing an assortment of clothes," Charlene said. "Some of them will range from a dress that most of our customers could buy to wear to church to ball gowns."

Charlene selected four outfits. "Take these to your dressing room, hang them up, and put on the Sunday church dress. We'll start with that and move up to the ball gown. Then walk slowly through the store, making sure your display card is always visible. If anybody asks you questions as to where they can find the dress, the information is on the back. Read it before you start out, but if you forget, just look at the card. There's also other information on the dress in case anyone asks."

Vera took the outfits to her dressing room, careful that nothing dragged on the floor. She closed the door behind her and jumped up in the air.

Vera saw some of the other models in passing as they scurried in and out of their dressing rooms. "Hi, I'm Vera Marshall. I just started today," was about all she had time to say. And all they had time to do was call their names and say, "pleased to meet you" before they were off to their next showing.

Vera felt like a movie star, not just any movie star, but her favorite, Dorothy Dandridge, walking around the store showing off Harrison's finest. Men and women stopped dead in their tracks as she came by, parting like the Red Sea to let her pass. Every so often a lady or gentleman would come closer to see the price tag and walk away. Vera smiled broadly throughout. Sometimes a customer wanted to feel the dress' material. Charlene told

Vera that if a customer wanted a feel, pull the skirt to one side and let her feel that.

When Vera put on the ball gown, Charlene said, "Spend a lot of time in the Fifth Avenue Shop, which is finer women's fashions, and the Gallant Gents' shop, which is our high end men's fashions. Those women can afford this dress, and the men who can afford it will be up here buying it for their wives or mistresses before you get back up to change your clothes."

Vera walked through the Fifth Avenue Shops to the "oohs" and "aahs" of women gazing at the gold lame full-length clinging sheath, gold pumps, and gold evening bag. Vera looked like the Greek Goddess Venus de Milo; one of the stylists from the beauty salon pinned her hair into a bun.

On her way to the Gallant Gents' shop, she heard someone behind her say, "Where can I purchase that lovely dress, young lady." She turned around with all the flair she had, leaning with one hip and sliding the other into place. She faced Velvet head on. "You look like 18 carat gold, baby," he said. "Soft, rare and high quality."

"Why thank you, sir," Vera said, not sure who could overhear them. She didn't want these people to know her business. "I wondered how long it would take you to show up," she whispered.

"Oh you did, did you?" Velvet said, laughing. "You're pretty sure of yourself aren't you?" he asked.

"Not me," Vera said, "I was pretty sure of you."

Velvet burst out laughing loud enough so that even more eyes turned in Vera's direction. "You sure are a sassy young girl," he said.

"I'm not a girl," Vera said, looking him dead in the face. "And if sassy means confident, then that's me."

She started walking away.

Velvet grabbed her arm and said, "Whoa, now, where're you going?"

Vera looked around nervously. She enjoyed playing with Velvet, but she couldn't play any longer. "Let go, Velvet. I'm working. I have to keep moving. I don't want to get fired my first day out. I can't stand here talking to you," she said, "unless of course you have some questions about the gown."

He let go his grip and said, "Why don't you tell me about it. And don't leave anything out. I've got nothing but time for you."

Vera ignored that last remark and started describing the dress, loud enough so that others could hear too. When she was finished, she said "thank you for listening" and started walking again.

"Now wait, honey," Velvet said, taking off after her. "Don't just leave me standing here."

Vera kept walking. "You're going to get me fired, Velvet, if you stop me from moving around. He trailed along right behind her, just like she wanted. Nothing like testing a man to see how much he really wanted you. She had this man following her around the store like he was a dog and she was a bone.

"What if I wanted to purchase that gown," he said.

Vera stopped and turned around. "The gown can be purchased on the 3rd Floor in Evening Wear. $49.99."

"But I don't know your size," Velvet said, looking at Vera's proportions like he wanted to measure her with his hands right then and there.

"Eight," she said, and walked to another department.

At 5:45, Vera's first day ended. Charlene congratulated her on a good first day. Three people had purchased the gold gown, and ten ladies bought the Sunday church dress. They even asked for the same accessories that Vera had on hoping, no doubt, to look like her when they put it all together.

Vera didn't see Velvet after she left him standing in the aisle, but she had no doubt that she would see him soon. She changed back into her clothes, walked down to the employee entrance and punched out. She started walking to Market Street to catch the trolley, but looked in the direction of the honking that all the employees heard as soon as they stepped outside. All heads turned in the direction of the white Cadillac Eldorado convertible sprawled across three slots in the parking lot. When Vera looked, she recognized Tony, the valet from Velvet's club, standing next to the car. He called out, "Miss Marshall, Miss Vera Marshall." Vera walked over.

"Velvet sent me," Tony said, raising his eyebrows as if to say, I don't approve, but I work for him, so what can I do.

"He said a lady fine as you doesn't need to be taking the trolley. She needs to be riding in style," Tony said. He used his hand to show Vera the car, as if he didn't recognize style when she saw it.

Vera just looked.

"Will you get in, Miss Marshall, or will you get me fired?" Tony asked with a sheepish grin.

"Can't stand to see a man beg," Vera said, lying. "I'll get in." Tony opened the door to the back seat. Even in the Cadillac's huge back seat, there almost wasn't enough room for her. A huge white Harrison's box with a gold ribbon took up 90% of the back seat. Vera opened the card on top with her name, and it read, "Wear it tonight."

She lifted off the box top, pretty sure of what was inside. The gold lame ball gown, size 8.

Vera tapped Tony on the back of the neck and asked, "What does your boss mean by 'wear it tonight.'"

"He wants me to pick you up tonight at 8 o'clock and bring you to the club," Tony said as he pulled out of the lot and on to Market Street.

"Just like that?" Vera asked. Oh no. Time to take this man to school even if he does own one of the biggest clubs in town. She leaned close to Tony's ear so he could hear every word over Nat King Cole's "Answer Me My Love" that played on the radio. "Tell your boss that I'm not going to be running the streets, sitting up in a nightclub, drinking liquor all night when I've got to go to work the next day—even if he did buy me this ballgown."

"Oh, so you're playing hard to get," Tony said.

"Who's playing?" Vera asked, as she sat back and watched the huge maple trees on Alfreda's street come into view.

CHAPTER 16

Tony dropped off Vera at Alfreda's to the stares of the neighbors she had yet to meet. While she didn't like Velvet's pretensions, she liked his car and took her time getting out. Head up, shoulders erect, she walked toward the door, leaving the gown on the seat.

She went upstairs, changed into a form-fitting white blouse, half unbuttoned, shirt tails tied in the front, black capri pants and walked back downstairs to fix her dinner. She was seated in the front room eating cherry pie and reading the latest issue of *Jet* magazine when the doorbell rang. She thought maybe it was Alfreda, too lazy to look for her key, so she opened the door. Velvet was leaning against the door jam, resting on one arm and one foot.

"I thought you liked the dress," said Velvet. He looked resplendent in a white linen suit, white leather shoes, and white straw hat with black brim.

"You thought right," said Vera. She eyed Velvet with one hand on the doorknob and one hand on her hip.

"Then why won't you wear it," said Velvet.

"I won't wear it on demand," she said.

"What demand?" said Velvet. He threw his hands up in the air like he was fed up. "I buy you a fancy dress and ask you to wear it to the club, to let me see you in it. What's wrong with that?"

He shifted from one side to the other and looked around at the neighbors out on their porches looking at him. Velvet raised his voice and said, "And do I have to stand out here in the street?" He looked around and now said in a whisper, "People know me, you know. Aren't you going to invite me in?"

Vera saw the crowd that gathered around Velvet's car. I don't even know these people yet, so I sure don't want them knowing my business before they know me, Vera thought. "Come in," she said, opening the screen door and letting him pass through.

Velvet walked into the front room, took his hat off like his Daddy always taught him to do in someone's home, and leaned against the sideboard waiting for Vera to ask him to sit down. She didn't.

"Back to your question," Vera said. "What's wrong is that I'm not at your beck and call just because you buy me a fancy gown. You can't throw stuff at me, Velvet, and expect me to jump. I may be young, but I'm not dumb."

Nothing beats a failure but a try, Velvet thought, and I'm one to keep trying. Sensing her mood, he said, "I didn't expect you to jump at nothing."

"Yes you did," Vera said. "Sending that car for me, having Tony deliver your messages." She walked to the other side of the room and looked at Velvet with fire in her eyes.

He liked that.

"If you want to ask me out, ask me yourself," Vera said. "Don't send somebody else to do the work for you."

"Oh, I get it," Velvet said as he put his hat down on the sideboard. He bowed like he was meeting the Queen of England. He got down on his hands and knees and said "Would you do me the honor of coming to the club tonight?"

Vera looked at him sincerely. Here she had one of the most successful nightclub owners on his knees, begging for her company. She had him just where she wanted him, for now.

"No," said Vera.

Velvet threw up his hands again in exasperation. "I don't get it," he said. "You just asked me to ask you out and then you tell me no." He wasn't used to any woman telling him no, especially a girl young enough to be his daughter. When he asked a woman out, the first word out of her mouth was "yes" and the second word was usually "sir". This young girl was breaking the rules.

"Wrong," said Vera. "I said if you want to ask me out, do it yourself. I didn't say that I'd say yes."

Thinking back, Velvet thought that's true. The girl was going to go and get literal on him.

"You sure are sassy for a young girl," he said.

"That's the only way to be, isn't it?" Vera said.

"Sassy will only get you so far, Vera," Velvet said.

Velvet smoothed the lapels on his coat. "You can't just be sassy. You've got to be smart. You've got the first, and I do like that in a woman. Let's hope you have the second."

He walked over to the sideboard to pick up his hat. "But I'm not one to beg, darling, or to stay where I'm not wanted. You're a fine woman who's bound to go far if you keep your head on straight." As he headed towards the door, he said, "Don't be a stranger around the club, honey, you hear?" He opened the door, turned to face Vera and said, "I'm a keep my eye on you."

Same as she did every day for the past week, Vera walked home from the trolley smiling and speaking to almost everyone she saw. She was happy; Charlene said that her first week couldn't have gone any better. When she walked into the house, she threw her pocketbook down on the sideboard and went straight upstairs to take off her dress and change into something more comfortable—a high class version of the house dress that most women wore, except hers had a halter top and a tight fit.

She looked in the refrigerator, pulled out the chicken legs she put in to thaw the night before and walked to the cabinet to get the flour, cornmeal, and spices she needed to fry the chicken. She started mixing them up when Alfreda came through the front door.

"God knows it's hot out there," Alfreda said. She pulled on the white handkerchief that stuck out of the side of her pocketbook all summer long and wiped her forehead. "I've got to take these stockings off before they burn my legs," she said, plopping down in the chair, throwing up her skirt and unhooking the stockings from her garter.

"So how's your second week going?" Alfreda asked.

"Just great," Vera said. "I modeled around the store most of the afternoon, even got to wear a sharp satin cocktail dress."

"Well go on gal," Alfreda said.

Alfreda pulled some papers out of her briefcase and spread them across the table. "Let's see," she said talking to herself. "Who do I need to see tonight?"

Vera threw some chicken into the hot oil and stood with her hands on her hips waiting for the first side to brown. As good as she felt about her day, she wanted to keep the good feeling going. Sitting home in Alfreda's empty house night after night with no one to talk to did not suit her. Going out, mingling with people, and flirting with men did. All she was going to get by being in that house alone was tired and frustrated. What was the point of living in town if you weren't going to out on the town. And besides, she wasn't used to being alone. Much as she hated to admit it, she missed her brothers and sisters and the energy that brought to four cold, bare walls.

"Can I go with you again?" Vera asked Alfreda in a soft voice like she knew there was something wrong in her asking.

"You wanna go out?" Alfreda asked. "How do you figure that you're going to go out drinking and partying get up and go to work tomorrow? Remember all the trouble you had last time?"

"I'm not gonna drink," Vera said as she turned the chicken. "I just want to get out of the house. It's boring when you're not here."

"Can't stand the sound of your own voice, huh?" Alfreda said.

"It's not that," Vera said. "It's that there's more out there than there is in here."

"That's for sure," Alfreda said.

After dinner, Vera put on a blue sateen linen dress with spaghetti straps and let her hair hang down in curls.

Alfreda just looked at her and said, "Let's go get what's ours to get."

Alfreda drove down City Line Avenue to Lincoln Drive, up Johnson Street to Germantown—another community of up and coming colored folks. When they stepped out, they went to Germantown Avenue. From the Club Nile at the north end to the Beehive at the south, Vera caused a commotion everywhere she went.

When Vera walked into the Club Nile, the group of men standing around the bar near the front door parted like the Red Sea. Alfreda walked through first.

"Don't stand around gawking, y'all," she said. "This here's my niece, Vera. Watch yourselves."

Alfreda knew who she had to see and started walking around the club, pulling out forms for people to sign and giving receipts to others for the dollar or two she collected.

All the men at the bar hopped off their stools. "Here's a seat for you Vera," one said. "Sit here, lovely," said another. "Let me help you up on the stool," said a third.

Vera examined each man quickly, and took the stool of the nicest looking one. No sense starting out the evening obligated to an ugly man, she thought.

"Here you go, darling," said the lucky man as he helped Vera up on the stool. "Can I buy you a drink?"

"Ginger ale," Vera said.

"Oh, a teetotaler," he said. "That's something we don't see too much of around here—a lady in a bar who doesn't drink."

"It's not that I don't drink," Vera said. "I'm not drinking tonight. I have to work tomorrow."

"Don't we all," he said.

Vera laughed.

As Alfreda went from table to table writing receipts, collecting money and signing up new customers, Vera stayed at the bar talking with the guys.

She quickly learned all of their names because they rushed to introduce themselves. She loved the attention and the bar talk.

Some of the men came on to her, but she played them off. Nobody really met her standards as far as looks went, so she kept things on the "let's be friends" tip, and they just talked. The men played the dozens with each other, hurling insults back and forth over Vera's head. They told jokes. They laughed. They talked about their jobs, their wives, and the world. Vera liked the conversation and the comedy.

"Come on gal, let's get out of here," Alfreda said as she approached Vera who was laughing with her group of admirers. "We have other spots to hit."

"I've never known you to be a party pooper," one of the regulars said to Alfreda.

"Hush up," Alfreda said. "If this is how you niggers party, you're pitiful." The party crowd howled with laughter.

Vera took a few gulps of her soda to finish it off. "It's time to go, fellas," Vera said. "But I'll be back."

"And I'll be waiting," said one of the regulars.

"Don't nobody want you," said another, and another round of the dozens began.

Alfreda and Vera left the Nile and went to another club about three blocks away. The only thing that changed was the location. Alfreda worked the crowd and Vera wowed them, drinking ginger ale as she went. But when Alfreda collected all the money she had to and signed up all the new customers she was going to, she took a seat at the bar, too, except she drank scotch and water, not ginger ale. Her stories were every bit as bold and funny and raunchy as the men.

When they got home, Vera said, "That sure was fun. I want to go out with you every night."

Alfreda said, "As long as you don't drink, I guess you'll be alright. You can go along with me whenever you want."

Vera continued her pattern of modeling to perfection every day and hitting the clubs with Alfreda every night. So far, she hadn't found a man who she was interested in although plenty of men were interested in her. She turned all those potential suitors into drinking buddies and she had them at clubs all over Philadelphia.

Friday night, as Alfreda put some hot sauce on Vera's fried flounder, Alfreda told Vera, "I've been keeping things quiet around this house for your benefit and out of some respect for the fact that you're my sister's child. But that shit's about to end. It's too damn quiet around here."

She pulled a fish bone out of her mouth before she went on. "Before you moved in, I told my usual crowd to lay low for a while. See, on the weekends, it's usually like party time at Grand Central Station around here with folks coming in and out. But now that I see that you like partying as much as I do, I think it's time to start it up again."

Vera knew she had made the right decision in coming to live with Alfreda. "Sound's good to me," Vera said.

"Good," said Alfreda. "We're going to party in here tomorrow night," Alfreda said. "I think you'll enjoy it."

CHAPTER 17

Saturday at work, Vera modeled in her first fashion show. She was one of the regular models, but she got more applause than all of the others, even the last model who was supposed to steal the show in a blockbuster outfit.

Charlene rushed to Vera's dressing room after the show. "You were fantastic. They loved you," she said.

"Thank you very much," Vera said. "I gave them by best." Which she had. She knew that some of the 400 women that she had admired for years on the pages of the *Elevator* would be watching her, and she wanted to make a good impression. Someday she would be one of them.

Charlene said, "I'm going to put you in the private showing rooms next week most of the time. You need to be before our best customers."

Vera left that day with her head so high in the clouds that somebody who didn't know her would think that she was high siddidy. She had all the more reason to party hardy and celebrate that night.

By the time Vera got home, Alfreda was setting up for the party. She pushed most of the living room furniture up against the side walls. "My crowd likes to dance," she told Vera, "so I've got to give them some room."

She put a plastic tablecloth on the dining room table. "No sense in using my good linen," she said. "The way these niggers get to spilling things after they've had a few drinks, I learned real quick to save the good stuff."

Arthurine catered all of Alfreda's parties because Alfreda wasn't going to take the time to cook for a crowd. Plus lots of times she didn't know

106

when the crowd was coming. If some of her friends drove by and wanted to stop in, Alfreda was ready to party and a phone call to Arthurine would get her all the food she needed. Arthurine arrived with two of her workers and foil-wrapped trays full of barbequed spare ribs, potato salad, greens, and corn bread. Alfreda set up the liquor up on the side table in the kitchen.

Alfreda pulled her records out from under the cabinet and put them on the table next to the large, floor model record player in the living room. As she did every time she had a party, she prayed her people didn't bump into it too much. She hated for her records to get scratched, but she always went out and bought more if they did.

As Arthurine got everything set up downstairs, Alfreda and Vera went upstairs to get dressed. Vera hoped that she would meet a decent man tonight. She hadn't gotten any since she left Billy Patterson in Ardmore, and it was long past time to find someone else to fill that void. All she wanted to find was a man who looked good in the face, had a body made for loving, money in his pocket and even more in his bank account, and entree into the world she wanted to inhabit.

At 9 o'clock, everything was ready.

Alfreda said, "Party time," and raised her glass of scotch and water.

"Amen to that," said Vera. She raised a glass of bourbon and ginger ale, her now favorite drink. When the bartenders at the Beehive suggested that she put a little bourbon in it after all those nights of drinking ginger ale, Vera obliged. That quickly became her drink of choice, except when she was at Velvet's because she liked a Slim Goodie as much as anyone else.

At about 9:15, the doorbell rang. Alfreda opened the door and let in three women and a man. The women were much like Alfreda—loud-talking and rough-acting. As the night went on, they started hanging on each other, but Vera thought it was because they were drunk. Then every few minutes for the rest of the night, more people arrived. Some came with paper bags holding their favorite liquors.

"Some niggers can be so particular," Alfreda said to Vera as she handed her a bottle to set on the liquor table. "Like they can tell the difference between Jack Daniels and Jack Shit after a few drinks." She and Arthurine, who was putting some more sauce on the ribs, fell out laughing.

It didn't take long for the house to fill with men and women laughing, loud talking, drinking liquor and greasing their chops on Arthurine's food. Alfreda put on some Dizzy Gillespie, and people rushed into the living room, two-by-two, to dance.

Vera noticed Tom as soon as he came in. The four drinks she had by then didn't slow her roll one bit. Tom was about 6'3" and the tallest man in the room. Skin the color of a dark chocolate bar. Hair slicked back, the light in the foyer making the peaks of the waves in his hair glisten like the sun did on the waves in the sea. Suit was sharp as a tack. Shoes polished like fine silverware, and so was he. A walk as smooth as cake batter.

Vera went over to get a drink when Tom was fixing himself one. He smelled her perfume before he saw her. He turned around and said, "I knew I smelled something sweet. Can I fix you a drink?"

"You sure can," Vera said. "Bourbon and ginger ale."

"Anything for a lady," Tom said as he mixed the drink and handed it to Vera.

"Haven't seen you around here," he said, eyeing her from her thick curly hair to her high heel wearing feet. "I'm Tom Stiles. And who might you be?"

"I'm Vera Marshall, Alfreda's niece. I moved in with her a few weeks ago," she said.

"I didn't know anything so lovely could come out of Alfreda's family," Tom said. "No offense, but she's not a whole lot to look at."

Vera laughed. "That may be true, but she's good people."

"Oh, I know that," said Tom. "Why else would she let these folks tear up her house like this?"

They both laughed. Count Basie's Orchestra was calling all boppers to the floor, so Tom asked, "Would you like to dance?"

"I sure would," said Vera.

They squeezed onto the makeshift dance floor, and Vera wiggled and shook with the rest of them. Tom liked every shimmy and shake. He took off his jacket as both he and Vera got hotter. When he heard Billie Holiday singing "Good Morning, Heartache", Tom asked Vera to keep dancing.

He wrapped his arms around her, inhaled the perfume she put behind her ear, and felt a rush between his legs. Vera moved her hands around Tom's back to feel the muscles sticking to that part of his crisp white shirt— freshly laundered, pressed and smelling like starch—that was moist with perspiration underneath. She liked what she felt as he got harder and harder. Tom moved his hands like he didn't know whether to rest them on the small of her back, or the tops of her shoulders or the mounds on her hips; he liked the feel of them all.

When the song ended, Vera's head was spinning—intoxicated from the bourbon and from Tom's feel and smell. He could see that she needed some steadying, so he took her arm and guided her to a corner. He propped her against the wall and kissed her, joining the other couples who were necking all around the room. Vera hadn't been kissed for a long time, so she came back at him with everything she had, surprising herself at how far she could thrust her tongue down his throat.

She wrapped her arms around his waist hard and held him tight.

When he got so hard that all he could think of was jerking off right there, Tom said, "If you live here, then we don't have to stand in this corner, do we?"

Vera loosened her grip and said, "We damn sure don't." She took Tom by the hand, and they walked upstairs. Vera led Tom into her bedroom and closed the door. Then she walked over to her night stand to get her diaphragm. She was drunk, but not so drunk that she'd forget to stop Tom's sperm from swimming up inside her.

Besides thinking that she didn't want to get pregnant, her only other thought was: I wonder if he is any good? No matter what else she thought Tom and his suave self could do for her, her overriding thought was whether he knew what he was doing.

"Look the other way, will you, honey, while I get this thing in," Vera said.

Tom dutifully obeyed, turned around, unzipped his pants and let them fall to the floor. He wanted to be ready when she was. Vera squatted and easily slid the diaphragm into place. She patted the edges with her finger to make sure the seal was tight. Then she turned around and saw Tom in his burgundy satin boxer shorts, facing the wall. The muscles on his thighs looked tough and sculpted like a long distance runner.

She tiptoed up behind him and ran her hands from the crook in the back of his knee up to the bottom of the boxers, using her fingers to press on each unyielding muscle until she moved her fingers around to the front of the boxers and felt around. Nice size, she thought, but what she said was, "Show time", as Tom spun around to face her.

He cupped his hands around Vera's behind and positioned her crotch right up against his. He held her there, tightly, while he pressed his lips against hers and thrust his tongue down her mouth. She gladly returned the favor until Tom quickly broke the suction that their mouths made, and he began kissing and licking her neck. He held Vera's behind tight with one hand and loosened the other so that he could squeeze each breast from the bottom as he kissed and licked it from the top, at the mound of her cleavage. Then he pulled his head back, released his tight grip on Vera's behind, and pushed her dress up to her waist with one hand. She already had the foresight to take off her underpants when she put on her diaphragm. He fell to his knees, stuck out his long tongue, and made it dance on her, quick and determined like a lizard's tongue when it's searching for food.

He licked and probed and sucked until he had tasted all of Vera. She held his head, gently at first, and then she pressed it hard into her, hoping that his tongue would go even deeper. When he pulled his head back, gasping for air, Tom said, "Not yet, baby. Not yet."

He cupped his hands back around her behind, lifted her up off the floor, and sat her on the edge of the bed. He dropped his boxers, and started thrusting into her.

Vera started to lay back, but he said, "Don't". He folded his legs up on either side of her, pulled her closer to him and took her right there on the edge of the bed. Vera moaned and moved with every thrust.

When his movements slowed slightly, Vera sensed that Tom's legs were giving out. She squeezed both arms tighter around his back and leaned back on the bed, making sure that he would lean back, too. He fell down on top of her, never missing a thrust.

When they finished, both Tom and Vera passed out and slept for about an hour. Vera woke up first, still a little groggy, and got dressed. She could hear the party still going on downstairs. She woke Tom up, thanked him, and helped him get dressed. It was time to talk.

"So what do you do, Tom?" Vera asked. He'd met the good-looking, good-loving hurdles. No sense beating around the bush about the other requirements she had if a man didn't meet those first two tests.

"I work at the shipyard, driving a dump truck," he said as he finished buttoning his shirt.

"Oh, really," said Vera. As fine as he was and as good as he felt, this was not the man for her. "Well, thanks for the memories, Tom," Vera said. "I better get back downstairs and see what's going on. Let's go."

She pulled him off the bed and practically pushed him out the door.

Vera walked quickly down the hallway as Tom said, "Wait a minute. When can I see you again?"

"Sorry, Tom," Vera said. "That wouldn't be possible."

He couldn't believe what he just heard. "Wait a minute," he said. Vera stopped and turned to face him. "You're going to screw me, not once, not twice, but three times and leave it at that," he said.

"That's about the sum of it, and you ought to be happy with that," she said, knowing that she did give him three good ones.

"I'm happy, alright," Tom said, "but couldn't I have some more? We were good together, baby, and it can only get better."

Vera turned around and kissed him just to shut him up. "Let's just leave it right where it is, honey. I enjoyed it and you did, too, but I know that was the liquor in me talking and nothing else. Now let's enjoy the rest of the party," she said. She walked away leaving him standing there dumbfounded, but knowing full well that he was happy with what he got.

When Vera went back downstairs, folks were sprawled all over the furniture and the floor in the living room and dining room. A small group sat at the kitchen table, devouring Arthurine's food. All the food in the dining room was long gone. Vera looked for Alfreda, and found her sitting in the kitchen, drinking her scotch and water.

"Some party, huh?" Alfreda said to Vera.

"Sure is," Vera said.

"Sit down and have a drink," Alfreda said.

"I sure need one," Vera said, as she poured herself yet another. She and Alfreda sat there drinking for the next hour while the party went on around them. Then Alfreda put her cup down and said, "It's time to get rid of these niggers. I need some sleep." She turned the lights on and shouted, "Party's over. Get the hell out!" She opened up the front door so there'd be no mistaking. Then she worked her way back to the kitchen, shaking the folks who passed out to get them to wake up and physically throwing out the door those people who were dragging their feet about leaving, which was almost everyone. But, no matter how rough Alfreda got, everyone left with a smile on his or her face. Alfreda knew how to throw a great party.

Come Monday morning, most everything about Alfreda's party was just a pleasant memory. Vera looked forward to going to work and getting away from the smell of stale liquor and cigarettes that permeated Alfreda's first floor. "Open up the windows and let it air out," Alfreda had said. "The smell will be gone in a day or two."

Vera enjoyed partying with Alfreda about as much as she enjoyed modeling. Now, she always followed the advice Alfreda first gave her: she ate before she went out to be able to have three drinks without getting drunk. Some nights, though, Vera lost count of how much she drank. Alfreda called Vera all kinds of stupid bitches as she tried to help her up the stairs to bed. Many nights Alfreda had to undress Vera and push her into bed.

Even though Vera set her alarm clock for 8 a.m., which usually gave her plenty of time to get to work, a few times she punched in late. But she always had an excuse. "The trolley was late," she'd tell Charlene, rushing in past the front desk and to her dressing room.

Some mornings Vera wore sunglasses to hide the redness in her eyes before the eye drops she put in every morning took effect. She was an expert with makeup, so most people never noticed the dark circles forming beneath her eyes. Vera thought she hid everything pretty well, except one morning, Irene, Vera's favorite beautician, said between turns with the hot comb, "You better slow down, girl. It's starting to show."

"What are you talking about Irene," Vera asked, never being one to peep her hole card and reveal too much.

"You're running the streets too much, baby," Irene said. Close to 60 years old, she called everybody baby. "Many's the morning you come in here with bloodshot eyes and bags underneath them. You didn't start out that way."

She put the hot comb down and took a drag on her cigarette. "You've got a pretty face, Vera. Don't ruin it out there running the streets," she said. Then she snuffed the butt out in the ashtray and picked up another section of Vera's hair. "What you want you've got other ways to get, baby," she said. "The Good Lord blessed you with a body and a brain. Don't start messing up both of 'em," she said as she ran the hot comb through Vera's hair.

"You're the only one who's noticed," Vera said, proud that she fooled everyone else.

"I'm the only one who's telling you," Irene said. "Don't think that I'm the only one who's noticed."

"I can handle it," Vera said.

"I've heard that before," Irene said, as she started combing Vera out.

CHAPTER 18

Vera's life settled into a pattern, although nothing she did could ever be called routine. Partying at the house on Saturday night. Sleeping it off on Sunday. Dragging her ass out of bed on Monday. Then every night, Monday through Friday, Vera sat at the bars and beer gardens all over town with her so-called friends. She kept looking for a man who was worthy of her time and energy. But when the liquor was talking, which was more often than not, she had no hesitation about having sex with men who didn't meet any of her standards, except the one about looking good.

Velvet's still was Vera's favorite club. One Thursday night, she went to the club in her red satin dress, strapless and slit on the side. She planned to see Michael Brown, who she met at the bar at the club last week. She was all up in his face then, practically throwing herself at the man until his resolve disappeared. He told Vera that he ran his own business, a janitorial service where he hired other people to do the cleaning, and he just managed the money. She hadn't heard of the business before, but it sounded good to her, and it looked like it worked for him—he had on the type of imported suit that Harrison's carried in the Gallant Gent's shop. She asked Velvet to give them a table in a dark corner in the back. Once they settled in, they kissed like they were the only ones in the room.

Michael told Vera that he had to go to Chicago to take care of some business, and he asked her to meet him back at the club the next Thursday. Vera baited her hook and planned to cast it. That Thursday, the club was packed like a size 14 woman in a 10 blouse—bursting at the seams. Every maid and chauffeur in someone's service had the night off. Vera squeezed her way in and looked around. It only took her a few seconds now for her eyes to get accustomed to the dark, smoky room. Her telescopic eyes immediately focused on Michael at a stool at the bar.

She walked over and tapped him on the back of the neck. He turned around quickly, knowing that the fingers that touched his neck didn't belong to a man. He saw Vera standing magnificently before him, jumped off the stool and kissed her on the cheek. "I missed you, baby. I'm glad you came," he said.

"I've been looking forward to it," said Vera. She kissed him back. With uncharacteristic honesty, she said, "I missed you, too."

He led her past the crowd at the bar to a table in the back. "Lenny, scotch on the rocks for me and bourbon and ginger for the lady," he said.

Michael slid his chair next to Vera's and put his arm around her shoulder. She leaned back, nestling in the curve of his arm like a baby bird in her mother's wings and waited for the drinks. "So how was your day," Michael asked, as he ran his fingers through one of her curls.

"Everyday's a good day," Vera said. "Sold a lot of dresses. Made Harrison's a lot of money."

He lightly massaged her neck as Lenny brought over the drinks. They took a few sips, leaned back, and watched a big, boisterous woman with a feathered headband and a dress with fringe in constant motion sing a raucous Bessie Smith song. Velvet liked to keep the place jumping on Thursday night. Michael and Vera half way finished their drinks when Vera felt Michael's hand being snatched off her shoulder so fast that she got a scratch from his fingernails. They both looked around and saw a woman standing behind them with a drawn switchblade.

"Either of you motherfuckers move, and I'll slice you," she said.

Vera was like a statue.

"Baby, put that thing down," Michael said, trying to calm her.

"Don't baby me, you no good, two-timing bastard. No wonder your stuff's so limp, you're giving everything to this bitch," she said.

"Uh . . . baby, you don't understand," Michael said. "You got it wrong."

"Shut the fuck up, you bastard. I got it right, all right," she said. "You think I'm going to let you divorce me for this bitch," she said as she waved the switchblade at Vera.

Vera couldn't believe what she just heard. "Divorce?" she said. She looked at Michael and said, "Are you married?" For a minute she was more shocked that he was married than that this crazy woman was standing so close to her with a knife.

"Of course he's married," the woman said. "Why the hell do you think I'm here?"

Michael stood up, put his hands up, and said, "Honey, put the knife down. You've been drinking," Michael said, trying to restore some order.

"Hell, yeah, I've been drinking. So the fuck what? I'll still slice this bitch if she doesn't leave you alone," the woman said.

Vera practically stammered, trying to control the rage the felt against Michael for not telling her he was married and against herself for not realizing it. "He didn't tell me he was married," she said. "I don't mess with married men. There's too many single one's out there."

The wife waved the switchblade in the direction of the door. "Then get the hell up, bitch, and get the hell away from him," she said.

Vera grabbed her pocketbook and pushed her chair back, more than ready to go. The back of the chair hit the wife in the stomach, and she stumbled over the chair. The switchblade came down first, cutting off a lock of Vera's hair and then cutting a nice, long, neat slice from the top of Vera's dress to about her midsection. Vera screamed, pulled her dress together, and ran towards the door. Alfreda heard screams, looked up from the paperwork she was completing, and reached in her pocketbook for her blade. She'd been in enough bars and enough fights to know that she'd better never walk into a bar without a blade. Alfreda saw Vera run past her screaming, crying, and dress ripped, and Alfreda ran out behind her.

Tony, on duty out front, caught Vera as she ran out, pushing her way past the people waiting in line to get in. He took off his jacket and threw it around Vera's shoulders as she alternately sobbed and screamed, "She almost sliced my face. She almost sliced my face."

Inside, Velvet told everyone, "Calm down. It's a domestic disturbance," not knowing for sure, but figuring that anytime two women were fighting over a man, one of the women had to be married to him.

As the bouncers held Michael and his wife, Velvet walked over to him and said, "Get the hell out of my club, nigger, and take that crazy-ass woman of yours out of here, too."

Frank sent one of the other valets to get Alfreda's car as he held Alfreda back with one hand because she wanted to go back inside and kick the wife's ass. When the valet brought the car around, he practically threw Alfreda into the driver's seat and the other valet hurried Vera into the passenger side. Alfreda tore off down Lancaster Avenue, cursing Frank for holding her back and asking Vera, "Are you ok, baby? Are you ok?"

Vera didn't say a word. She just hugged Tony's jacket to her shoulders and cried the whole way home.

The next morning, Vera called in sick. "God blessed you with a body and a brain," she remembered Irene saying. "Don't mess them up." If that blade fell a few inches to the left, she would have a scar on her face that would put an end to her modeling career and change her life forever. Still in shock, she pulled the bathrobe around her and headed downstairs to get something to eat.

There on the living room couch in plain view, acting as if they were the only ones in the house, which they usually were, was a sight Vera had never seen before. Arthurine was sprawled out on the couch, arms over her head, legs up in the air with Alfreda's head in between them, tongue flapping and licking and twirling and sucking, while Arthurine moaned in ecstacy.

"Oh, my God," Vera shouted, quickly putting her hand to her mouth as if that would keep the shock inside her.

Arthurine didn't hear Vera, but Alfreda looked up, lips moist, and said, "Now you know, baby," and went right back to work on Arthurine. No need to stop now, she thought. Time to get it while the getting is good. Vera turned around, ran back upstairs and started throwing her clothes in a suitcase. She was going back to Ardmore.

Vera was crying and throwing clothes in the trunks when Alfreda knocked at the door. "Let me in, Vera," Alfreda said.

Vera didn't budge. "I'm leaving, Aunt Alfreda," Vera said behind the closed door.

Alfreda hung her head as she pressed her hand against the door, waiting to be invited in. "I won't stop you Vera, but let's talk," Alfreda said.

Vera wiped off some of the tears, opened the door, and went right back to packing without looking up.

"That's what I am baby," Alfreda said. "I came to Philly because I couldn't hide it any more," she said, looking at the floor. She walked over to Vera's closet so that she had to look at her, even if she was looking down and all she saw was her feet. "I tried to hide it from you, too, and that wasn't right either."

Vera sighed and put down the blouse in her hand. "What you do is your own business, Aunt Alfreda," Vera said. "It's just that I'd never seen anything like that before. Heard about it, but never seen it."

Alfreda said, "Don't hold that against me, Vera."

"I don't," Vera said, as she continued packing. "It's just that I can't live my life with all that . . . with all this. Lord knows I've got my wild ways, but even they've gotten too wild for me. Last night I almost get my face sliced. And this morning, I find out my aunt likes women and so do her friends." Vera continued, "No offense, but I can't imagine me ever being with another woman, and I know that sooner or later, one of them is bound to try me. I just figure that the men want to try me, so I guess that the women would want to, too. No offense, but I don't want to have to hurt anybody to get her to leave me alone, do you know what I mean?" Vera asked.

"I know," Alfreda said. "I've had to stop some of them already." Two or three of her friends had already asked Alfreda if Vera went that way.

Vera sat down on the side of the bed, tired, like she was laying the weight in her head and her heart on the bed with the weight on her bones. "You need your own place back, Aunt Alfreda. I'm in the way here, and I can't keep up. You were right. This going out every night and running around is hurting me. People at the store are starting to notice, and I can't have that."

"I don't want to say I told you so, but I did," Alfreda said. "But you had to learn for yourself."

Vera closed up the suitcases and said, "You're right about that. I learned."

"Let me help you with these," Alfreda said as she helped Vera close one of the big trunks. "When you're ready, I'll drive you back home." Alfreda wiped the tears from her eyes.

"I liked your company, Vera, and I like your spunk," Alfreda said. "Watch yourself and you'll be all right," Alfreda said.

"I intend to," Vera said. Then she headed towards the bathroom to wash herself clean.

CHAPTER 19

Welsh Road was almost deserted. The Haverford College bus had let off its workers a few hours before, and most of the other members of the working class had trudged in from their jobs, hands full with afternoon newspapers and metal lunch boxes, paper bags with maid's uniforms neatly folded, or food from the green grocer around the corner for that evening's dinner. At 6 o'clock, everybody with any sense was inside eating dinner.

When Alfreda's Cadillac rolled down the street, Vera looked around. She was happy that no one was around to see her return, tail between her legs, like a dog who just got spanked. Alfreda put the gear in park, turned off the ignition, and both she and Vera got out. Vera walked around to the trunk and met Alfreda there.

"I just want to thank you for taking me in and helping me out," Vera said.

"Glad to do it baby," Alfreda said. She picked up one of the suitcases and said, "Emma sure will be surprised to see you home."

"I just hope she doesn't say 'I told you so'",said Vera, as she walked towards the steps.

"Give her time, baby, give her time," said Alfreda. She followed Vera up the stairs."

Little noise came from the Marshall dinner table because all of the serving dishes were back down on the table after being passed around from one hungry mouth to another. No one talked because food filled everyone's mouth. The kids closest to the door heard the loud thumps on the porch floor when Vera set down the suitcases so she could open the door.

Valerie looked up from her mashed potatoes to see who was coming in. She shouted, "Vera! Vera's here."

One-by-one, the Marshall children pushed their chairs back from the table so fast that they almost fell over. Kids scuffled away from the table and ran straight from the dining room through the living room to the front room.

"I'm home," Vera shouted, putting on a face full of smiles, holding her arm out to hug the brothers and sisters who ran towards her.

Emma and John sat at opposite ends of the table, motionless as their children moved all around them. They looked at each other, eyes wide.

"The girl is home," John said to Emma.

"I'm not surprised," said Emma as she put her fork down. She slowly lifted herself out of the chair and walked over to John's side. He rose to meet her and they walked to the front room together.

"I'm home, Mom," said Vera, gently pushing her brothers and sisters to the side, walking towards Emma, looking directly into her soft eyes. Vera wrapped her arms around her mother's sturdy, comforting frame and laid her head down on her shoulder.

Alfreda stood in the doorway looking her sister straight in the eyes. She didn't say a word to her. There was plenty of time for that.

"You got more bags out there, Alfreda?", John asked.

"A whole carful," Alfreda said. "I'll help you with them." Alfreda turned and walked away, and John followed her.

Emma patted Vera on the back and said, "You home to stay, honey?" Vera could only shake her head yes.

"I'm glad," Emma said.

Emma held Vera's arms and helped her stand up straight. She told Valerie, "go on in and fix Vera a plate," handing Vera off to her sister.

Alfreda reappeared at the door, carrying another bag in. Emma wasn't surprised that Vera returned, but she wondered just what incident set her off. Now was not the time to find out. She walked over to Alfreda and gave her a hug.

"Come on in and get something to eat," she said. Alfreda looked at her quizzically, like she was waiting for the other shoe to drop.

"No questions asked," Emma said. "At least not tonight."

Alfreda nodded, took Emma's outstretched hand, and walked back into the kitchen with her. No questions asked.

After Emma put all the younger kids in bed and the older ones went on their own accord, she sat on her chair in the living room, waiting for Vera to come down. She knew that she'd come. She knew that what Vera needed most of all now was her mother's love. All through dinner Vera avoided the younger kids' questions as to why she came back home. The older ones knew not to ask, that if Vera came home, something didn't go right. And Emma and John just tried to make it like she never left. But Emma knew Vera needed her. She didn't need her often, but when she did, Emma knew it. After all, she was her first born and that first surge of maternal instinct was a powerful one.

Predictably, Vera came down the stairs in a bathrobe she left at home and didn't dare take in town—chenille with a broken belt loop, hem frayed from being stepped on, and the seat worn out from being sat on.

Vera sat on the couch nearest Emma.

"Do you want to talk?" Emma asked. She ached for her daughter as only a mother can ache when her child is taught one of life's lessons.

"It just wasn't what I thought, Mom. That wild life works for Aunt Alfreda, but it doesn't work for me. I had to get out," Vera said as the tears started falling.

Emma extended her hand and Vera rushed over, kneeled down and laid her head on Emma's lap. "Get it all out," said Emma, as she patted Vera's back and let Vera use her apron to catch her tears. "Get it all out and then forget it honey. Don't let it hold you back. You just keep on."

"Yes, Mom," Vera said, and she cried for the next half hour.

The next morning Vera woke up as soon as John knocked on the door with his familiar, "you chillun get up." She found it comforting. She dressed quickly and ate breakfast quickly, anxious to get out of the house. As she walked to the trolley stop, she couldn't believe that she was walking those same streets that she had walked all of her life, seeing the same people that she had seen all of her life. The only thing different that day was that the swing that she usually had in her stride was gone.

Since the swing was gone, if anyone looked at Vera from behind, he'd figure that he was looking at just any girl in Ardmore—well, almost. Except for the rounded, perfectly shaped behind that drove men crazy, Vera Marshall walked just like any regular colored girl in Ardmore, something that she never figured that she was. She said hello to the people she passed, but it was only half-hearted.

"Nice to see you," she would lie. It's not nice to see the same old thing. This was the neighborhood she wanted to escape, the streets she wanted to leave, not to walk again and certainly not to walk on with the intentions of catching a trolley.

As she approached the trolley, Vera saw Mrs. Martin, who taught Vera in Sunday school when she was young enough that Emma and John could force her to go. Mrs. Martin looked twice when she saw Vera in the crowd. "What are you doing back in Ardmore?" she asked.

You'll never know, thought Vera. "I just decided to move back home. I can save more money that way," Vera said.

"Just like Alfreda to charge you to stay at her place," said Mrs. Martin, assuming that was the truth behind Vera's lie. Mrs. Martin grew up with Alfreda and heard all the stories about her wild ways, even spread a few herself. "It's better for you to be home anyway. Young girl like you doesn't need to be living on her own."

You got that right, or at least half right, thought Vera. She wondered whether her problem was age or circumstance. Either way, it didn't matter. The end result was that she was back home.

As the street car left Ardmore, Vera looked out of the window at everything she didn't want. She wanted to get out, the same thing that she wanted every day since she was nine years old. Her father had helped her escape then, and it had all seemed so easy.

Unlike most nine-year-olds, Vera hated the summer. Summer meant work, not play, and what nine-year-old wanted to work. But it was early morning, and her job was about to begin.

She walked into the first of the four rooms, one right after the other, shotgun style, on the first floor of her family's twin house and plopped into a club chair in the front room. Her black leather Mary Janes moved back and forth, kicking the chair's pock-marked wooden leg. She twirled one of her two-inch thick shoulder length pigtails and looked at the window, watching the dancing shadows and light and ignored the motion, clatter and laughter that seven younger brothers and sisters generated.

"Vera, get me a diaper," Emma called out as she wiped off her eighth baby's behind. Vera could block out her brothers and sisters, but she couldn't block out her mother. Vera jumped out of the chair and ran into the back room, the one right before the kitchen. She grabbed a diaper, ran back and handed it to Emma, who now stood in the dining room, snapping another child into a high chair.

"Vera, come feed this child his cereal while I go change the baby," Emma said as she disappeared into the front room. After Vera spooned the last bit of cereal into her youngest sister's mouth, she wiped a few dribbles of barley mush from the corners of the baby's mouth with her pink bib, the satin bow fraggled after the constant washing.

"Vera, take these children outside for awhile. I can't stand any more crying," Emma said. Vera gathered up every child who could walk and marched them around the block, hoping that by the time they got home, the younger ones would be ready for a nap and Emma would leave her alone for a few minutes.

One morning, John bent over his plumber's tool box, preparing for another day of work when Emma called out, "Vera, go get the baby's bottle together." He watched the smile leave Vera's face as she jumped up from the floor beside him and rushed into the kitchen to warm up the baby's bottle on the stove. She moved quickly, but not sprightly, as she struck a match and lit the burner. She stood with her hands on her hips, waiting for the water to boil, lips poked out, spirit gone.

That wasn't the Vera he wanted to see. That girl with her lips poked out wasn't the high-spirited girl who loved to laugh, play dress up, trick her friends into playing the games that she wanted to play, run up and down Welsh Road, stopping to talk with her neighbors—no matter what their ages, examining everything that interested her, and challenging everything that didn't seem right.

"Leave her be, Emma," John said. "She's only a child herself, and you have her working like she's grown."

"Leave her be?" Emma asked, as she strapped her two-year-old in the high chair with one hand and put a pacifier in her one-year-old's mouth with the other.

"Somebody has to help me with these children," Emma said. It didn't occur to her to ask John to help with the children. She never once saw a man "babysit" his children, let alone put a diaper on one. "The oldest has to help with the youngest. That's the way it's always been."

John straightened up, looked at Emma and said, "Not around here. Not all the time, at least. I'm taking Vera with me. She needs to get out."

Emma looked at John as if he had lost his mind. "Get out and do what? Watch you work?" Emma said. She thought about the musty, dirty basements and boiler rooms where John spent most of his time on plumbing jobs. "That'll be mighty boring to a nine-year-old girl. But go on and take her. She'll be so scared of all those spiders and mice, she won't mind sitting in the house here helping me with these children."

Vera sprinkled a few drops of formula on her wrist and knew that the bottle had warmed just enough. She walked towards the dining room to give the bottle to Emma.

When Vera walked by John, he put his hand out to stop her. "Hold on, Vera," he said as he fastened the clasp on his tool box with the other hand. "How'd you like to go out with me today?"

Vera's eyes got tight, and she looked at John like she didn't quite understand what she heard. "Where?" she asked.

"To work, that's where," John said.

"You mean I don't have to stay here and help Mom?" she asked.

"Not today," John said. "You can come with me. I've got a job up in Devon, and I need some company on the ride."

Vera didn't believe that her mother would let "her little helper", as she called her, out of the house unless the other kids trailed behind her. "Mom said I could go?" Vera asked.

"She sure did," said John. Then he stared at Vera, wondering why his daughter felt that she had to check with her mother before she believed something that he said.

"Then I'm going," Vera said, smiling broadly, her lyrical emphasis on the word "going". "Let me run and give Mom the bottle, and I'm ready." Her whole face smiled as she handed Emma the bottle.

"Pop said I can go with him today," Vera said, still not quite sure that Emma really would let it happen.

"He told me," Emma said as she nestled the baby in her arms and put the nipple in her mouth. "Have a good time." No sense in scaring her now, Emma thought. She'll be plenty scared later, sitting in the basement, wondering what's crawling around her, trying to get on her skin.

John walked into the dining room, his ever present tan cotton cap in one hand and tool box in another, his wiry frame bent over from years of carrying the heavy tools. "Come on, Vera. Let's go," he said.

Vera walked behind him, as close as she could get without stepping on his feet.

"No fair," shouted her brother Bobby. "Where's Vera going?" he asked. Because if Vera wasn't there to help Emma, as the next oldest, he'd have to do it, and he had better plans for the day.

Vera stuck out her tongue at him and said, "I'm going to work with Pop." She stuck out her chest, too, as if that meant something.

Bobby pushed one of his brothers off his leg and stood up. "I want to go, too."

John walked right past him. "You'll get your turn when your time comes. Today, it's just Vera and me."

Just like old times, Vera thought. Before the rest of you kids were born, and I never got Mom or Pop to myself again.

Vera bounced down the front steps after John. He threw the toolbox in the bed of his third-hand Ford truck with the letters "John Marshall, Plumbing and Heating" painted on both doors. He opened the passenger door for Vera, and she climbed up on to the first step, which was over a foot off the ground. She scooted into the seat, smoothed out her dress like Emma taught her a real lady does when she sits down, and smiled as John climbed in the driver's seat beside her. She kicked the heel of her Mary Janes at the bottom of her seat as John started up the engine and rolled down Welsh Road.

John and Vera turned left on to Lancaster Avenue, Main Street on the Main Line. When Vera saw the Ardmore train station on her right, she said, "Old Maids Never Wed and Have Babies."

"That's right, baby. Don't you forget it. You take the train, and you get off after Wynnewood." John and Emma had taught Vera the names of the important stations on the Main Line of the Pennsylvania Railroad the way that most people on the Main Line learned them. Take the first letters of Old Maids Never Wed and Have Babies, and you'll have the station names: Overbrook, Merion, Narberth, Wynnewood, Ardmore, Haverford and Bryn Mawr.

When they reached the intersection of Lancaster Avenue and Sugartown Road in Devon, Vera noticed what looked like a thin tombstone with the markings, "14M to P."

"What's that, Pop?" she asked.

"That means 14 miles to Philadelphia," John said.

I wonder how many miles to Ardmore, thought Vera. But it didn't really matter. She was far enough away from 479 Welsh Road not to be bothered with any kids.

John turned left onto Sugartown Road, and the scenery immediately changed from business to residential. A large stone house dominated the hill on the left, and a smaller one just like it was squeezed in closer to the road.

"What's that, Pop?" Vera asked.

"That house there they called La Maison—a fancy French word that means 'the house'", John said as he looked straight ahead. He'd seen so many large mansions in close to 30 years of plumbing on the Main Line that they didn't phase him at all.

"Why's that little house there?" Vera asked, eyes wide.

"That there is what they call the carriage house," John said. Before Vera could ask "what's that", John answered, "the carriage house is where the people live what work on the cars and tend the grounds. They make sure that nobody goes up to the big house, lessen of course the big man or misses wants them to."

Vera looked at him, eyes wide. She didn't exactly understand why they needed a whole separate house for that, but she thought they were lucky to have it. They traveled down the road for two more miles, crossed a small stone bridge, and John turned to the left into a driveway.

"We're going to stop at the carriage house right there," he said.

Vera sat up straight in her seat and looked down the hill at the white plaster house with the six-foot wide porch that wrapped around on all sides and the little carriage house that looked just like it. John pulled up next to the carriage house, and Seth Johnson, who lived right down the street from them, walked outside.

"Right on time, John, as usual," said Seth.

"The early bird gets the worm," John said. Or in this case, enough money to feed eight kids and a pregnant wife for the next few days.

Seth walked closer to John's truck and rested his hands on the open window. "I see you have some company today. Good morning, Vera."

"Good morning. Mr. Johnson," Vera said, leaning forward so that she could really see him.

John said, "I want to get the girl out of the house more, so I figured she could ride with me. She won't be a bother."

"Of course she won't," said Seth. "I know you and Emma have given her proper home training. She's welcome here anytime, far as I'm concerned." Seth walked over to the wrought iron gate leading to the main house. He pulled the heavy gates to either side and waved for John to enter.

John drove down the winding driveway. As he did, Vera looked out of the window at a little pond at the bottom of the hill and another little house right next to the stream that fed into it. She made a note to ask John about that later.

John parked in the back of the house, next to some other trucks and a few tractors. He helped Vera out of the truck and then walked back to the open flatbed to retrieve his tool box. "Come on, honey. Let's go," he said. He walked to a small white door in the back of the main house. He knocked three times and waited. Vera stood quietly with her hands folded, but head turning in every direction, looking at all the lush green grass down the hill, perfect, she thought, for rolling down in the summer or sledding down in the winter.

After a few seconds, Scott Benjamin, who served on the Trustee Board with John at church, opened the door. He wore a black suit with a white shirt, black tie, and white apron around his waist. "Come on in, John," Scott said. "That old burner is steaming up this place something awful. Giving off heat in the middle of July. And the misses still wants me to wear this jacket," he said, flapping the lapel to cool himself down.

As John walked in, Vera marched in behind him. "Good morning, Mr. Benjamin," she said.

"Why good morning, Vera. I didn't even see you standing there," Scott said.

John said, "Just brought her along for the day. The child needs to get out, and Emma has her taking care of the other kids all day."

Scott laughed. "I know Emma didn't want to hear nothing about you taking her little helper away."

"Didn't want to, but had to," John said. Scott laughed again. John walked toward the stairs that led to the basement. He paused, turned to Scott and asked, "Do you have a chair that I can use down there? Vera's going to need something to sit on."

Scott wiped his hand on a tea towel and walked over to a small wooden table in the middle of the room. "Here. Take this one. It ain't the misses good chair if they put it back here for us to use."

"Don't I know it," John said. They always gave the help the worst and tried to convince them that it wasn't that bad. John hated being in service to rich white folks like he was when he first came up North. That's why he learned all he could about plumbing when he worked in service on the Walthrop Farm in Haverford and left out of there as soon as he could do plumbing work as good as any outside plumber they called in.

"Always have something of your own," John's father told him one day when he surveyed his 50-acre farm in Port Deposit, Maryland. That was one bit of advice that John followed. He opened up his own plumbing business as soon as he left the farm. Mrs. Walthrop surprised him by demanding that the Lower Merion Township Board of Supervisors give him his plumbing license when they didn't want to because he was colored. But she wanted that new bathroom with the gold fixtures, and she wanted John to put them in. She knew for a fact that even though he was colored, he was better than any other plumber on the Main Line.

John opened the basement door. The steps immediately changed from polished and finished wood, gleaming and smooth, to unfinished wood, bare, rough and bumpy. John switched on the light and told Vera, "Stay here 'till I come back." He took the chair down and placed it under the light, not too close to the oil burner, but not too far away from him. He walked back upstairs, picked up his toolbox and said, "Let's go. Hold on to the rail, baby."

You don't have to tell me to do that, Pop, she thought. Even with the lights on, the basement was dark. When Vera reached the last step, John put out his free hand and led her around the dirt floor to the chair. "You sit here. I won't be too long," he said. "And keep your feet up off the floor." No telling what's running around here, he thought.

Vera sat down and looked at the pipes, exposed wires, wooden beams and peeling paint. She felt like she was on an adventure, nothing like what she felt at home. She watched John work and amused herself by counting the pipes, or singing songs, or just making rhythms while kicking the heels of her shoes on the chair.

Vera felt a lot of emotions down in that basement, but not one of them was scared. Not that day or any day that John took her out.

She quickly turned into John's little helper as she learned the name of all the tools in John's tool box. She figured that the more help she was, the more likely John was to take her out. It soon became a familiar sight to see John from behind, head under a sink, arms adjusting pipes, and Vera sitting on the floor next to him, rummaging through the tool box every time John said, "Hand me the packing nut, will you, baby?" "Can you get me that 3/8 inch swagging tool?"

John took Vera to some of the finest estates on the Main Line—Inverness and Oaks in Radnor, Casselberry in Berwyn, Tarleton in Devon, and Highland in Wynnewood. The domestic help had a lot of say in the operation of those households, especially after years of trusted service. When the estate needed a plumber, the head butler or head housekeeper hired one. Since John was a friend who worked on their own homes, they hired him.

Vera's pigtails constantly swung from side to side as she turned her head walking down the 12-foot wide hallways in these estates. She looked at all the exquisite furnishings, like the 20-foot mahogany bar built into the hallway at Inverness and the polished oak dining room table with 30 chairs at Casselberry.

John usually had no problem getting permission for Vera to wait in the kitchen or the yard while he finished his work. He knew maids, housekeepers, cooks, laundresses, chauffeurs, butlers and grounds keepers at every estate on the Main Line.

People who lived in Philadelphia were always surprised to hear a colored person say that he lived in Ardmore, or Bryn Mawr, or Haverford, or any of the other towns. What they didn't understand, but what every well-bred society matron did, was that if the help didn't live in, they had to live close by to be available to meet the employer's every demand.

So, when John was called to fix a heater at the Newsom's estate in Haverford, he first went into the kitchen to ask his neighbor, Cassie Bond, if Vera could sit in the kitchen. The answer always was yes. Light-hearted Vera was as welcome as a day off. Before John fixed the leaking faucets at the Passat estate in Wynnewood, he walked around back to the garage where Vernon Thomas, head usher at the church, kept Passat's fleet of motor cars in top order. Vera spent many an hour in that garage peering over the steering wheels and pretending to drive Fleetwood Cadillacs and Lincoln Continental limousines as Vernon waxed them to a blinding shine.

It got so that every day, Vera asked John if she could go with him. "Not today, baby," said John every other day. "We'll go tomorrow." And they did.

John liked having Vera with him. She asked questions about everything, and when he answered, she'd ask more. One day, as they drove down the long winding driveway at the Inverness estate, Vera asked, "Why do these people have such big houses, and we don't?"

John answered, "Because they have a lot of money."

"Why don't we have a lot of money?" she asked.

John paused before answering that one. He thought that he could tell her that they didn't have money because they weren't white, that his father was a slave when the fathers of those who lived in the big estates built, ran and took millions of dollars from the Pennsylvania Railroad Company, and that colored people started ten steps behind white people anyway. He could tell her that a colored man had to work twice as hard as a white man just to have half as much. But he didn't want Vera to think that, at nine years old, the cards already were stacked against her and that if she just stayed even, she was doing better than most.

So he said, "We just don't. That's all. But we do the best we can, and that's all we can do." He drove past the estate's sloping green fields and turned the corner onto Darby-Paoli Road.

Vera twirled her pig tail, kicked the seat with her foot, and thought: something's not making sense here. "But Pop, that's not right," she said. "Why just do the best you can? Suppose that's not enough? Shouldn't you want to do the best you can . . . until you can do better?"

John eased his foot off the accelerator, took his eyes off the road for a minute, and looked at Vera. The child's got a point, he thought.

"Vera, honey," he said. "I hadn't thought about it that way before. But I think you may be right."

He took her hand and said, "I don't want you to just settle for what you've got, although what you've got is not bad. But if you want more, you go get it. Don't beat yourself up or tear yourself down if you can't do any better, but don't stop there, either." He went on, "You do the best you can, but only until you can do better. And why shouldn't you do better? You work for it, honey. You work for it."

"Just because the white folks are the only ones living like this today doesn't mean that the colored folks can't live like this tomorrow, God willing," John said, chuckling that his little girl got him thinking. "Do the best you can . . . until you can do better. I like that, Vera," he said, as he patted her on the knee.

As the trolley rolled closer to Philadelphia, Vera pressed her eyelids together and pulled at the corners where her eyes met the bone in her nose. Weary and worn, all Vera could think was that Pop got her here. He showed her that there was a better way and that all she had to do was work for it. She got away and she worked for it, but she failed.

Maybe she wasn't as smart as she—and everybody else—always thought she was. Maybe the Daniels *were* better than the rest of us. Maybe she couldn't rise above her circumstances. Pop helped her escape out of the house before, but she didn't see anybody else who was going to lift her out of that twin house in working class, colored Ardmore, not even herself.

When the trolley pulled into the terminal at 69th Street, Vera walked like a zombie to the Market-Frankford line to catch the subway. She sat in silence with her hands folded neatly on her lap as the El moved from 69th to 52nd Streets. At 52nd Street, she got off and joined the throng walking down the street towards Harrison's. She was just one of the crowd.

As soon as Vera walked into the models' dressing room, she saw Charlene sitting at a table in the back, discussing with one of the dressers the outfits that the models would wear that day.

"Excuse me, Charlene," Vera said, approaching the table.

Charlene looked up.

"I'd like to give you my new address," Vera said.

"Moving on up already?" said one of the other models who overheard Vera. Vera was surprised because she thought she kept her voice as low as her mood. But she ignored the other model.

Charlene could tell by the downcast look on Vera's face that she didn't want every one else in the room to know her business, so she said, "Come up to my desk. You can fill out a change of address form there." She turned to the dresser and said, "I'll be right back Elizabeth."

Vera followed Charlene to her French provincial style desk at the front of the room.

"You can just put your address on here," Charlene said, getting a good look at Vera's eyes. The sparkle was gone.

Vera took the paper and started filling it out. Tears welled up in her eyes as she wrote down the address that she thought she'd never have to use again.

Charlene took the paper from Vera and read it. "Moved back home?" she asked Vera with a whisper.

"Yes," said Vera softly.

Charlene touched Vera's arm lightly. "There's nothing wrong with that, Vera. In fact, sometimes that's best." Charlene thought it was pointless to caution Vera now to get more rest and to stop drinking because it was starting to show in her bloodshot eyes and feigned late trolley arrivals when everybody who took the same trolley got to work on time. She liked Vera, and she was a good model who sold more dresses than anyone. No sense in rubbing it in.

Vera took a handkerchief out of her pocketbook, turned her head so that the other models couldn't see her, and wiped a tear from her eye. She turned back around and said to Charlene, "Thank you," and walked back to get dressed.

All day long, Vera went through the motions, walking up and down the aisles, smiling sweetly, and holding up price and designer signs. The minutes dragged on until her 6 p.m. quitting time. She punched out, and took the subway and the trolley in silence.

"I'm worried about Vera," said John as he changed into his bed clothes. "The child just goes to work, comes home, and mopes around the house, looking like she wants to cry if anybody says anything to her."

Emma said, "She's just trying to find her way, John," Emma said.

"But I feel so bad for her," said John. "Vera never let anything get to her. And now she's letting this thing with Alfreda drag her down and hold her back. It's just not right."

"Only God knows what's right," said Emma. "But one thing I know is that Vera won't stay down too long. She ain't no bottom-feeding fish, sucking up people's leftovers. She's one of those fish that's always jumping out of the pond, trying to see what else is out there."

CHAPTER 20

Vera dragged herself up the steps to 479, threw her pocketbook on a little wrought iron table on the porch, and sat down on a rocking chair outside. Sounds of children laughing and screaming, adults talking, and dishes clanging pushed through as the Marshalls made it to the table for dinner.

She wasn't hungry and wasn't in a hurry to go inside. She didn't want to talk to anybody and didn't want to be around them either. She longed for her nice quiet room at Alfreda's and the luxury of thoughts she didn't have to share. The only place she could get any peace was on the porch at dinner time.

She leaned back, closed her eyes and rocked. Just as she started to block out the sounds from inside the house and all the thoughts from inside her head, Bobby walked around the sidewalk leading to the back of the house and looked up at Vera on the porch. He was hungry, but didn't want to startle her by walking on the porch. So he called out, "Getting some shut eye?"

Vera stopped rocking and quickly opened her eyes. "Just resting," she said. "Just resting."

Bobby walked up on the porch and sat down on the rocker next to hers. Emma called out from inside, "Bobby, come on in. We're ready to eat."

"Go on, Mom," he said. "I've got something to do out here. You all eat without me."

"Good. More for me!" Milton yelled. Bobby could tell that it was the younger ones who broke out in laughter. He ignored them and turned to Vera. "What's wrong with you, Vera? You've been moping around since you got back from Aunt Alfreda's. You're not the Vera who left out of here a few months ago."

"And I never will be her," Vera said. "The Vera that left out of here thought that she was living her dream, but it turned out to be a nightmare."

Since she brought it up, Bobby thought it was time to ask the question he wanted to since she came home. "So what happened in there?" he asked.

Vera leaned her head back and closed her eyes. "Nothing except too much drinking, too much partying, and too many men—and women. Aunt Alfreda's living a life that was too fast, even for me," she said. She sat up and shook her head in disbelief. "And now here I am back home sitting on the same old porch with the same old people. No offense to you, Bobby."

Still, she turned to him and said, "I just never thought I'd be back here."

"But you can always leave again," Bobby said.

Vera laughed to keep from crying. "Yeah, but when? I left, and now I'm back. After talking so much, after being so big, bad and bold, I'm back. Right back where I started."

"Not exactly where you started," Bobby said. "You're working. You got a good job. You're making good money. I'm sure you'll get promoted and start making even more money. That is how it works, isn't it?"

Vera got up and walked to the other end of the porch. She leaned over the railing so he couldn't see the tears forming in her eyes. Much as she loved Bobby, she wasn't ready to let him see her cry.

"But I was right there, Bobby. Right there with the people I thought were doing something. Except I found out that they weren't doing nothing or that I didn't like what they were doing, after all this time wishing, hoping, planning and scheming to be one of them," she said. "It's shaken my confidence. It really has."

"Your confidence is shaken?" Bobby said, incredulously. "Girl, you must be kidding. Look here," he said, trying to get her to turn around.

She looked, and he put out his fingers, ready to count off, "First of all, you're beautiful. You've always known that, and that hasn't changed."

"Yeah, but . . ." Vera interrupted.

"No buts, let me finish," Bobby said.

"Second," he said, thrusting out his middle finger, "you're smart as a whip, and you know that," he said. "And third," he said, sticking out his ring finger, "you've got more ambition than anybody in Lower Merion. There's no way in hell, excuse my French, that you're going to spend the rest of your days staying up in here." He pointed to the house with his thumb.

"Snap out of it, Vera," Bobby said. "This isn't the life for you, and you've always been right about that. Just because things didn't work out with Aunt Alfreda doesn't mean that they never will. Mom warned you about staying with her, but we all knew you wouldn't listen. Now you see for yourself. The whole set up wasn't bound to work. It's not your fault."

Vera looked at Bobby, and she thought back. It wasn't her fault that that woman came at her with a knife—she didn't know that man was married. It wasn't her fault that she saw Alfreda and Arthurine on the couch—they should have stayed up in Alfreda's room. The truth is, what happened wasn't anybody's fault. It just was, that's all. A part of life she had to see. A lesson she had to learn. A path she had to follow. A plan she had to work. But sure as she stood there, she knew that only the punks let one mistake hold them back. And she was no punk. If she was anything, she was all woman. And a woman had to be woman enough to pick herself up, cut through the bullshit, and keep on stepping. Alfreda had showed her that.

Vera took a deep breath and elevated her carriage to full modeling stance. She looked straight at Bobby and said, "You're right. It damn sure wasn't my fault." She picked up her pocketbook and said, "Come on. I just got my appetite back. Let's go eat." She hugged Bobby and said, "Thanks, little brother." She flung open the screen door and announced, "I'm home, and I'm hungry." She threw her hat and pocketbook on the table beside the door, told Milton to move over and got a chair for her place at the table. Her place, at least for now.

The sun shone brightly on Vera's face as John went down the hall banging on doors yelling, "You chillun' get up." Instead of immediately jumping up and rushing to the bathroom, she stayed in bed for a few minutes to feel the sun's warmth.

"I feel yellow today," she announced to everyone and no one because none of her sisters were awake yet.

She walked over to the closet, and selected a yellow linen sleeveless dress with a yellow rose in the center of its white belt. Vera looked on the top shelf of her closet at the hatboxes arranged with a description of each hat on the outside so that she didn't have to disturb any of them to find out what was inside.

She selected a yellow straw hat, wide brim, with a yellow and white striped ribbon tied around it. She looked at the purses hanging from the back of the closet door and selected a white patent leather.

"Perfect," she said as she laid the clothes on the bed and went off to get washed up.

"Good morning, Mom," Vera said as she walked into the kitchen where Emma was preparing breakfast.

Emma stood up straight and took a good look at Vera. Vera's eyes sparkled and her stance was confident. Her shoulders were straight up instead of hunched over as they'd been for the past few weeks. Hand on hip. Head held high.

"Well don't you look pretty," Emma said, thinking that it was about time. As much as she picked at Vera for dressing like a tramp and acting way too grown, she missed her spirit these past few weeks.

Emma turned to stir the oatmeal and asked, "You feeling better?"

"The best, Mom," Vera said, popping a piece of bread in the toaster.

God does answer prayer, Emma thought.

On her way to work, Vera shouted "How you doing?" across Welsh Road to Mrs. Thompson who was walking in the opposite direction. "Beautiful morning, isn't it," she called to Tommy Preston as he drove by.

"It ain't just the morning that's beautiful," he called back.

"You got that right, sugar," Vera said, switching her hips as she walked along at a brisk pace.

Waiting for the trolley, Vera joined in conversation after conversation, chatting about the weather, accepting compliments for her outfit, and catching up on the latest about who is seeing whom.

When she got off the El at 52nd street, she stopped a minute and straightened her hat. If there was a mirror on the street, she would have checked it out to see how fine she looked. She clutched her pocketbook firmly under her arm and headed toward Harrison's.

"Woo-wee," said a man sweeping the sidewalk as she passed.

""Here's to you too, honey," Vera said.

"You're bright as the sun and twice as hot in that yellow, baby," a man called out from a bench.

"Don't get too close or you'll melt," she said and laughed.

Standing in line to punch in, Vera spoke to everyone. "Hey, how ya doing? Lovely day, isn't it?"

Charlene was sitting at her desk, looking over the day's schedule when Vera arrived.

"Good morning, Charlene," Vera said, approaching the table.

"Well, good morning to you. Don't you look like summer in that outfit. Very nice," Charlene said, admiring the way Vera put it all together.

"You bought that last month, didn't you?" Charlene asked.

"Sure did," Vera said as she smoothed the skirt with her hand. "Fine fashions for women by Gigi de Paris."

"You can walk the floor in that same dress this morning—fresh off the rack, of course," Charlene said. The girl certainly had style.

"Of course," Vera said.

"But, we'll use your hat," Charlene said with a smile. "No sense messing with perfection."

"That's what I always say," Vera said as she sashayed down to the dressing room to wait for someone to bring her a carbon copy of her dress.

That day, Vera practically waltzed around Harrison's floors. She smiled and laughed and chatted up the dress.

"Perfect for a church social," Vera said to a group of women standing near the cosmetics counter.

"Can't you see yourself walking in the park in this one," Vera asked a group of women fingering blouses on the fifth floor.

"It's a lucky fellow with a lady in yellow," Vera said through a smiling mouth to men looking at suits in Gallant Gents.

By the time Vera got back upstairs to change back into her own dress at lunchtime, Fine Women's fashions had sold out it's entire stock of that dress, two in every size from four to sixteen.

"You sure got some style," Charlene said, rubbing her hands in glee over the sales figures.

"It's all in the presentation," Vera said as she headed back to her dressing room.

For the next few weeks, Vera broke all of the Harrison's sales records that she set before. Every time she wore a dress, it sold out. The buyers started asking Charlene to let them know a few days in advance if Vera was going to wear one of their dresses so they could stock up. Vera started showing the other models how she did it when they asked, as they all did.

Half the time the men couldn't even describe the dress that Vera was wearing or any of the accessories. All they noticed was that whatever she was wearing sure looked good. Nine times out of ten, the men told the sales girls, "I'll take whatever that brown-skinned gal was wearing," since Vera was the darkest model Harrison's had. "Head to toe, just wrap it up," they'd say.

More times than Vera wanted, which was no times, men showed an interest in more than what she wore. "How about your number, honey." "You name it; you got it". "Care to join me for lunch?" "How about a drink when you get off?" Vera heard it all. And let it all roll off her back.

It's not that she wasn't interested. Sometimes, she'd look at a man and feel the heat rising that had nothing to do with the temperature outside. Sometimes, she imagined herself lying next to a man as he kissed her from neck bone to her ankle bone. Sometimes, she looked at a man's lips and wondered if they felt as soft as they looked. Sometimes, she wondered how she could have kept her legs closed ever since she left Alfreda's house.

But every time, her erotic daydreams were interrupted by the vivid picture of a steel switchblade falling an inch from her face. And she knew that if that happened, she'd lose her job modeling, and that was about all that she had at this point. A modeling job at Harrison's and a 400 dream. She didn't want to lose either one.

One day, Vera was standing on the second floor balcony overlooking the first floor men's department modeling in a pink chiffon dress with a scoop neck, butterfly sleeves, pink satin shoes, and a three-strand pearl necklace with matching earrings. She looked over at the men's department, as she did every time she stood there, and raised an eyebrow. Lou Addit, her friend from Ardmore, stood there fingering ties. And Donny Butcher, the 400's most eligible bachelor, stood right next to him, looking at the ties Lou showed him.

Addit's was the biggest colored funeral home on the Main Line, and Butcher's was the biggest colored funeral home in Philadelphia. Lou and Donny were the oldest sons, in line to take over the businesses from their fathers. Vera didn't know that they were friends, but she should have suspected it. Water seeks its own level, and so does money.

Vera made herself a mental note to stop by Addit's on her way home.

CHAPTER 21

Addit's Funeral Home and Florist Shop, a whitewashed clapboard formerly a single house, dominated the corner of Spring Avenue and Chestnut Lane. It was built on the hilly side of the corner. If you sat on the front porch that wrapped around three sides of the house, you could see for four blocks in either direction. Every colored person in Ardmore went to Addit's sooner or later. It was the only colored funeral home in town. Addit's took care of everything—the casket, the flowers, and even the preacher for people who didn't have a church home. Mr. Addit made a fortune burying people, although Mr. Butcher made at least twice as much burying all the folks in town. But like most businessmen, Addit never passed up an opportunity to make money. Since he sold floral arrangements for the funerals and since there was no other colored florist in Ardmore, he opened up a little flower shop, too. People entered a door on the left for funerals and a door on the right for flowers.

Lou Addit, Jr. worked in the flower shop for a few hours every afternoon. As the heir to the family business, his father required him to know all aspects of the business. Lou got more dates than the average average-looking guy in Ardmore because all of the girls knew that he had a secure future.

Vera walked up the steps, opened the door marked "Florist", and found Lou behind the counter.

"Hey, Lou, how ya doing," Vera said, as she closed the door.

"Vera," Lou said, stepping around from the counter. He stretched his arms out and said, "You're a sight for sore eyes, girl." He hugged her, stood back and took a good look. "I heard you were back. What brings you back to this one-horse town?"

"Just trying to save some money. City living was too much on my salary," she said. Lou didn't need to know that she never had to pay for anything she didn't want to in town.

"Well, it's good to see you," he said. "Haven't seen you since you graduated."

"I've kept a low profile," Vera said, walking from flower bin to flower bin, smelling the flowers like she really gave two hoots about them.

"How are you going to keep a low profile, good as you look," he said.

"It isn't easy, believe me," Vera said, and they both laughed.

"As a matter of fact," she said, fingering some daffodils in front of the desk, "I saw you this afternoon at Harrison's."

"This afternoon?" he said. "I didn't see you. Why didn't you say something?"

"I was working up on the second floor while you were down in the men's department looking at ties," she said. "I'm a model there."

Lou stepped back. "Get out of here, girl," he said. "You're one of the famous Harrison models?" He couldn't believe it because he had seen many a model there, but never one as dark as Vera.

"Sure am," she said. "Top seller too. I wear a dress, and it seems to sell out."

"No wonder," Lou said. "Who wouldn't want to look like you?"

"You flatter me, honey," Vera said, smelling a rose.

"You flatter yourself," Lou said.

Vera examined every petal on a bin of gladiolas so Lou couldn't detect the real interest in her face. "Wasn't that Donny Butcher I saw you with?" she asked.

"Oh, Donny. Yeah. Sure, that was him. My ace boon coon. Do you know him?" Lou asked, moving flowers from one container to another.

"Not personally," said Vera, "but I know of him. And who doesn't? He's in the *Elevator* every week." She put her hands out in front of her like she was reading a paper. "Donny Butcher, Jr., son of Mr. Donald Butcher, Sr., proprietor of Butcher's Funeral Home, and his lovely wife Harriet, attended a garden party at the home of the lovely Edna Nixon . . . . Seen on the arm of the beautiful Caroline Chewson was Donny Butcher, heir apparent to the Butcher Funeral Home . . . . Blah, blah, blah. Blah, blah, blah."

Lou laughed. "You sure got that down. My man is always in the paper."

"And always on some girl's arm," Vera said.

"The ladies love him," Lou said, laughing. "I tell him just to give me his leftovers."

Lou looked at Vera. "Don't tell me you're interested in him, too?"

"He's a good looking man, honey, but I don't run after nobody," Vera said. "You know that. I don't have to."

"Well, that's what I thought," Lou said, reassured that at least some things didn't change.

"No harm in looking though, and he's not bad on the eyes," Vera said.

"The way those girls in town run after him, you'd think he was the last man in the 400," Lou said. "He is rolling in the dough, but one woman to him is just the same as the next."

That's because he hasn't met the right woman yet, Vera thought.

"Looks like all those cotillions and coming out parties don't make you a real woman," Vera said.

"They damn sure don't," Lou said. "The way some of those girls look, you've got to wonder what they're coming out of."

They both laughed.

Vera selected an arrangement of yellow daylilies, white carnations, baby's breath, and a few white roses.

"Next time you come in the store, look for me," Vera said.

"I'll do just that," Lou said, ringing up her purchase.

Vera walked home knowing that it was just a matter of time.

It was party time at the Robinson-Welburn Lodge Number 794. Most evenings, the Lodge was open only to its members—the colored Free Masons in Wayne, Devon and Berwyn. A few times a year, the good brothers rented out their meeting hall to one of the many social groups looking for a spot to hold a party. Tonight, folks up and down the Main Line prepared to head to the Lodge for the Thanksgiving Ball given by the Top Men of Distinction, a social club for colored young men, ages 17-25.

Hazel's House of Beauty on Spring Avenue in Ardmore was so crowded that Vera could hardly squeeze her hips past Miss Elaine's desk at the front door.

"I have a one o'clock, Miss Elaine," said Vera, as she counted four women sitting and two standing, waiting their turns to be transformed. "I can't be sitting up here all afternoon waiting for Hazel to do my hair."

Each of the six hairdresser's chairs held a woman whose hair was either wet, smothered under a plastic cap, or dried and sticking out all over her head like Frankenstein's Bride. Vera knew that Hazel and her girls, good as they were, couldn't do all those heads by 5 p.m. She had no intentions of being in the group that was going to get out of there late, rush through dinner, dress in a hurry, and hope that they wouldn't miss their rides to the ball.

"I'm a regular customer, so I don't expect to wait. You see me in here every week, not just when there's a big dance, like some of these other women who straighten her hair in their kitchens 50 weeks of the year," said Vera, loud enough so that Hazel could hear her.

Hazel turned away from the head she was shampooing, dried her hands on her white overcoat, and hightailed it over to Vera. Vera was one of her best customers, and she rightly figured that Hazel wanted to keep her happy. The beauticians at Harrison's styled Vera's hair every day, but every week Vera went to Hazel for the heavy maintenance—coloring, cutting and straightening as needed.

"Now hush, Vera," said Hazel, patting Vera's arm. She whispered, "You know I'm going to get you in and out. Next bowl that opens up, I'll have Carla shampoo your hair. Soon as she's finished, I'll drop whatever I'm doing and take care of you. It should only be a few minutes."

"I hope so, Hazel," said Vera. "It's so crowded in here, I can barely breath."

Hazel said, "The day of the Top Men of Distinction Ball is the best day for my business, next to New Year's Eve. Same thing at the barber shop. We're doing so many heads that the sidewalks on Spring Avenue look like the runway at a hair show."

Vera laughed, and Hazel walked back to her client, whose hair by now had matted up to one-half its size and was in desperate need of the hot comb. Hazel took the comb off the hot plate, rolled up her sleeves, and went to work.

Vera looked around the shop and realized that she recognized everyone. A few months ago, that would have depressed her. Today, it was somewhat comforting. Ardmore was home, for now, but she had a plan to get out. When she looked back at the manicurist's table where Florette was filing somebody's nails like she was using a chainsaw, Vera was shocked. Phyllis Daniels was next in line, patiently waiting her turn with her arms and legs properly folded in front of her and her back upright. Her hair clung close to her head in thick curls, and it still fell down past her shoulders, a rare sight in that beauty parlor.

Vera couldn't believe that Mrs. Daniels let her daughter get her hair done down on Spring Avenue with the common people. That family always went in town and got their personal services from other high-yellow folk who weren't smart enough or fortunate enough to be doctors or lawyers or dentists. Either Phyllis got some newfound independence now that she was dating Bobby or her parents had lost their minds. Vera was going to find out which. She tucked her pocketbook under her arm and strolled to the back of the shop.

"Hey, Phyllis," said Vera. "I sure am surprised to see you here. I thought you got your hair done in town?" She really wasn't asking a question, but she expected an answer.

"Oh, hi, Vera," said Phyllis, in one of the softest voices Vera ever heard. Phyllis stood up to greet her and said, "I usually get my hair done in town, you're right. We had car trouble this morning and couldn't get into the city. Father called Miss Hazel—she's one of his patients—and begged her to let me in."

Vera said, "Well, Hazel's the best hairdresser I know of, and she did a right fine job on your hair. It looks beautiful. But then again, it always does."

"Thanks," said Phyllis. "I think she did a great job, too. Maybe Mother will let me come again."

"Since you just had to get your hair done today, I guess you're going to the ball tonight," Vera said.

"Yes I am," Phyllis said.

"I'll see you there then," Vera said.

Phyllis looked surprised. "Oh, not that ball. Not the ball that everyone here seems to be going to," she said, waving her arm around the shop. "And Bobby, too," she said with a hint of sadness. "I'm going to the Links ball in town."

I should have known, thought Vera. "I didn't think your parents would let you party with us up at the Lodge," Vera said, not commenting maliciously, but honestly.

"No, they wouldn't," said Phyllis, sadly. Although she wanted to be at that ball with Bobby more than anything, but there was no way her parents would let her miss the Links ball and all the eligible young men there for a fake meeting with a cover so that she could be with Bobby.

"I'll tell Bobby that I saw you," Vera said. Then she whispered in Phyllis' ear, "If you get bored with the 400, stop by. We'll be partying till three, four o'clock."

Hazel waved her hands like she was directing traffic and when she finally caught Vera's eye, she motioned for her to sit in the chair in front of the shampoo bowl.

Vera walked over, and Hazel immediately asked, "Who do you want to look like today?" Every time Hazel did Vera's hair, Vera wanted her hair to look like some movie star's, even the white ones. Thank goodness Hazel saw a lot of movies, or she wouldn't have known what Vera was talking about.

"Dorothy Dandridge in *The Bright Road*."

By seven o'clock, Vera was dressed, fed and ready to go. Nobody took a date to the Thanksgiving Ball because too many good-looking folk of both sexes went to be tied down to any one person. Even the most homely girl would get some play that night. On Welsh Road, Delila, Bobby, Vera, Paul and his older brother, Carl, piled into the third-hand Buick that Carl bought with his money from his job at the Autocar plant to make the uncomfortable but exciting journey up Lancaster Avenue.

The same scene repeated up and down the Main Line: on Prescott Avenue in Bryn Mawr, Buck Lane in Haverford, Highland Avenue in Radnor, and Mt. Pleasant Street in Wayne. Nubile men and women in their Saturday go-to-party clothes crammed into anything on four wheels and headed to Berwyn.

Lancaster Avenue was practically deserted that far up. There were fewer stores, fewer cars, fewer lights, and fewer people than down in Ardmore. But at the intersection of Bridge Road and Lancaster Avenue, the floodlights outside the Lodge shined like a lighthouse guiding the folks to their spot to party.

CHAPTER 22

Two Men of Distinction took turns at the front door of the Lodge, welcoming and inspecting every guest as he or she arrived. Jimmy Bennett was on duty when Vera stepped out of Carl's overstuffed Buick.

"Lawd have mercy. Here comes Vera Marshall," Jimmy said to his partner on the door. "She sure looks fine tonight."

And she did.

Vera borrowed a dress from Harrison's Fine Evening Wear Department. It was fire-engine red, of course, a color that no one could ignore. The material was satin, but the bodice was decorated totally with red sequins that flickered as she walked under the bright lights. Against Emma's protests, the only thing covering Vera on that chilly November night was a sheer crepe scarf thrown around her shoulders. Vera answered Emma's protests by saying, "There will be so many people in the car, Mom, that all that body heat will keep me warm." Warm, but not warm enough, Emma said, as Vera walked away.

"Good evening, Miss Marshall," Jimmy said, sarcastically emphasizing the "Miss" as Vera approached. "You look good enough to eat," he said, remembering how good she tasted when he did. "I hope you'll save me a dance tonight."

Vera looked at Jimmy and said, "That liquor has finally fried your brain because you seem to have forgotten that you're the fish that I threw back. Tonight, my hook has somebody else's name on it."

"Lucky man, whoever he is," Jimmy said, fingering his goatee and staring at Vera's rear as she passed him by.

Inside, the party had already started. Twenty tables lined the room, and at least 15 of them were full. Vera staked out the free table closest to the dance floor, although she knew that she'd be noticed wherever she sat.

Her eyes scanned the room to see if Lou Addit had arrived yet and if his "ace boon coon" Donny Butcher was with him. A lot of folks were there, but Lou and Donny weren't among them. Vera poured herself a shot of bourbon from Carl's flask, filled the glass with ginger ale from the set-up on the table, sat back and waited. Fifteen minutes later, she sprang into action.

When Lou and Donny entered, they did what all the men did: walked around the perimeter of the dance floor, directly or surreptitiously checking out the women. Vera watched as they made their promenade. She'd seen Donny's picture probably 100 times in the *Elevator*. She knew he was fine, but even in the dim light at the Lodge, she could see that he was even finer. He was about 6'2" and with a body that you wouldn't call slim, but muscular and well-proportioned. His hair was wavy, and he had a thin moustache. His skin looked to be the color of coffee with a touch of cream or the soft golden brown of a deer's fur.

When Lou and Donny reached the table next to Vera's, she stood up, walked over to the other side of the table and bent over to talk with her cousin Margaret. True, Margaret couldn't really hear what Vera said over the noise of Spencer Little's Band of Renown, but Vera didn't care. What she really wanted to do was let Donny Butcher get a good look at her from head to toe.

Vera was still standing when Lou and Donny reached her table. Lou placed his hand on Vera's shoulder and said like a gentleman, "Good evening, Vera."

Vera turned around and said, like she didn't know who it was, "Oh, Lou. It's you. Nice to see you."

"Nice to see you, too, girl," said Lou. He stepped back, took a good look and said, "You sure look good." Donny stood at Lou's side, checking out Vera and breathing heavy, if only to himself.

"Vera, I'd like you to meet my friend, Donny Butcher," Lou said, patting Donny on the back. Vera extended her hand, like any lady would. Donny took it and squeezed it and said, "The pleasure is all mine."

If everything goes according to plan, it will be, Vera thought.

She looked Donny directly in the eye, smiled and said, "It's a pleasure to meet you, too, Donny." Then she immediately bent down to talk with Margaret. She positioned her chest to show just enough cleavage to make Donny want to see more.

Donny took another good look at Vera. Hair flowing, shape showing. She got his hormones flowing.

"Would you like to dance?" he asked, extending his hand for Vera to take it, somehow knowing that she would.

"I'd be happy too," Vera said, taking his hand and standing straight up. Donny led her past the tables and standing bodies crowded around the rim of the dance floor to a free spot about a foot square for them to dance in.

Vera started shimmying and shaking and twisting her high heels into the wooden floor. Donny showed a few moves of his own as he tried to keep up with her. The band was so loud, it didn't make sense to try to talk because you'd just look like a fool mouthing words, so Donny and Vera smiled at each other. All through the song. The band segued from one song to another, and Donny and Vera kept dancing and smiling.

Finally, Spencer Little, the band leader, announced, "We're going to adjust the pace and slow it down a taste," and the band played Nat King Cole's rendition of "You Stepped Out of a Dream."

Donny put his hand out again and walked closer to Vera. "May I?" he asked.

"You certainly may," Vera responded.

Donny wrapped his arms around Vera's waist, and she wrapped hers around Donny's neck. He inhaled deeply and let the sensual mixture of Oriental spices in Vera's perfume fill his head. It was nice to smell something besides the Chanel No. 5 that all the women in the 400 wore.

"You certainly are a beautiful woman," Donny said, sliding his hands down her back.

"Thanks for the compliment," Vera said.

He leaned back and looked her in the face. "I'm sure I'm not the first one who has told you that."

"No you're not," Vera said, "but I like hearing it from you as much as I like hearing it from anyone else."

Donny laughed.

Vera subtly followed Donny's movements so that he got a chance to feel every part of her body. He felt as good as he looked, and she did, too.

When that song was over, the band played another slow drag. Donny and Vera stayed together like they were two crayons melting in the heat that permeated the Robinson-Welburn Lodge.

Jimmy Bennett stood on the sidelines watching Vera and Donny. With every sip of the scotch and water in his hand, he became more jealous. He shifted from one foot to another. He cocked his head back, jutting out his chin. He squinted his eyes and shot dirty looks like they were darts. He moved his head from side to side like he was looking at the situation from different directions. He stroked his goatee like he was pulling out hairs. Every time Vera stroked Donny's neck with her fingers, Jimmy remembered how Vera used to stroke him and build him up until he was ready to make love to her for hours.

"To hell with that shit," he said to no one in particular.

The band stopped playing, and Donny and Vera separated.

"Can I get you drink?" Donny asked Vera.

"I'd love a bourbon and ginger ale," Vera said. Switching from one foot to the other, trying not to be too obvious about her discomfort, Vera said, "Why don't you bring that over to my table? I have to make a little visit to the ladies room," she said.

"Back over there?", asked Donny, nodding his head in the direction of the table where Delila and Margaret and two men they had finished dancing with were just sitting down.

"Right over there, where we met," Vera said. "I'll be back in a few minutes, depending how many ladies are lined up. You know how women are," she said, laughing, and she headed off towards the bathroom.

As Vera closed the ladies room door, Jimmy Bennett strolled over to the door, leaned against the wall, and waited.

A few minutes later, Vera opened the door, with a fresh whiff of Mitsuoko and a fresh coat of Max Factor's Red Desire lipstick, and walked towards the dance floor and her table. With every step she felt that she was one step closer to hooking Donny Butcher.

Vera's mind was on Donny when she felt somebody's hand on her, jerking her arm.

"Wait a minute, baby," Jimmy said as Vera turned around.

She took one look at him and pulled back her arm. "Don't pull on me, Jimmy," Vera warned him. "What do you want anyway?"

He moved in closer and practically spitting in her face. "You," he said.

"Get the hell out of here," Vera said, as she stepped back. "You smell like a still," she said and turned away.

"Wait a minute, wait a minute," Jimmy demanded, tugging at Vera's arm again.

Vera spun around with disgust in her eyes. "I said don't touch me, Jimmy. Now leave me alone, or you'll be sorry."

Jimmy threw his hands up in the air and moved back. "Hold up now, baby," he said. "No need for you to talk to me like that." He moved from side to side.

Trying to steady his drunk ass, Vera thought.

"Uh, baby, I just want to tell you that I want you back. Come on here with me. You know we were good together."

Vera shot back, "Were good together. Emphasis on were," she threw up her hands. "I'm through with you, Jimmy. Been through with you, and you know it."

Then she sniffed. "And besides that, your breath stinks. You smell like you've been soaking in liquor." She turned around and started walking away. Jimmy followed her.

It took Jimmy until he got to the middle of the dance floor, to realize that Vera insulted him. He raised his voice and said, "You used to like it. Used to like everything about me."

He rubbed his crotch and said, "Used to couldn't get enough of this right here. You know you want it baby, because, God knows, I still want you." Then, with the same filthy hand he used to rub himself, Jimmy reached out to grab Vera and caught hold of her dress. Like any drunk unaware of his strength, Jimmy pulled so hard to get her to turn around and face him that as Vera spun around, the zipper on her dress ripped open.

By now, half the room was watching the scene unfolding on the dance floor.

. "I'll be damned," Vera said. She reached around behind her with one hand to feel the ripped dress. This isn't even my dress, she thought. That made her even more mad.

With her other free hand, Vera reared back and smacked Jimmy dead across the side of his face. Jimmy was stunned for a second, but he'd been in too many fights not to have quick reactions. He raised his left hand in a fist and reared back to punch Vera.

Before he could bring his fist to her face, Bobby, Paul and Carl were on Jimmy like white on rice. Bobby caught Jimmy's hand in mid-swing and pulled it behind his back. Carl leaped on Jimmy and knocked him down. And Paul groped for Jimmy's other hand to stop him from hitting Bobby and Carl.

Sonny Bennett, Jimmy's brother, and two guys that Jimmy hung with ran up on the floor and shoved Bobby, Paul and Carl to get them off Jimmy. No one knows who threw the first punch, but soon enough, fists were flying and punches were landing. Everyone in the hall looked at the dance floor now.

Charlie Long nearly knocked over his chair, as fast as he ran out to the floor to help his cousins—Bobby, Paul and Carl. Their third cousin once removed, Fletcher Taylor, quick took up the rear guard and started fighting off any other Bennetts or their relatives who wanted to get in the mix. Before you could say "Jack Robinson", almost every male in the room was on the dance floor backing up his boys.

The colored community on the Main Line was so small that almost everybody in the room was related to somebody else in the room, so when their blood relatives got pulled into the fight, they got pulled into it, too. If the parents taught their kids nothing else, it was to stick up for family. If one son came home beaten up, the other better come home beaten up, too. Family loyalty aside, other folks in the room used the fight as an occasion to kick the ass of someone they've been wanting to kick for the longest, just on G.P.—general principle.

Vera and the other women in the room stood on the sidelines watching the fight erupt and rooting for their men. People screamed, tables were turned over, and chairs flew as folks tried to get out of the way of the bodies in the fight as they moved around the hall, knocked into tables, and fell back into the crowd.

Donny Butcher had just gotten Vera's drink from the bar when the fight broke out. He missed the preliminaries and looked up only when the Marshall and the Bennett men started fighting. He couldn't believe how fast the fight escalated and how soon the hall was pure chaos.

"Yo, man," Donny said to Lou. "Let's get the hell out of here before the cops come."

"I'm with ya, man," Lou said. "These country cops out here don't play. Before the night's over, these niggers are going to be underneath the jail." Lou knew everyone out there fighting, but he had no interest in getting involved in it. He wasn't related to anyone out there, and his Daddy would have his head if he was out here rough-housing.

"Let's go," said Lou, putting his drink down and looked around for an exit. They'd have to go through the fight to get to the door, and Lou wasn't having any of that. But there was a window with a screen not twenty feet away from them. All those folks in one room drew some heat, so the windows were open, even in November. Lou quickly pushed out the screen and climbed out. Donny followed right behind him.

Vera, wondering what happened to Donny, caught a glimpse of him jumping out the window as she looked around the room.

Unbeknownst to everyone, the janitor at the lodge had called the police when the fight took in more than ten people. He figured that there was no sense in calling the cops and getting those young men in trouble with Johnny Law if they were going to take it outside or if it was going to burn itself out. But this fight kept growing and growing. When the boys started messing up the Lodge's furniture, he figured it was time for the cops, because then his job was on the line.

Donny and Lou jumped into Donny's Cadillac, hit the ignition, turned left out the parking lot, and hightailed it back down Lancaster Avenue towards Philly just as the Easttown Township police turned the corner onto Lancaster Avenue and into the parking lot.

CHAPTER 23

All along Lancaster Avenue, police cars with lights flashing whizzed by them. Tredyffrin Township police from Wayne. Radnor Township police from Radnor. Lower Merion Township police from Haverford and Bryn Mawr. Easttown Township police called for backup from police departments up and down the Main Line. Colored folks fighting and rioting took more than one police department to handle.

Paul was just about to take another swing at Tommy Bennett when the cops arrived. Six Easttown Township Police—the entire police department, the two on duty and the four dragged out of their beds who were on call every time there was a dance at the Lodge—rushed in the door, billy clubs in the air, bullhorn in the sergeant's mouth yelling, "Break it up! Break it up!"

More people started screaming and yelling. "The cops are here." "Cool it. It's the man." "Johnny Law, Johnny Law!" One by one, the guys stopped fighting as the police pushed their way into the center of the crowd.

"Break it up, break it up," the cops yelled as they pulled one body off of another, stood between arms that were ready to swing and their targets, and tried to talk some sense into hotheaded men. In a few minutes, the dance floor was crowded with police from all the Main Line townships. The cops formed a ring around the outside of the guys who were fighting to keep the perpetrators inside.

Once the cops got all the guys cooled down or at least stopped all the fighting, Sergeant Lotello of the Easttown police said, "Does somebody want to tell me what happened here?" He got no answer and said, "Any of you boys want to talk?"

Nobody spoke.

"Who started this thing?" he asked, walking around the ring of cops, looking the brawlers in the eye.

Silence. The guys may have just beat the tar out of each other, but they know that even if they just did, they weren't going to turn anybody in to the white cops. The few colored lawyers on the Main Line hardly got a good chance to defend the colored boys who got in to trouble, with judges who didn't listen and evidence that suddenly appeared. And the white lawyers could care less about one more nigger getting locked up, so as much as they didn't like someone, they didn't want to send them off to the white folks justice. They'd take care of their own. They knew that as small as the colored community was on the Main Line, they'd see that person again and they'd deal with them in their own way.

The sergeant pushed between a few of his men and called out, "Any of you ladies have any idea what happened here?"

The women just looked back at him, shook their heads and shrugged their shoulders. They knew better, too.

Lotello threw his hands up in the air and said, "Where's the janitor that called us? Somebody better start talking around here."

He hit his billy club into the palm of his hand. "Somebody better talk or we'll carry the lot of you in," he said. Looking around the room at the group of men in uniform ringing the dance floor, nobody doubted that they had the paddy wagons to do it.

"I'm right here," said the janitor as he put up his hand and squeezed his way to the middle of the dance floor. All of them boys didn't need to get in trouble for that one troublemaker, the janitor thought, so he realized that it was time to talk.

"Alls I know is that man right there," he said, pointing at Jimmy, "ripped that lady's dress," he said, pointing at Vera, "and started to punch her."

"She slapped me first," Jimmy said, sounding like a child telling on his sister to his mother. Like the cops cared to hear that. A man hitting a man who hit him first was self defense; a man hitting a woman because she slapped him was a 352—assault, pure and simple.

"Is that Jimmy Bennett?" said Keith Sweeny of the Lower Merion police department. He stepped out of the circle to take a closer look at Jimmy. Since nobody had bothered to turn on all the lights, Sweeny flashed his flash light in Jimmy's face. "Might have known you'd be involved. Isn't it enough, you causing trouble in Lower Merion, you have to come on up here to Berwyn?" he said.

"So you know this fellow," Sergeant Lotello said.

"Sure do," said Sweeny. "Locked him up a few times. Drinking and carrying on. Suspected of some petty theft, but never proven. Yeah, I know him real well."

"Can't have no man hitting on a lady," the janitor said, as Vera looked over at the sergeant with her head held high as a lady would, even one with a ripped zipper.

"So I take it the rest of you were just watching?" the Sergeant said to the men crowded in the middle. "How come no one owns up to hitting anybody when I see black eyes and busted lips already?"

Still, silence from the men in the middle.

"All right," said the Sergeant, frustrated and tired. "Since it seems like I'm not going to get anything out of you colored boys, I'll go with what I have."

He walked over to Jimmy. "What'd you say your name was boy?"

"Jimmy Bennett. B-E-N-N-E-T-T," said Officer Sweeny because Jimmy didn't open his mouth.

Lotello said, "You, Jimmy Bennett. Seems like you started this mess. Didn't your mama ever tell you don't hit a lady?" The ladies in the crowd laughed.

"You come on with me. Looks like we're going to get to know you here in Easttown Township, too," said the sergeant.

"And for the rest of yous," he said, waving his billy club at the crowd, "this party is over. Get on home and back to where you came from. If there's ever any more mess like this in Easttown Township, we'll take you all in, whether you tell us what happened or not. Because once we get yous to the station, we'd get some of yous to talk and that'd be all we need."

He turned completely around the circle with his billy club straight out and said, "Now get the hell out of here."

He didn't have to say it twice. The folks were out the door before the cops were. Grabbing their purses and bags, piling back into the cars in the parking lot and heading down Lancaster Avenue, thinking of the stories they'd tell with glee for the rest of the year until the next Top Men of Distinction Ball.

Bobby threw his jacket over Vera's shoulders to cover up where the dress was ripped.

"You all right?" he finally got a chance to ask.

"I should be asking you," she said, touching his swollen lip.

"Nothing that an ice bag won't cure," he said.

"And you, Paul," she said, looking at his black eye. "I'm a buy you a great big old T-bone."

Carl rubbed his sore jaw and said, "Jimmy Bennett ain't got the sense he was born with. How does he think he's going to mess with you with all of us up in there?"

"How can he think when he's full of liquor," Vera said. "Even when he's not, he has trouble." They fell out laughing.

"Thanks, guys, for coming to my rescue," Vera told them.

"How could we not?" said Carl. "Uncle John would whop our behinds if he heard any different, and I'll chance a whipping from Jimmy Bennett for one from Uncle John any day."

"You got that right," said Bobby, and they all laughed.

The Marshalls talked all about the fight all the way back to Ardmore. Who hit who with what. Did you see Paul drop Sonny Bennett to the floor? Did you see Bobby spin Jimmy around so fast he fell on top of Paul who was lying on top of Randy Dinger? They laughed and rehashed all the way home.

Vera told them that Jimmy got jealous because she was dancing with Donny Butcher of Butcher Funeral Homes.

"What was he doing out there with us? Slumming?" asked Delila. "We're not in the 400 crowd he runs with."

"And he ain't nothing like the crowd *we* run with," Vera said. "He jumped out the window at the first sign of trouble. What a punk. He didn't even join in, after he had just spent the last half hour dancing with me, up close, too. I would think that he, of all people, would come to my defense."

"Maybe he was afraid of messing up his pretty boy face," said Carl, laughing.

"Well, I know one thing," said Vera. "I don't want no man who ain't, if you know what I mean."

"I know what you mean, girl," said Delila. "Can't stand a man who runs from a fight."

"You got that right," said Vera as she leaned back and threw Donny Butcher out of her mind as easy as he jumped out of that window.

"Man, we got out of there just in time," Donny said to Lou as they watched the police cars speed by.

"No question about it," said Lou.

"Those boys were fighting like somebody was talking about somebody's Mama," Donny said, laughing.

"What happened back there?" Donny asked. "I'm at the bar getting a drink for that fine Vera, and next thing I knew, those boys were banging heads."

"You didn't see it?" Lou said.

"Naw, man," Donny said. "I was trying to get the bourbon and ginger and get back to that fine thing."

Lou said, "The whole thing was a fight *about* that fine thing. Her crazy old ex-boyfriend grabbed her and ripped her dress. So then she slapped him. Then he pulled back like he was going to hit her. So her brothers and cousins jumped on him, then his brothers and his boys jumped on them, and then everybody got into it. You aren't going to have that many related folks out there fighting without the rest of their family getting into it. I don't know what it's like in the city, but out here, blood is definitely thicker than water."

"So that big fight was about Vera?" Donny asked.

"Sure was," Lou said.

Donny laughed. "Well, she sure's worth fighting for. That's about one of the finest women I've seen in a long time. Long legs, long hair, big breasts, and a butt that'll make you want to smack your momma. I've got to see her again, man," Donny said. "Can you get me in touch with her?"

Lou said, "She works right down there at Harrison's as a model. She saw us when we were in the store the other day."

"Oh she did, did she," Donny said. "I know we didn't see her because I would have remembered."

"That's right," said Lou. "She was on the second floor looking over the balcony while we were looking at ties."

"I'll be damned," said Donny, as he turned down Spring Avenue to drop off Lou.

Monday morning Donny dressed in his finest suit—undertaker's black of course, with a red jacquard pattern tie, white shirt, and a black fedora with a red band. He shaved carefully and splashed cologne on his cheeks and rubbed it on his neck so Vera could smell sensual musk when she got close.

At 11:30 a.m., Donny opened the front door to Harrison's. He looked around the first floor as far as he could see, but didn't see Vera. He was only going to wait 15 minutes for her to show up before he went upstairs to ask Mr. Harrison, an old friend of his father's, to find Vera for him.

Donny looked at the men's cologne to see if there was anything there that appealed to him. He looked over at men's accessories to see if anything new had come in. After about five minutes, he figured he might have more luck going upstairs to the women's department, especially since Lou told him that when they were in the store last, she was on the second floor.

Donny took the escalator upstairs and walked through the pink trellis that was the entrance to Fine Women's Fashions. Two sales girls rushed up to him.

"Can I help you sir?" said one, and "Is there anything I can get for you, sir?" said the other simultaneously. The salesgirls in that department were required to read the *Elevator*'s society pages every week to recognize the faces of the customers in the 400, to know when the colored society required new clothes, and for what occasion. They both recognized Donny Butcher. But Mrs. Harrison trained them not to call their society customers by their names unless they were formally introduced; even though their pictures were in the paper on a regular basis, they still deserved their privacy, and at Harrison's, they would have it.

Before they could offer him a private showing room to look at dresses for the woman in his life, he said, "Nothing, thank you. I see what I'm looking for."

CHAPTER 24

Vera stood at the end of the department showing a group of women a green silk suit with a cluster of red holly berries, pinned above the left breast. She let them feel the smooth fabric. "Perfect for holiday entertaining," she said. She turned from side to side, tilting the green wide-brimmed felt hat with the red ribbon and matching holly berries around the brim. Vera was smiling and so were the ladies in her little audience.

She obviously enjoys her job, he thought. Donny snuck up behind Vera.

"Where can I buy that dress, because I met a lady Saturday night who would look fantastic in it", Donny said.

Vera turned around smiling, but dropped the smile when she saw who it was.

"$49.99. Fine Women's Fashions," Vera said. She turned around to the women in front of her, said, "Good day ladies," and walked away.

Donny stood there looking dumbfaced, and then realized that he had to go after her.

"Hey, wait a minute," he said.

Vera turned around only to say, "Hay is for horses," and walked away.

When she got out of the department, she headed toward the elevator. By this time, Donny was practically running after her.

"I meant, Vera, wait," he said. But she didn't stop. Neither did Donny.

They both got on the waiting elevator. Vera held up the price card so that all the other passengers could see it and said, "Fine Women's Fashions. Perfect for a holiday get-together."

If Donny wanted to talk to her, he had to follow her to the first floor. As she stepped off the elevator and headed over towards women's cosmetics, Donny caught up with her.

"Whoa, slow down. What's the matter, Vera? I was talking about you. That lady I met Saturday night was you and that dress does look fabulous on you," he said, looking her up and down.

"Yeah, that lady you met and left Saturday," she said. "I saw you and Lou jumping out of the window just as things were heating up. You didn't even bother to come to my defense."

Donny held up his hands. "Whoa. Wait a minute. I didn't even know what happened in there until Lou and I were half way back to Philly. All I knew is that some local yokels were starting a riot, and I wasn't going to wait for the cops to get there. City cops are bad enough, and Lou said that country cops are worse."

"You expect me to believe that?" Vera said. "Some crazy jack rabbit gets mad at me for dancing with you, and you expect me to believe that you don't know anything about it?"

"It's the truth," Donny said, raising his eyebrows like Vera would fall for that innocent look. "I was over at the bar, getting your drink, and the next thing I knew, all hell had broken loose."

"Yeah," she said, "and you hightailed it out of there just like I'm going to do now." She turned on her green suede three-inch heels and walked away.

Donny ran after her.

"Hold on now. Why don't we discuss this over lunch?" Donny said, as he admired the way she looked from behind in that tight, A-line skirt.

Vera turned around and said, "Mr. Butcher, I have to work for my living. I can't stand here and talk with you just because you want to talk, nor can I have you following me around while I'm trying to do my job. I'm not interested in having lunch with you today, tomorrow, or ever. In fact, I'm not interested in you. And now I'm going to walk away from you without a care as to what becomes of you the same way you did me Saturday night."

Donny just looked. Vera walked away and this time, he let her. Self-assured and smiling to himself, he thought, she's playing hard to get. I'm up for the game, he thought.

But what he didn't know was that Vera wasn't playing.

Vera was steaming. So much so that she couldn't finish her walk around the store. She headed back to the model's dressing room.

One of the other models, Mary Carroll stood outside her dressing room, dressed in her street clothes, ready to go to lunch.

"What's wrong with you?" she said as Vera stomped down the hall, mumbling to herself about some "no good bastard", "he has a lot of damn nerve".

"You know that Donny Butcher I told you about this morning," Vera said, holding her price card on her hip.

"Yeah, I remember," Mary said. "The dream man who jumped out the window."

"Well, I just had to tell him off downstairs," Vera said. Waving her price card in the air, she said, "I can't believe that he's that arrogant to think that I would still want him. Who does he think he is? Forget him, who does he think *I* am," Vera said. "He comes telling me that I look fabulous in this dress, like I don't already know that, like it's not my job to look fabulous, like I'm supposed to fall all over him."

She put both hands on her hips and shifted her weight to one foot like she was getting ready to read Mary Carroll. "I set him straight. Told him I was gonna leave him the same as he left me Saturday night, jumping out that window," she said. "I know he thought I'd fall for him, since I'm sure Lou told him I was a plumber's daughter."

She walked up and down the hallway outside of the dressing rooms, letting her anger burn off. "I bet he wouldn't treat any of those 400 chicks like that. He was sorely mistaken to think that I would fall in line just because he asked. I may want a man from the 400, but that's what I mean. A man, not a little boy who jumps out of windows at the first sign of trouble."

Mary figured it was safe to talk then. "I guess he figures that all the money he has, he doesn't have to get involved in someone else's fight and that he can jump out of any window he wants," Mary said.

"Well, like I told him, he can keep on going," Vera said. And I guess I'll have to keep on looking, she thought.

On Tuesday, Vera modeled swim wear. It had become very fashionable for women in the 400 to take a Caribbean cruise during the winter, or at least to go to Florida. And so like the stores downtown, Harrison's carried a small selection of cruisewear. Even though most shoppers weren't thinking about going anywhere but home to wrap their Christmas presents, Mrs. Harrison believed that Harrison's should cater to those customers who could afford to go away and inspire those who couldn't. Charlene liked the opportunity to do something different than the usual holiday entertaining outfits. Vera wore a navy blue tank suit with a flared skirt with white waves rising and falling over the hem. Her long brown hair was wrapped in a navy blue turban with a white carnation on the side. She even carried a white beach ball with navy stripes. On her feet, white leather mules with an open toe revealing bright red nail polish on her toes.

She and Mary stood in the middle of a large child's sandbox next to the first floor elevator. Vera spotted Donny before he spotted her, but Charlene gave the models strict instructions not to move out of the sandbox—even if they were cold and wanted to walk around to warm themselves up. Vera was stuck.

She turned in the opposite direction from Donny, but he just walked around to face her. She turned back again, and Donny walked back to face her. He joined the small crowd in front looking at the two lovely ladies in bathing suits in November.

"Excuse me, Miss," Donny said to Vera. "What can you tell me about that swimsuit?"

"$9.99. Cruisewear in the Casual Shop," said Vera. She turned around so that the people on the other side could get a good look.

Donny moved over to the other side.

"What type of fabric is it," Donny asked in his most sincere voice, so Vera would think that he really cared.

"100 percent cotton," Vera said.

"And how does one care for that fabric," Donny asked.

Vera shot him a dirty look.

"You know, I mean, should you hand wash or what?" Donny asked.

"All fine things should be hand washed, sir," Vera said.

Donny held up his hands. "Then all I need is a bar of soap," he said. Everyone around him laughed. Vera didn't.

Donny pressed on, "What style do I ask for if I want to purchase that suit for a special lady?"

Vera wanted to roll her eyes, but couldn't because other customers were looking. "The Catalina," she said. He pulled out a notepad from his coat pocket and wrote it down.

"Now maybe you can help me with the size," Donny said. "The lady I have in mind is about your size, although I must say, she looks nothing like you."

Vera looked over his head as she said, "Size 8."

"Thanks," he said, writing that down, too.

"Just one more question, Miss," Donny said, knowing that she'd have to listen.

"Would you like to have lunch with me?" he asked.

"Absolutely not, sir," Vera said. The crowd laughed at his humiliation.

Vera was in the dressing room changing into her street clothes for lunch when she heard a knock at the door. "Come in," she said.

Charlene opened the door, holding a small pink Harrison's box with a huge white bow.

"A package for you," Charlene said.

"From who?" Vera asked.

"I don't know," said Charlene. "There should be a card underneath all that ribbon."

Vera took the box, said "thank you" and lifted up the ribbon flower. No card. She opened the box anyway and found a card with her name handwritten on the envelope. The card read, "If not lunch, how about the Bahamas?" It was signed "Donny".

On her way out to lunch, she carried the box to gift wrap.

A clerk with the name tag "Katherine" said, "Can I help you?"

"I'd like to send this to Mr. Donny Butcher at Butcher Funeral Home. And I'd like it delivered today," Vera said.

"Certainly. That would be no problem," Katherine said, taking the box from Vera's hands. She set the box on the counter and said, "Do you need a gift card?"

"No," said Vera. "I already put the card inside."

At the bottom of Donny's card, Vera had simply written, "No."

The next day, in the dressing rooms, Mary said, "Girl, you're crazy turning down that fine Donny Butcher. Even if Mr. 400 jumped out the window, it's clear that cat likes you, Vera. Putting up with that crap you dish out and still coming back for more."

Vera said, "Pl-e-ase, Mary. He may be fine, but he ain't dandy, if you know what I mean. And besides. I was looking for a man when he came along. Another will come along soon, trust me. They always do."

"Well, you probably got that right," Mary said.

"If Donny Butcher knows what's good for him, he'll leave me alone and go on back to those 400 girls who keep running after his punk ass," Vera said.

She tilted her dark brown mink beret to just the right angle and said, "Time to go." Vera was modeling a brown wool crepe suit with a boxy jacket and mink trim around the 3/4 length sleeves. The A-line skirt didn't even have a walking split in the back. She wore brown leather pumps with sensible 1" heels and an old-lady-going-to-church handbag slung over her wrist. Even she was bored with the outfit.

Vera called out to Charlene and said, "What are you trying to do to me? No man will be looking at me in this get up. You know I'm trying to catch a man, and you have me wearing this." She ran her hand down both sides of the skirt.

"I thought you'd already been caught," said Charlene, as she looked over yesterday's sales records. "Besides, Mrs. Harrison wanted to tone things down after yesterday's swimsuit promotion. Can't show your flesh all the time, she said."

"I'll show it if they want to see it," Vera said. Then she whispered in Mary's ear, "But I'm glad she's off that crazy cruisewear kick. I'd like to freeze my butt off yesterday." She and Mary laughed as they walked out the door.

Vera decided to show the suit at the hosiery counter. A sensible suit would appeal to sensible ladies selecting sensible hosiery.

She sashayed to the aisle next to the hosiery counter, stuck out her right foot, smiled and held up her sign. "Ladies Dresses. Fourteen ninety-nine. Perfect for church," she said.

One by one the ladies at the counter turned around to look at Vera. She walked back and forth down the short aisle. As she turned around to show the dress to a lady behind her who called out, "What kind of material is that, sugar?", she looked over at the aisle near the escalator. Donny Butcher was leaning against the railing, hat cocked to one side, just looking. Vera expected him to say something or to come over. He did neither. He just stood there, looking. When she looked back in his direction, he was gone.

CHAPTER 25

When Vera arrived the next day, Charlene pulled her to the side. "You've got a special assignment today," Charlene said. "I know you love the floor modeling, but we've got a private showing lined up for you. Seems like the ladies of the LaDeDa Social Club are interested in picking their spring toilettes today. They want to see 11 dresses, including evening wear, at noon. And, they specifically requested you as their model of choice."

"Eleven outfits?" asked Vera. "What are they going to do while I change?"

"Eat lunch, I guess," Charlene said. "Although I'm not handling the luncheon arrangements. Mr. Harrison himself is getting personally involved."

"Well, well," said Vera. "Do you think I've hit the big time?"

"I'd say so," said Charlene. "Now let's go select the outfits. They must fit perfectly. Any alterations will have to be done right away," she says, dragging Vera by the hand down to the wide open dressing room.

Upstairs, Donny stood up from his seat across from Mr. Harrison's hand polished mahogany desk. "I can't thank you enough, Mr. Harrison," he said.

"Anything for a Butcher, you know that," Mr. Harrison said, running his hands down his suspenders. "Now don't you forget to give your Dad and Mom my best."

"I'll do that sir," Donny said, opening the door. "Thanks again."

"Your purchases are more than thanks enough," Mr. Harrison said. He couldn't remember the last time he'd seen a man so smitten.

At 11:45, Vera and Charlene took their places behind the curtain in the private showing room. Charlene quickly reviewed her cards and the order of the show as Vera smoothed her hair in place. Every strand must be perfect. Denise, the dresser, was arranging the outfits in order, knowing that she couldn't take too long to dress Vera between dresses since she was the only model in the show.

At noon, the ladies behind the curtain figured that the ladies in front of the curtain had arrived, although they wouldn't dare look. Mr. Harrison told Charlene to start the show precisely at 12:15.

At 12:15, Charlene pushed the curtains open and stepped out. She looked around the room and stopped. There were no ladies sitting at tables having lunch and chatting. The only thing she saw were 10 empty tables and Donny Butcher sitting at the end of the runway at a table, alone, with a tall beverage glass in his hand.

Charlene said, "I'm sorry. There must be some mistake. I think I'm in the wrong showing room." She wanted to call him Mr. Butcher, but even she didn't dare—unless he introduced himself. Before she could turn and walk away, Donny raised his hand to stop her.

"You have a model back there named Vera getting ready to model eleven outfits?" he asked.

"Yes, I do," said Charlene, still in shock.

"Then there's no mistake," Donny said.

"But I thought this showing was for the ladies of the LaDeDa Social Club," she said, still puzzled.

"Nope," said Donny. "Just me. Mr. Harrison's just doing me a little favor, if you know what I mean."

Charlene looked at Donny, dropped the puzzled look from her face, and said, "I see what you mean." She knew that Vera was going to be mad; she'd heard the talk about Donny Butcher. But she had to do the show, mad or not. Charlene only knew of one way to prepare Vera for this.

She said to Donny, "Excuse me for one second, sir," and went back through the curtain to where Vera stood, ready to go on.

"What's going on?" Vera asked, tired of standing motionless in her best model stance ready for the curtain to open up.

"Just keep your head up and smile," Charlene said. She patted Vera on the arm and went back out front. She walked over to the podium said, "We're ready now," and launched into her fashion show commentator voice, "Good afternoon and welcome to a Spring Cavalcade of Fashion at Harrison's."

She pressed the button on the podium that automatically opened the curtains. The huge pink velveteen curtains trimmed in white and gold tassels swung open to reveal Vera standing in the middle of the stage in a suit with gold buttons; pink, green and yellow checks; a pink leather handbag, pink pumps, and a yellow felt hat.

Vera looked out and saw only Donny sitting at the table, sipping a drink. In her shock, the only thing she remembered were Charlene's words, "Keep your head up and smile." She turned around to show the complete outfit, heard Charlene describing it, and started walking down the runway, head up, smiling.

When she got to the end near Donny, Vera whirled around and headed off in the other direction as if she didn't see him. She used her runway training, which was to look over the audience's heads, don't look anyone in the eye, and keep your cool at all times. She paused at the beginning of the runway and went back behind the curtain as Charlene finished describing the outfit.

"Damn, that man sure is persistent," Vera said to Denise as she unbuttoned the jacket.

"What man are you talking about?" Denise asked.

"That Donny Butcher," Vera said. "That man who's been after me for the past week. He got Mr. Harrison himself to arrange this fashion show with me just for him," she said, now pacing around the dressing room in her underwear.

"Just him sitting out there. It ain't no ladies social club. Just a man who's hot in his pants for me," she laughed. "Now don't that beat all." She paced back and forth. "I'll fix him though."

"Keep still, girl," Denise said. "I've got to get you in and out of these things. One man or a hundred, Mr. Harrison arranged a fashion show, and you'd better give that man a good one."

"Well, that's all I'll ever give him," Vera said.

"Doesn't matter," said Denise. "Just get back out there and do it."

Vera walked back out in an ecru linen dress with a white lace collar, perfect for a spring luncheon. She paraded up and down the runway in dresses, suits, evening gowns, cocktail dresses. When she walked out in an evening gown or cocktail dress, Donny said, "Ump, ump, ump" or "Lord have mercy," or "My, my, my, you sure look good."

Vera kept her head up, looked over Donny's head and smiled. She even found herself smiling, not because Charlene told her to, but because she was enjoyed this little game of cat and mouse.

For her last outfit, Vera modeled a full-length evening gown that had a large hoop skirt, but was strapless and cut low in the front. She had a mink stole draped around her shoulders. Charlene instructed to stand on the stage as she wound up the description.

" . . . and thank you for coming to Harrison's for a Spring Cavalcade of Fashion."

Donny put down his drink, stood up and clapped. Vera bowed as Charlene held her hand out to her.

Then Charlene pressed the button that automatically closed the curtain and Vera disappeared.

"I hope you enjoyed the show, sir," said Charlene. "Do let me know if there is anything I can help you with."

"I've taken care of everything with Mr. Harrison," Donny said, picking up his hat and placing it on his head. "Good bye now," he said and walked out.

As soon as the door closed behind Donny, Charlene pressed the button to automatically open the curtain. "That's some man," she said to Vera, who stood there shaking her head. "He set this whole thing up just to see you," she said. With a touch of envy, she added, "I never had a man that determined to have me."

Vera paced around the stage. "That man had a whole lot of nerve, getting us to put on a fashion show just for him."

"Well, technically," said Charlene, "it was still a fashion show."

"Did he buy anything?" Vera asked.

"No," said Charlene.

"All that work just so he can have me prance around for him," Vera said. "The nerve of him."

Charlene gathered her cards together. "I'm sure he paid mightily for the privilege. Mr. Harrison wouldn't take you—a top-selling floor model— off the floor for nothing. I guess if you've got money, you can get anything," Charlene said.

"Not everything. It'll take more than money to get me because if that's all it took, he would have had me by now, as much money as those Butcher's have," Vera said, as she laughed. But Donny was persistent. Maybe he wasn't so much of a punk. And he sure did look good sitting there in that form-fitting suit, sipping that drink. She enjoyed strutting her stuff for him, if only to let him know what he was missing.

That evening, the Marshalls were inside, eating dinner, causing a commotion, as usual. Donald and Valerie argued back and forth about whose turn it was to wash the dishes. Milton picked at Cynthia and grabbed food off her plate. They hardly noticed the noise outside their door.

"Quiet down, everyone," Bobby said, holding his hands out and waving them down in a shushing motion. "I think somebody's at the door."

He walked over and opened the door. Sure enough, a man with a driver's uniform and cap stood on the front step. "Is this the residence of Miss Vera Marshall?"

"It is," Bobby said.

"Is Miss Marshall home," the driver asked.

"Depends on who's asking," Vera yelled from inside.

"I think you better come here Vera," Bobby said. "This is something you want to see."

The kids at the table rushed to the door because if there was something to see that Vera would want to see, they wanted to see it, too. They had to get right in front or else they wouldn't be able to see a thing. Vera strolled over with the rest of the girls and looked outside.

Half of Welsh Road was gathered around three long black Cadillac limousines double-parked in front of the Marshall's and the next two houses. As soon as Vera walked through the crowd on her porch and to the top of the stairs, one of the back seat limo doors opened. She recognized the man who got out as one of the Harrison delivery boys. He carried a large pink Harrison's box with a white ribbon.

"May we go inside with the packages?" the driver asked.

"Sure," said Vera. No sense in all of Ardmore knowing her business. She opened the door and led the driver inside to the living room. The delivery boy easily walked up the sidewalk and the steps, but he had to fight a crowd to get to the front door.

"Perhaps the lady should have a seat on the couch," the driver said, pointing to Emma's good plastic slipcovered couch. "We're going to need room to put down the packages."

Packages plural, thought Vera. That means there's more than one.

"I'm game," said Vera, sitting down.

"Y'all get out of the way and let the man in," Vera said to her brothers and sisters who crowded around the door. The brothers and sisters made a path. The delivery boy brought in the box and laid it on the floor in front of Vera. He took off the bow, which was just taped to the top of the box, and opened it. He picked up the red rose that laid on top of the wrapping tissue and handed it to Vera. He smoothed open the tissue to reveal the first suit that Vera wore at Donny's private fashion show—the yellow, green, and pink checked suit. The delivery boy placed the box at Vera's feet and stood next to the driver.

Then another delivery boy walked in, opened the package, handed Vera the rose, pulled back the tissue and revealed the second outfit that

Vera wore that afternoon. One by one, nine more delivery boys came in, opened their boxes, handed Vera a rose and displayed the dresses—causing her family to move onto the stairs to make room for the delivery boys but also to get a good bird's eye view of all of those fine clothes laid out on the floor.

The eleventh delivery boy carried the largest box. He opened it and showed Vera the ball gown *and* the mink stole she modeled last. He handed Vera the eleventh rose and stood back. She was impressed, all right, but she pretended not to care. At least not yet. She stood up and counted the roses. "One, two, three." She counted until she reached eleven.

"Only eleven. Where's the twelfth rose?"

Before the delivery boys could answer, the front door opened. Donny walked in holding a red rose with a big pink satin bow around it, ribbon trailing two feet behind him. All the women in the house, Emma included, caught their breath as this fine-looking man in a navy blue suit, blue and gold tie, black shoes, and black hat walked in. The girls closest to the door smiled as they caught a whiff of his aftershave. Donny walked straight up to Vera, bent down on his knee and said, "Forgive me, Vera." He took her hand, kissed it, and looked deep into her eyes.

Vera paused for a few seconds, and then a smile started working its way across her face. Then she laughed so loudly that Emma almost rushed over there and put her hand over her mouth. She couldn't believe that Vera was so rude to this nice young man.

Vera got herself under control before Emma could move. "Get up, honey," she said. "You sure know how to apologize. I like that in a man."

Donny stood up and so did she. He still held on to her hand. She looked him straight in the eyes and said, "You're forgiven," and hugged him with all the strength in her arms.

Everybody in the house applauded.

CHAPTER 26

Vera and Donny started dating immediately. He liked her spirit, her humor, her drive, her looks and her body. She liked his position in the 400, his looks, and the way he made her feel when she gave her body to him. Far from being the punk that she thought he was, Vera quickly concluded that Donny was a bit of a rogue, and she liked that. He was in the 400, but he still had a touch of the street in him.

They went to society parties and balls, but they also went to the clubs like Velvet's where they sometimes saw Alfreda working the room, still collecting a dollar a week from her customers. Vera loved Donny's social position, but she genuinely loved him, too. And she loved it every time Donny pulled up to Welsh Road in his big black Cadillac because that meant that she was one step closer to getting away.

Vera caused quite a stir in Donny's world. She never could slip in anywhere unnoticed. Neither could Donny because everyone in colored society recognized his face from the *Elevator*. The combination of Vera and Donny together was something to behold. Vera was always turning heads, and Donny was always catching eyes. When Donny and Vera entered a ball or party, there wasn't a couple that looked finer.

And Vera was happy. This was the closest she had ever come to being a part of 400 society. She liked going to homes with china that you could see through when you held it up to the light and crystal that resonated if you pinged it with your finger. She liked going to ballrooms with large crystal chandeliers, fresh cut flowers on the table, and the finest dance orchestras in town.

The women in the 400 liked to look at Vera on the store floor or in a fashion show, but they didn't want to look at her across the table as a guest at a luncheon or dinner in their homes with one of their most eligible young bachelors at her arm. They drew these lines: Vera was a woman of questionable background, uneducated, had to work for a living, and a little too flashy for their prim and proper tastes. Vera didn't say much at those social events, but she didn't have to. She never said much to women anyway, and there were always plenty of men around to talk with when Donny walked away to get her a drink or something to eat.

Donny's sister Mary and his mother Harriet were the most horrified of all. But Donald Butcher, Sr. liked Vera; he liked her spirit, and she seemed to make Donny happy. And if the boy was happy, that was good enough for him. Donald Butcher didn't pay any mind to Mary and Harriet's feelings because he didn't get where he was in his business or personal life relying on so-called female intuition.

One of the 400's biggest social events was the May Pole Ball. It was held every year on the Saturday before Memorial Day, and it was sponsored by the Philadelphia Chapter of Hansel & Gretel, a group of 400 mothers who organized a club for their children so they could associate with other 400 children and not be forced to play with children of the "wrong" background.

The Ball was held at the Mayfair Hall in Mt. Airy. It was the only facility open to colored folks that was big enough to hold the 500 guests that attended every year and that had ceilings high enough to accommodate the elaborate May poles that formed a centerpiece on each table. The Hansel & Gretel Mothers always guaranteed 500 guests because every year the ball sold out and there was a waiting list of people who hoped to get in if the hall would just squeeze in just one more table, which, of course, it never did.

The Butchers had a prime table at the ball ever since it began. Harriet Butcher was in the initial group of five mothers who founded Hansel & Gretel and started the event. The Butcher table was in the first row, right in front of the bandstand. Harriet, with her hair piled on top of her head in a bun that all the 400 matrons wore because it was the closest thing they could get to a crown on top of their heads, always sat facing the bandstand so she could see everyone as they got up to dance or came into the room.

Yet, she was protected enough by the tables behind her so that anyone who wanted to talk to her had to make an effort to walk through the other tables to do so. She liked it that way, for fond as she was of the other Hansel

& Gretel mothers, most of the other guests at the event were NOKD—not our kind, dear, as she told Mary.

Especially that Vera Marshall.

"I don't know what has possessed you, Donny Butcher," Harriet said to him one day at the dinner table. "Dating that girl."

"I know," said his sister, Mary, pointing down below Donny's waist.

"You don't know nothing, Mary," Donny said.

"Anything," Harriet corrected him. "Good heavens. That girl has even got you using bad grammar."

"Anything," Donny repeated. "You don't know anything, Mary." Donny barely tolerated Mary and her ways. She was everything he didn't like about the circle into which he was born. She immediately wanted to know what someone's father did before she decided whether that person was good enough to know. She literally looked down her pointed nose and flung her long straight hair at anyone who didn't meet her standards. To please Mary, a person didn't have to just run in the 400 circles; he or she had to be born into them.

"You are embarrassing the family, bringing that working girl into our circle," Harriet said. "Why, just the other day, at the Pierce's party, Catherine Pierce came up to me and said, 'Isn't that girl with your son a model at Harrison's' and I couldn't lie. She's not the first one to ask that. Oh, no. Everybody knows it."

"They're not asking because they don't know because they've all seen her at enough fashion shows. Who could miss her, really? They're asking because they want me to know what they know," Harriet said, stabbing her prime rib and letting juices ooze out with every sentence. "Of course, I had to say, 'Yes, she is a model at Harrison's.' So Catherine says, 'Well, I don't know their family name. What does her father do?'"

"Of course I was mortified, so I tried to put a positive spin on it. So I say, 'She's from the Main Line you know.'" Harriet rolled her eyes and said, 'Then, Catherine says, 'Then we should know her family. Tell me again, what does her father do?' knowing full well that I didn't even tell her once what he did."

"So I say, 'he owns and operates a very successful plumbing business.' And she says, 'Oh really, then I'm sure Noreen knows him', takes her drink and walks straight over to Noreen Daniels," Harriet went on.

"Meanwhile, I'm trying to have a pleasant conversation with Attorney Clemens' wife when Noreen comes over, stands so she must be recognized, and says, 'excuse me, Harriet, but I thought you should know.' Like I didn't know what she would say next. To my absolute mortification, *again*, Noreen says, 'That Marshall girl's father is just a plumber. And his business, if you can call it that, is just he and his son—a no-account who had the nerve to come sniffing around my daughter Phyllis.'"

"Then she touches my arm and says, 'Harriet, darling. You have to be careful of those Marshalls. They're not our kind, although they obviously want to be because they keep coming after our children. And they do breed like rabbits. Mrs. Marshall had ten children, not that they all lived, but the ones that did were all crowded up in a little row house.' Then Noreen had the nerve to say, 'I thought you would want to know' and walks away, leaving me standing there with Attorney Clemens' wife looking at me. So I say to her, 'You know young men. I'm afraid my son is sowing his wild oats,'" Harriet said.

Donny heard enough and threw his fork down. "Mother, I'm not a horse."

"Then don't act like one," Harriet snapped back. "For heaven's sake," she pleaded. "Come to your senses."

She shook her head and said, exasperated, "All the nice girls we try to fix you up with, you're not interested. Every single girl at that party wanted to be on your arm, and you're walking around with that low-class woman who dresses like a harlot."

Donny said, "She doesn't dress like a harlot, mother. She has a nice figure. She shows it off. What's wrong with that? After all, she is a model. And I'm sure that those girls wished they looked half as good in their clothes as Vera does. Half the time Vera's not wearing clothes that are any different than what anyone else has on. She just has more to pack inside them, and, sometimes, what she's packing spills over the top," he laughed.

Mary rolled her eyes. "You are so disgusting," she said.

Harriet shook the spoon at Donny as she paused in the middle of getting herself another helping of mashed potatoes. "You'll soon see, Donny. That girl is no good. She's after nothing but your money, and thank God we've put most of it in trust so that you can't spend it all on her anyway."

"He spends enough," said Mary. She was always angry that Donny got more of a monthly allowance than she did because, according to her father, a boy needed more money because he had to pay for dates and such.

"Don't you worry about what I spend my money on," Donny said to Mary. "At least I get something out of it, some enjoyment. You spend yours in a vain attempt to look beautiful, and that money goes right down the drain."

"Hush, now," said Harriet. "Just watch out for yourself, young man, because we're watching you."

"What else is new," said Donny, rolling his eyes and taking another helping of meat.

"Sit still and let me get it," said Valerie. She was trying to fasten the strap on Vera's sandals, but Vera kept turning from side to side to adjust her necklace, to make sure that it fell at the exact middle of her cleavage.

"As soon as you and Donny start necking, it's going to get out of place anyway," Valerie said.

"True. But it must be perfectly in place when Donny first sees it," Vera said. "I don't care what happens to it after that. In fact, if he doesn't get messed up after some groping and tugging, I'll think that I'm slipping."

The girls broke out in laughter. Valerie and Patricia were gathered in their bedroom to help Vera get dressed. Valerie touched up the few strands of hair that came loose from Vera's french roll since she left Hazel's House of Beauty. Patricia made sure the seams on Vera's dress were straight, and then she zipped her up. Vera had to squeeze into the dress, just a little. She wanted it tight enough to show what needed to be shown, but not so tight that she couldn't move freely.

Their dressing duties now completed, Patricia and Valerie laid across their beds admiring how beautiful Vera looked. They dreamed of the day when they would go to a ball as fancy as the May Pole Ball. Once Valerie got the strap secured, she stood up, stepped back and said, "There. Finished. Now let's have a look at you."

Vera stood up, smoothed her dress as she always did when she rose, and got into her model's stance.

"Gorgeous," said Patricia.

"You've done it again," said Valerie.

For Vera was truly beautiful. The dress was red satin. Straight and narrow. Strapless with a heart-shaped neckline. Around the neckline were what looked like hundreds of tiny white pearls that merged into the bud of a daylily in the center. Hundreds of more tiny pearls were sewn straight down the middle to the hemline as the flower stem. White Alencon lace formed a bustle on the back of the dress. It was accented with tiny white pearls and shimmering white sequins. Vera wore full length white gloves. Her pearl necklace ended at the center of her cleavage with a diamond-like stone. The earrings matched.

"Oh, yea," said Patricia. "That necklace will be knocked off track as soon as you get into Donny's car."

"Speaking of which, he ought to be here in two minutes," Vera said, looking at the clock on her dresser. Donny was nothing if not punctual.

No sooner had she said that than the doorbell rang. The girls ran to the hallway to make sure it was Donny. Vera heard John say, "Good evening, young man. Come in. Have a seat. I'll go get her."

The stairs creaked as Pop walked up them. He saw the girls' heads hanging over the railing. "Tell Vera Donny's here," he said to them for show's sake, because he didn't have to tell them what they already knew.

Valerie stuck her head in the bedroom door and said, "Show time."

Vera walked out and down the stairs. She was well versed with making an entrance walking down the stairs because she did it every day. Donny looked up expectantly and was not disappointed.

"You look beautiful," he said as Vera stepped off the last step. He walked over to her and gave her a peck on the cheek. Anything more than that could wait.

Donny opened the small square book in his hands and took out a wrist corsage. He knew by now there would be nowhere to pin a carnation on Vera's dress—she was partial to strapless to show off her bosom, and he had no problem with that. He lifted the corsage with its simple presentation of miniature red roses and baby's breath, took her hand, and gently slid the corsage on her wrist. The corsage was simple because he didn't want anything to detract from Vera, not that he had yet seen a bunch of flowers that could take anything from her.

"Thank you so much," Vera said as she returned Donny's peck on the cheek. Her kiss was as tender as her feelings for him.

"Enough of that kissing," John joked. "You younguns get on out of here and have a good time." John was proud of Vera. After all her wildness, he thought she had finally settled down. This Butcher boy kept her attention longer than any other man did, and, besides, he seemed like a good man. He was down-to-earth and had the breeding and good manners that were hard to hide. And any man who was going to be running his own business and making his own living, instead of looking for someone to give him something—like a job—was good enough for him.

John liked the self-made man. It wasn't Donny's money that John respected; it was Donny's ability to make his money independently, not subject to the whims of an employer. And the one thing people were always going to do was die, so the boy had a steady pool of customers.

Patricia handed Vera the mink stole that Donny bought her the day she modeled all those outfits for him. Even though it was 70 degrees outside, every woman at the ball would show up in a mink stole. As small as the stoles were, they weren't really made for warmth anyway. Vera handed the stole to Donny, who gently put it over her shoulders, patted her back, and said, "Let's go."

CHAPTER 27

The cars disgorging passengers at the Hansel & Gretel Ball were not the usual assortment of coaches that you see at a colored social event. These folks drove Cadillacs and Lincolns, not Chevies and Fords.

Donny and Vera sat in his black Cadillac in the line of cars waiting for a valet to take the car and park it.

"I just have to say it again," said Donny, looking over at Vera. "You look beautiful."

Vera took his hand and squeezed it. "You don't look too bad yourself."

A man in a tuxedo walked up to Donny's car, opened the door, and said, "Good evening, sir. Welcome to the May Pole Ball." Simultaneously, another tuxeoded gentleman opened Vera's door and welcomed her. He escorted her around to Donny's side, where he took her arm, and they started in.

The two co-chairs of the Ball stood at the front door welcoming guests in a receiving line. The line served two purposes. One was to welcome guests as any well-bred person does at his or her home. The other was to make sure that a Hansel & Gretel mother personally inspected every one who walked through the door. They believed that since all the guests knew they'd be scrutinized, they would dress up to their standards and behave themselves accordingly.

Donny and Vera waited in line. Already, heads turned in Vera's direction. When they reached the front of the line, Donny didn't wait for the ladies to introduce themselves because he knew them both. "Good evening, Mrs. Nixon and Mrs. Agnew. I'd like to present my friend, Miss Vera Marshall," he said.

The ladies looked at Vera and actually hesitated for a moment before putting out their hands in greeting.

"Oh, my. Good evening, Miss Marshall," said Mrs. Nixon, raising her eyebrows and actually lifting herself up a few inches so she could literally look down on Vera.

"Good evening," said Vera, ignoring the slight completely and moving graciously to the next lady.

"Good evening, Miss Marshall," repeated Mrs. Agnew. "That red dress certainly looks bright next to your skin color."

"Well, red *is* my color," said Vera. She quickly turned on her high heel and showed Mrs. Agnew her peplumed behind before she could say anything else.

When they walked a few feet away, Donny looked at Vera and laughed. "You're giving these ladies a time already. The night is young. Save some. Because the way we're being stared at," he said, looking around the room, "it's going to be a long night."

Harriet Butcher, never one to be fashionably late, was already at her table holding court. She wore a long-sleeved sky blue crepe gown, showing no skin anywhere, except her neck, face and hands, all of which were the color of the inside of a banana. Donny led Vera to the table. Harriet ignored their arrival, as she wished she could ignore Vera all night, by refusing to interrupt her conversation with Mrs. Pointer to greet Vera.

"Nice to see you, Vera," said Mr. Butcher. "My, my. You sure look lovely," he said as he held her hand and stood back. "Turn around so I can see that beautiful gown." Vera obliged and turned expertly as any model would.

"Doesn't she look gorgeous, Harriet," he asked, forcing her to look up.

Harriet turned her head for a second and then said in a voice as flat as a pancake, "Fine, dear," and she went right back to her conversation.

"You look lovely, too, Mrs. Butcher," Vera said, making sure Harriet knew that even though she had forgotten her manners, Vera hadn't forgotten hers.

Harriet didn't thank Vera for the compliment because once she turned her head, she had dismissed her. Donny might have brought that girl to the ball, but Harriet figured that she didn't have to ack like she was there.

Vera stood next to Harriet, motionless for a few seconds, waiting for her to acknowledge her compliment, but it didn't come. "Come on honey, I want to introduce you to a friend of mine," Donny said after he called out to one of his friends a few tables down, more happy to see him than he's ever been. He knew that his mother was ignoring Vera, and he wanted to separate the women before Vera forced the issue.

Vera opened her mouth like she was going to say something. She wanted to say, "I'm standing right here until that wench acknowledges my presence." Or, "I'm going to get in that woman's face until she acknowledges my compliment like the lady she is supposed to be." She tapped her feet like she was thinking when, all of a sudden, she said, "OK, Donny. Let's go."

As they walked away, Donny said, "Don't worry about Mom. She doesn't like any of the ladies I go out with unless she picks them out herself, and I've never been interested in anything she wanted."

Vera just walked on with Donny, but thought, well, Mrs. Queen Bee better get used to me because I'm not going anywhere.

Donny and Vera worked just about every table with people under 30. The men were glad to see Donny because he was like a brother to most of them; they played in the sand boxes as toddlers and partied in each other's basements as teenagers. And every one of them liked the way that Donny partied and who he partied with. The women were glad to see Donny because, even though he was with Vera, they figured that as long as he was still single, they had a chance.

As more people in the ballroom started drinking, more couples hit the floor to dance to Johnny Dee and the Softones Band. Donny and Vera were right out there, doing the bop and causing heads to turn.

Dr. and Mrs. Daniels had a table in the third row from the dance floor. Although Mrs. Daniels was an active member of Hansel & Gretel now, she wasn't in the original founding group. She was accepted as "one of us" though once she survived the scrutiny of the other members and was voted in without hesitation.

Ned Daniels sat at his family table with his mother and father and some girl from Howard University who thought she was doing something by dating a doctor's son, even one as simple as Ned. Ned turned his chair around to look at the dance floor. He put his very dry martini down on the table and sat forward in the chair to make sure that his eyes were not deceiving him. He found out at several Howard fraternity parties that he couldn't hold his liquor and hoped that his drinking that night wasn't affecting his eyesight. He focused on the lady in the red dress who was bopping and lindy-hopping all over the floor.

"It can't be," he muttered.

"What is it, darling?" Noreen asked. "I'm sorry Ned. I didn't hear you."

"I said it can't be," said Ned in a louder and more irritated voice.

"What can't be dear?" Noreen said. "You look like you've seen a ghost."

"Vera Marshall at the May Pole Ball?" Ned said incredulously. He sat so far forward in his chair to take a look that he almost fell to the ground.

Noreen looked on the dance floor. "Oh, my, yes," she said, practically faint of breath. "That girl is showing up everywhere. Donny Butcher has disgraced his family with her."

"She's dating Donny Butcher?" Ned asked. What a lucky dog, he thought. He's getting everything I couldn't.

"She certainly is," Noreen said with indignation. "But I made sure that Harriet knew that girl was not our kind. Imagine, a plumber's daughter here, trying to fit in. She's just making a spectacle out of herself. Donny will come to his senses after he's had his way with her enough times."

The thought of Donny having his way made Ned even more jealous. "I wonder if he knows what kind of woman she really is," Ned said.

"Of course he does," said Noreen, exasperated at Ned's stupidity. She talked to him like the child she still thought he was. "Why do you think he's with her?"

Because he's no dummy, thought Ned. Because he's getting what I never could. Because she's probably showing him things that these 400 girls can't even dream about. "She's only after his money," Ned said. "And she's so common, it will be him today and somebody else tomorrow."

The band slowed down and played The Platters' rendition of the ballad, "Only You". Couples moved together, found the most comfortable way to wrap their arms around each other, and moved slowly together in rhythm. Donny held Vera tightly and didn't just let his arms rest in one spot on her back or neck like any proper man would do.

He rested in one spot for a while, massaged her back, her neck, and then whispered words in her ear that caused her to touch his back and neck with her fingers, lightly, like a feather, and then with a little more pressure, like she knew just what points to press on him to put a smile on his face. Ned hated the thought of Vera pressing Donny where he wanted her and feeling her feather light fingers up and down his legs until they came to rest on his groin.

Ned blinked his eyes several times as his heart beat faster, the bulge between his legs started to swell, and he shifted in his seat. The thought of Vera still infuriated and excited him. He stood up from the table, said "Excuse me", and went to the bathroom to think and to relieve himself in a way he was all too accustomed to doing. He still hadn't found a girl at Howard who would go all the way with him, doctor's son or not.

In a few minutes, Ned returned to the table refreshed. He knew exactly where the Butchers were seated, everyone did, and he decided to stop by their table with his date on their promenade. Every couple did the Grand Promenade, walking the outer edge of the dance floor to pay homage to the grand dowagers.

Ned approached the Butcher table only when he saw Donny and Vera seated there. "Good evening, Mrs. Butcher," Ned said, nodding appropriately at Harriet.

"Why hello, dear," Harriet said. "How nice of you to come up from Howard for the ball."

"Wouldn't miss it for the world," Ned said. "This is my friend, Angelique," he said, pointing to the girl, which was her cue to nod her head in acknowledgment.

Usually the Grand Dames introduced the other guests at their table. It was sort of a contest to see who could have the most interesting and prestigious collection of guests. Harriet set about introducing her guests to Ned, but when she said, "You know my son, Donny," who was in deep conversation with Vera and not paying any attention to Harriet, figuring that he'd met everyone there he'd wanted to meet anyway, Ned interrupted and said, "And I know his date, too. Vera Marshall of the Ardmore Marshalls. All twelve of them."

No matter how deep she was in conversation or what else she was doing, Vera always knew when someone was talking about her. She looked up.

"Good evening, Vera," Ned said. "What a surprise to see you here."

"Hello, Ned," Vera said without emotion. "I'm surprised to see you, too," refusing to let him think that she thought she was out of place. "I thought you'd be in college studying, not up here partying," she said. Donny looked up, too.

"Even though I am in summer school, some families have traditions that must be followed, and the May Pole Ball is one of them," Ned said.

"You always did try to follow in your father's footsteps," Vera said. Donny smirked. Hazel looked at Vera with wide eyes. She couldn't believe that this girl was talking like an impudent to a Hansel & Gretel son.

"What better footsteps could there be," Ned said. "Of course, you wouldn't know anything about following in your father's accomplished footsteps, now would you?"

Donny knew an insult when he heard one, so he stood up and threw out his chest like he was ready for a fight. He never liked Ned. Donny teased him constantly as they grew up in Hansel & Gretel, from the first time Ned showed up at one of the youth meetings in short pants and it wasn't even the summer. While the other Hansel & Gretel teen boys tried to get out of going to every tea or recital or dramatic reading that the mothers dreamed up to inject them with some culture, Ned eagerly supported every one. He often showed up early to help set up tables and chairs, like currying favor with the mothers was going to help him get closer to the daughters and secure his place in the 400.

Ned tried to make the other boys look bad because that was the only way anybody would think that he was any good. A couple of the boys threatened to kick Ned's ass, but when the Milquetoast pantywaist told his mother, all of the other mothers lectured their sons on how they'd take away their keys to the Cadillacs if the mothers ever heard of fisticuffs applied to Ned. And now Ned had the nerve to insult his date? Oh, no. Donny wouldn't have it.

"Watch yourself, Daniels," Donny said.

"I might say the same to you, Donny," Ned said as he grabbed Angelique's arm and positioned her body between his and Donny's, figuring that Donny would never hit a girl. "You and Miss Marshall enjoy yourself," he said as he pulled on Angelique's arm and started to walk away.

"We always do," said Donny. He put his arm around Vera's shoulder and squeezed it.

Donny and Vera enjoyed themselves so much that they danced almost every number.

Harriet tried to ignore her son, but she couldn't. Several times, Donny and Vera all but cleared the dance floor with the wild style of dancing that they preferred.

Donny's friends eagerly stood back on the sidelines, made a little circle, and gave Donny and Vera a chance to work out. They liked watching Vera dance and wished that they were taking her home that night instead of Donny.

"Run and get me a cool drink, will you darling," Harriet asked Mr. Butcher as she fanned herself with the Chinese silk fan she purchased at Harrison's accessories counter. "I'm perspiring so just watching that boy make a spectacle of himself. If I hear one more comment about that woman tonight, I'll scream."

"Well, don't scream too loudly because Miss Marshall is not a woman who goes without comment," Mr. Butcher said as he got up from the table and walked over to the bar.

From across the room, Ned watched Mr. Butcher leave the table. Harriet shook her head almost as violently as she shook her fan. Ned decided that now was the time to strike.

"May I, Mrs. Butcher," Ned asked, pointing to the chair next to hers.

"Oh, of course, child," Harriet said, almost lost in the sight of her son sliding that woman beneath his legs. "Sit down."

Ned pulled out the seat, looked over at the dance floor and said, "Vera is putting on quite a show, don't you think?", knowing full well that's what she thought.

"On my, yes," Harriet said, embarrassed to look at them.

"Vera always has been quite the . . . how shall I say it." He paused. "Exhibitionist."

"I expected the more common boys on the Main Line to fall for her type, but I never expected that one of our kind would," he said, setting her up. "I just hope that Donny learns what type of girl she is before it's too late."

Harriet asked, curious as to how this young man would answer, "Too late for what?"

"Well, she's always wanted to be in the 400," said Ned. "That's all she talked about in high school. How she was going to find some rich guy, trick him into marrying her and spend all his money."

Mary slapped her fan down on the table. "I knew it!"

Sensing victory in the air, Ned pressed on. "And she gets any man she wants because she does things that decent girls never would do until they married. Everybody in school knew it. As a matter of fact, any Negro on the Main Line can tell you about Vera Marshall," he said.

"Oh my lands," said Harriet. She touched Ned's arms and said, "Will you please talk to Donny? Will you tell him what you know?"

Ned sighed. "I'm afraid Donny wouldn't listen to me, especially once she starts letting him have his way with her."

Harriet's shoulders slumped in disappointment.

Ned moved in for the kill. "But there's a way for him to see for himself."

"Mary, dear. Do listen to what Ned has to say," said Harriet.

Ned bent in closer like he was going to whisper. "Now here's what I propose," he said, as the cabal formulated their plans.

CHAPTER 28

Two days later, the Marshalls sat in the back room watching "I Love Lucy" on television. Everybody was laughing as Lucy made yet another attempt to get into show business, everybody but Bobby. Vera looked at Bobby, who was leaning back on the side chair, digging his fingernails into the chair arms like he was trying to keep himself from sinking down any further. She knew that he was really trying to keep himself from falling into the abyss that was created when the principal at Ardmore High School blew a hole in his dreams.

She wished that she could do something to cheer him up, but he had lost two things that were dear to him in one day: Phyllis and his plans to go to college. Actually, he had one taken from him; the other he gave away.

The principal gave the chemistry prize to Morgan Hamilton, even though Bobby's grades were higher. As Mr. Texton explained to Bobby, the principal, over Mr. Texton's strenuous objections, factored in classroom attendance for the first time in the history of the chemistry prize. Bobby had missed about a month of school in the winter when a bad case of strep throat turned into rheumatic fever. And although he kept up his stellar grades, the attendance factor was enough to move the prize from his hands to the hands of Morgan Hamilton, whose great-grandfather founded the Philadelphia area's premier oil company.

The Hamiltons sent their children to public schools to toughen them up and help them understand the mentality of their future employees. They also made generous annual contributions to the school so that their children's grades never suffered, even if they should have. So when the principal figured that he could pay back the Hamiltons by giving Morgan the chemistry prize, he figured—why not? What did a colored boy need with a college education? Most of them still ended up working in the post office, and who needed four years of college for that?

So even though Fisk University in Nashville had accepted both Bobby and Phyllis, he couldn't go. Bobby and Phyllis planned to get far enough away from the Daniels' so that the family couldn't drive down for the weekend and disturb them. When he told Phyllis that he didn't get the prize, he also told her that it would be better to break up now than three months from then when she went off to Fisk and he stayed home to work in the family plumbing business. He figured that it wouldn't be as hard to break up sooner rather than later.

But Vera knew that Bobby hurt as much now as he ever would. He helped her snap out of it when she returned from Alfreda's and the pain of her lost dream seemed too much to bear. Now, she wished that she could help him, to come to his aid like she did so many times before.

Just as she was thinking of how she could get those two back together again, the phone rang. Valerie got up to answer it. She tapped Vera on the shoulder instead of yelling above the sound of the radio, an act for which the rest of the family would surely cuff her.

"For you, Vera," Valerie said. Vera jumped up. "Take your time. It's a girl, not lover boy," she said.

"Shut up," said Vera, jokingly, wondering who it might be. Not many girls called her. She held the phone to one ear, put a finger in the other so she could hear, and said, "Hello."

"Hello. Is this Vera?" asked the voice.

"Yes, it is. Who's calling?" she said, truly wondering who this woman was. She didn't get too many calls from women.

"Vera, this is Mary Butcher," she said.

Vera almost dropped the phone. She took the phone off her ear for a second as if she didn't believe what she just heard. Why would Mary call her? She knew that the woman didn't like her. In an instant, she thought something was wrong with Donny.

"Yes, Mary," Vera said. "Is Donny alright?"

"Yes, of course," Mary said. "Donny's fine."

"Oh," said Vera, "I just thought that you were calling about Donny" not saying what she was thinking, which was "because I know you couldn't be calling to talk with me."

"In a way, I am calling about Donny," Mary said. She cleared her throat and then began, "I know we haven't exactly been on the best of terms."

Vera thought, you got that right. We haven't been on any terms, not that it bothered her because she and Donny were doing better than ever. Vera just mumbled, "Uh, huh."

". . . and I think it's time to change that," Mary continued. "it's clear that Donny is serious about you, and I think we should get to know each other because, who knows . . . we might be family one day, and I think Donny would like us to get along."

Vera smiled. So Donny's been talking about her to the family. She knew things were going good, but maybe she didn't know how good. Vera could care less whether Mary thought they should get to know each other better, but if that's what Donny wanted, she'd go along with it.

"Well, that's mighty nice of you, Mary," Vera said, stifling the laughter that wanted to rise through her mouth. "What do you have in mind?"

"I'd love to meet you for lunch one day," Mary said in a voice so sweet it must have given her a cavity. "I come to Harrison's often, as you know, so it's nothing for me to meet you there for lunch."

"Well, why don't we do that," said Vera. What a change, she thought, because every time she saw Mary in Harrison's, she either walked in the opposite direction so she didn't have to speak or tried to pretend that she didn't see her. Some days, Vera wouldn't let Mary get away without speaking. She'd walk right up on her, stand right in front of her even, and say hello or nod her head directly at her so that even her "well bred" ass had to acknowledge her presence.

"Can we meet next Monday at noon in the Silver Dining Room?" Mary asked.

"That's fine with me," Vera said.

"Great," Mary said. "I'll see you then. And please don't tell Donny that we're having lunch. I'd like to surprise him afterwards. So can this be our little secret?"

"That's fine with me, too," Vera said. "Goodbye."

"Goodbye," said Mary. She hung up the phone, and when she was sure that Vera had hung up, Harriet did the same thing on the other line.

Mary walked into the living room where Harriet had just hung up the phone and said, "Step one done." Harriet smiled at Mary and said, "Good job, dear."

"So today's the big day," Bobby said to Vera at breakfast Monday morning between scoops of oatmeal. "The day you get accepted into the family," he said, laughing.

"Well, it had to come eventually," said Vera.

"Oh, did it?" Bobby said, egging her on.

"Of course," said Vera, with a twirl of her arm and a smile on her face. "You know I'm irresistible."

Ken McNamara smelled Vera's perfume as she walked by the table in the corner of the Silver Dining Room where he was hiding. He recognized the Mitsuoko. Every one of his female classmates at Howard Drama School—and some of the men—wore that perfume now. They thought that it gave them an air of Far Eastern mystery, of sensual sophistication—something that all those aspiring actresses wanted. As if that made it any easier for them to get parts.

He tried to give off that air himself by dressing in avant garde French clothes, always wearing an ascot around his neck and collecting smoking jackets which he wore around campus like they were fraternity sweaters. He figured that he must have given off the right air and achieved the right look because that pre-law egghead hired him for this job. This would be the easiest $100 plus expenses that he ever made.

That perfume took him out of character for an instant. He closed his eyes, thought of himself as the Negro Cary Grant, took three deep breaths, and he was back in character. He looked across the room where a waitress placed two salads before Vera and Mary. He would wait until they were eating their main course.

"It must be interesting being a model," Mary said to Vera as she stabbed a tiny cauliflower floret with her fork.

"Oh, it's very interesting," said Vera, pushing the food around on her plate, trying not to eat all of the salad like she really wanted to. She had read somewhere that society ladies never ate all of their food, and although that went against everything that Mom and Pop taught her and everything her stomach told her, she didn't want Mary to think that she was so uncouth that she'd eat all the food off her plate.

"It's about the only work I'd ever wanted to do," Vera said.

"You're so lucky," Mary said, lying. "Sometimes I wish Daddy would let me work. If I made my own money, I could do exactly with it what I pleased. Now I have to beg Daddy for money if there's something I want between allowances. I've asked him for an allowance as big as Donny's, but he always says that girls don't need as much money as boys." She poked out her bottom lip and pouted.

God give me strength, thought Vera, to sit here and listen to this. Complaining that she can't work when somebody is giving her money? That she couldn't believe. The rich *are* different, she thought, and honey, I can't wait to find out how different.

"I guess your parents don't want you working while you're in college," Vera said. "But won't they let you work when you graduate?"

Mary laughed. "When I graduate, I'd better have my MRS degree, or I'd better not come home. None of the girls I know go to college to get a degree. Most of them go with no intentions of even finishing. They go to get married, plain and simple, and everybody knows it," she said. "At least everybody in our circle," she said, unable to pass on getting in that dig at Vera.

"That's a lot of money to spend just to get a man," Vera said, not being one to accept an insult, even from someone she hoped would be her future sister-in-law.

"Mummy and Daddy say it's money well spent," Mary said, smugly.

"Well, then," said Vera, "I imagine it is," as if what "Mummy" and "Daddy" said was the word.

That's a fine looking woman, thought Ken. No wonder some rich guy was taken with her. She's the kind of lady to make you want to spend your money. Maybe I could keep this gig going long enough to get a piece of her, he thought.

The waitress served Mary her turkey platter and Vera her shrimp scampi. Vera ordered one of the most expensive things on the menu to show Mary that she could afford to pay for it. Mary tried to make pleasant conversation with Vera, and Vera tried to keep up her end of the conversation without insulting Mary, like she really wanted to do. The girl had what she wanted— the money and the prestige that came with the Butcher name—so Vera tempered her tongue. Donny liked her just as she was, but Mary didn't, and if it meant putting on airs to have Mary give Donny a good report, that's what she'd do. At least for today.

The girls managed to get a few fork fulls into their mouths when Vera noticed one of the finest looking men she'd seen in a long time walking up the aisle behind Mary. He had on a navy blue suit with a paisley tie in burgundies, maroons, golds, greens and navies. His dark brown shoes glistened in that way that freshly and expertly shined shoes do. His hair, in rippling waves, glistened, too. His moustache hugged the top of his full lips, and it was trimmed in a perfectly straight line. When he licked his lips, just as he got to Mary's chair, Vera wished that she could have felt what that tongue did.

He cleared his throat, "Umph. Excuse me for interrupting your lunch," he said, looking right at Vera and bending over a little bit so that she could see his long black eyelashes that curled up at the end.

As he said that, Mary looked around, and said, "Ken! How are you! Whatever are you doing here?"

"Just visiting some friends in town and thought I'd come over and do a little shopping," he said. "I saw you as soon as I walked in and thought I'd come over and say hello."

"Well I'm glad you did," Mary said. She touched his arm and said, "Oh, Ken. Let me introduce you to Vera Marshall. She's one of the models here at the store."

He bent over, took Vera's hand, and kissed it with those soft, full lips. "I've noticed some lovely models since I've been here, but none as lovely as you," he said.

Vera's hand tingled. "You flatter me," she said, meaning it. "It's nice to meet you," she added, meaning that, too.

Ken pointed at the two half-eaten plates. "I see you're in the middle of your meal. I won't hold you up any longer."

Mary acted flustered. "Well, where are you sitting? Are you eating with anyone?"

"I have a table over there," he said, pointing in the corner.

Mary looked around. "Oh, nobody sits over there," she said, as if he had committed the cardinal sin. "Come and sit with us." She looked at Vera and said, "You don't mind, do you Vera?"

"Not at all," Vera said, smiling at Ken. "I'd be happy to have him join us," she said, hoping that Mary didn't catch how she meant it.

The waitress brought a chair over for Ken, and he sat down. Vera learned that Ken was in his last year at Howard Law School and looking to move to Philadelphia when he graduated to practice law with his uncle, whose name she didn't recognize, but who apparently had a lucrative practice because Mary said that he was so busy, he'd missed all the 400 balls and lunches over the last few months. Ken said that there was a lot more money to be made in Philadelphia than in Elmira, New York, where he was from, even though his father, the town's colored doctor, begged him to come home and take care of the legal business for all of the clients he had. Mary said that as successful as his father was, she wondered why he didn't go home, too. It seemed to her that there truly was a lot of money to be made in Elmira.

"I don't want to be a big fish in a small pond," said Ken. "I'd rather be a big fish in a bigger pond."

Vera liked what she heard.

After Ken's main course arrived, Mary excused herself to go to the ladies room. As soon as she left the table, Ken looked over at Vera and said, "If you're the type of woman I can expect to meet in Philadelphia, I can't wait to move here."

Vera sat back and took a sip of her tea. "You won't meet any women like me here." She continued, "In fact, you won't meet any women like me anywhere." She looked straight into his eyes and said, "I'm one of a kind."

"I can see that," Ken said. "And you look like my kind," he said as he fingered his tie. "Yes, you certainly do."

"How would you like to have dinner with me tonight?" he asked, as he leaned closer to her, pretending that she couldn't hear unless he came close. She took a deep breath, inhaled his patchouli and musk cologne, and came to her senses, in spite of herself.

"Can't do it, honey," she said. "I'm seeing someone. In fact, Im seeing Mary's brother."

"My, my," he said, leaning back. "The famous Donny Butcher, the heir apparent to the Butcher fortune?"

"One and the same, if you say so. He's a good man, and I love him. You're a little too late, although, God knows, you would have been my type," she said.

"Would have been," he said, mockingly. "Is all hope lost?"

"I'm not about to blow a good thing," Vera said.

"Well, let me ask you something," Ken said, again leaning closer to Vera. She looked at the bones and veins and smooth coffee brown skin on the back of his neck. She wondered how soft it would have felt if she could run her fingers across that smooth brown skin and feel the baby soft hairs that marched in a line up to the bottom of his freshly cut hair.

"Are you engaged yet?" Ken asked.

"Not yet," Vera said, "but soon."

Ken laughed. "Soon! What does that mean? Is that man crazy?" This time he touched her arm. "If I was that man and you were my woman, there'd be no question about soon. I can see right now that I would have snatched you up and made you mine a long time ago."

Vera was moved by that bit of flattery. There was no denying that what the man said was true. Soon is now, she thought. Just what was Donny waiting for? She knew he loved her, and, for the first time, she could say that she truly loved a man. But Ken hit a nerve, and she didn't want to show it.

"I know he loves me, and I know he wants to marry me," Vera said. "I can wait, and it won't be much longer."

Ken laughed again. "You don't look like the kind of woman who waits for anything," he said. "You look like the kind of woman who goes out and gets what she wants."

"But what you don't seem to understand, sir, is that I've got it," she said, getting a little irritated.

"Not until you've got that rock on your finger, you don't," he said. He took her hand in his and said, "And I'd put a nice one, right there," pointing to her ring finger. "Let me try this," he said, undefeated. "How about if I can arrange things so that it doesn't look like a date, so maybe your reluctant fiancee doesn't know."

"I told you, I'm not interested," she said, knowing that she was. Suppose Donny didn't marry her? Then what? Here's a fine looking lawyer coming to town, and I can get first crack at him. No telling who'd be trying to get their paws on him by next spring. And she wasn't getting any younger. She was almost 20.

"You give private showings of those dresses, don't you? I saw a sign downstairs," Ken said. He rubbed his chin, "Suppose I got a private showing. Then we could talk."

"Just you and me and the moderator," Vera said. She imagined that Charlene wouldn't be too thrilled with this because she was getting mighty tired of all of those men who asked for a private showing with a model when what they really wanted was a date. Still, Charlene never turned down a private showing, but the models had to work extra hard at the ones that were set up by "gentlemen callers." If a man didn't buy at least $100 worth of clothes, Harrison's didn't make any money off of it. Sometimes the models tried too hard to be nice to the men at these showings. Harrison's was becoming known as *the* place in Philadelphia for men with money to go to get a nice-looking date, or mistress, depending on their status.

"If you want me to show you some outfits, I'd have to show them to you," Vera said. "But don't get your hopes up." She raised her perfectly arched eyebrow.

"I already have," he said.

Mary returned from the ladies room, wondering just how far Ken got with Vera. She acted like nothing had happened in her absence except polite conversation. As Ken finished his meal and the girls finished their desert, Vera announced, "I'm sorry to have to leave you two, but I must get back. I have a showing this afternoon."

Mary stood up and walked over to Vera's side of the table. She hugged her and almost knocked Vera off balance. "It was so nice of you to come," Mary said. "I feel much better about everything, and I hope you do, too. Donny will be so surprised." She clapped her hands together with glee.

Vera smiled. Thank God. A good report leads to a big diamond. "I'm glad we got to talk, too, Mary. Let's do it again sometime," she said, knowing that's the last thing she'd want to do with her free time.

"It was nice meeting you, Ken," Vera said, sticking out her hand for a handshake. He took the hand and held it momentarily. "I hope to see you again when you move to Philadelphia. We could use a good lawyer like you."

Ken stood on his feet, and his 6'2" lean, fine brown frame towered over Vera. "Promise you'll call me if you ever get in trouble?" he said, with the devil in his eye.

"I can usually handle whatever trouble I get into, but you can bet that I'll call you if I need you," she said as she shook his hand and walked away.

As soon as Vera disappeared around the corner of the Dining Room, Mary hit Ken on the arm and practically shouted, jumping up and down in her chair, "Tell me what happened! Tell me!"

CHAPTER 29

Noreen Daniels sat in the living room having her afternoon tea, today Earl Gray brewed exactly according to the directions on the loose tea can, complete with one cucumber and cream cheese sandwich on white bread, crust removed and cut into three sections, and two shortbread cookies.

Phyllis sat at the dining table, reading from the *Autobiography of Frederick Douglass* and writing notes in a three-ring blue notebook.

The living room console radio which Noreen inherited from her mother was tuned to Caroline Devereaux's "Ladies' Tea Talk", as it was everyday at 3:15 p.m., for Noreen followed Caroline's instructions exactly. By the time Caroline said, "Pull up your loveliest side chair, pour yourself a cup of tea, pick up a crumpet and take 45 minutes for yourself, ladies," Noreen was seated with all her necessaries beside her.

Caroline's show was timed precisely to give the ladies a 45-minute break before they, and women all over America, rose at 4 p.m. to begin preparing dinner for their families. Uncultured ladies took their breaks listening to soap operas; ladies of refinement, like Noreen and her friends, took their breaks with Caroline.

Caroline's topic today was "Twenty Ways to Serve an Artichoke," and the guest was talking about how to properly peel the leaves when Ned walked in breaking Noreen's blessed concentration.

"At last, at last," Ned said, plopping down in the chair next to his mother.

"Must you, dear," Noreen said as she put down her teacup—Lenox's Autumn pattern, of course, heirloom china that had been in the Daniels family since 1919 when the pattern was introduced. "Caroline's on," she said. Young people, she thought. How quickly they forget the things that are important to their parents.

"Oh, Caroline," said Ned, having a flash of recognition. "What's she talking about today?"

"If you must know, dear," Noreen said, not even attempting to hide her irritation, " . . . artichokes."

"Oh, mother, you know everything there is to know about artichokes," Ned said, rolling his eyes.

"One can never know everything," Noreen said.

"Well, I can't imagine what Caroline has to say about artichokes that is more important than what I have to say about Vera Marshall," Ned said.

"Vera Marshall," Mrs. Daniels said, raising her voice. "I can't believe that you are here bothering me about that Marshall girl. Really," she said, exasperated. "I thought I taught you better than that."

Phyllis heard her mother yell Vera's name, and she looked up from her studies of the life of a runaway slave. Why would her mother be talking about Vera? But when she peeked around the corner and saw Ned sitting in the chair, waving his hands, smiling and acting like he was excited, she closed the book, put down her pen, pushed out her chair, and walked over to the door, making sure that she was hidden from her mother's and Ned's view.

" . . . and when Donny finds out, that will be the end of that little relationship," Ned said, clapping his hands together.

"Oh, my. I certainly hope so," Noreen said, wiping the tears of laughter that fell down her eyes. "Well, son, I didn't think it could be, but that was worth your interrupting Caroline." She pointed to the tray and said, "Have a crumpet, son. You certainly deserve one."

Phyllis shook her head. Ned's pettiness never ceased to amaze her, but even she was surprised at his obsession with destroying Vera. Phyllis tiptoed back to the dining table, pulled out her seat, and pretended to be reading more about Frederick Douglass.

Well, Ned wasn't going to get his way this time. Not if she had anything to do with it. She never would have had that sweet relationship with Bobby if it wasn't for Vera. Ned tried everything he could to deprive her of her happiness, and Vera did everything she could to help her get her happiness with Bobby. Even though she and Bobby broke up, she always got along fine with Vera, the few times she'd seen her on the streets of Ardmore or in Harrison's. Vera gave Phyllis her happiness, and now Phyllis was going to help give Vera hers.

"Believe it, dear," Harriet Butcher said as she stood in the door of Donny's bathroom. "I just talked to her not five minutes ago."

Donny's voice was somewhat muffled as he called out from behind the shower door. "You and Mary want to have lunch with me and Vera and, how do you say, bury the hatchet?" Donny said.

"Yes, dear," said Harriet. "It's high time that we got to know this girl better. Mary had lunch with her last week and said she was positively enchanting."

That she is, thought Donny.

"It's time for me to get to know this girl," Harriet said, "seeing as how your relationship seems to be getting more serious. If you insist on seeing her, as you apparently do, the least I can do is get to know her. After all, maybe some of our culture will rub off on her." She couldn't resist adding that.

"You can't change her, Mom," Donny said, sticking his hand out and grabbing a towel. He walked out of the shower and looked at his mother. "You have to just try to love her, Mom, and believe me, that's not so hard. She kind of grows on you after a while."

"Please, dear," said Harriet. "Nothing grows on me. The very thought makes me think of moss or warts or horrid moles. Or better yet, leeches."

Pulling on his pants, Donny said, "I mean she'll get into your affections. Is that a better way to put it?"

"Better, but not best," Harriet said. Harriet thought that Donny might truly be heartbroken when he found Vera in the clinches of another man, and that thought made her a little sad. Even she could see that he truly loved her and would be hurt at her betrayal. She didn't relish the thought of having a heartsick Donny moping around the house, even for a few days. He was her son, after all, and she hated to see any of her children hurt. But this was a necessary wound. And better to have it happen now, before they married, rather than after, when her betrayal would cost the whole family money.

"We'll all leave in an hour," she said.

Charlene moved in place behind the small podium in the Park Avenue Suite to begin Ken McNamara's private showing. "Good afternoon, Mr. McNamara," she said. "Welcome to Harrison's. I hope that you find today's fashions to your liking."

Like it or not, she thought, at least buy something.

"We have a fine selection of lingerie and at home wear for that special woman in your life," she continued. Whomever the lucky lady is, she thought. That sure is a good looking man.

"Our model today is Vera," she said, as if he didn't know, as if he didn't demand that it would be Vera or no one.

Hearing her name, Vera opened the door behind which the models waited and walked out on cue wrapped in a peignoir that was almost entirely black lace with a black satin ribbon for a belt. Vera walked seductively to the middle of the room, stuck out a foot nestled in black satin mules with marabou feathers around the toes and lightly tugged at the end of the bow belt. The robe parted down the center, she caught the belt with both hands and opened the robe to reveal a black lace negligee split up the left side. She paused long enough for Ken to get a good, hard look or, as she said to the dresser, a look to get hard.

Ken sat in a chair at the back of the room with his legs crossed and his hat in his hand. As he ran his fingers around the hat brim, he leaned his head to the side and smiled at Vera as she came closer. Vera smiled back and ended the smile by drawing her lips up into a perfect, pouty, bow. Ken shifted in his chair at the thought of those luscious red lips on his or any other part of his body.

She disappeared behind the door and returned a minute later in a baby blue satin bathrobe with matching gown. "This outfit is L'Air Blue," said Charlene. "One hundred percent satin with mother-of-pearl buttons down the front of the gown." As she said that, Vera opened the bathrobe to reveal her perfect figure offset to its finest. Ken shifted in his chair again to hide the erection that was getting harder and bigger by the minute. As Charlene said, "The bottom of the robe is trimmed in . . .", someone knocked at the door.

Charlene said, "Excuse me, sir. This must be very urgent because our staff is instructed not to interrupt a private showing except for the utmost emergency." She put her cards down on the podium, reached over and opened the door. Neither Ken nor Vera could see who knocked on the door. Charlene bent over so that her body was halfway out the door, and then said, "Excuse me, sir. Something came up that I must take care of. Can you wait for a few minutes?"

He looked at Vera, still with her gown open, and said, "Certainly. Take all the time you need."

Charlene closed the door, and Vera stood there, bathrobe open, looking at Ken. Ken jumped out of his seat and stood not a foot away from Vera.

"You sure look good," he said, running his finger around the hat brim with increasing velocity.

Vera smiled and said, "Thank you. You look pretty good yourself."

Ken figured that was his opening. He moved in closer and put his arm out and around Vera's waist, pulling her to him and bending down as if he was going to kiss her.

"Wait, wait, honey," said Vera. She pushed him back ever so gently and smoothed her gown with her hands. "I'll lose my job if I mess up this outfit," she said. She took his hands in hers and ran her fingers over his muscular hands.

"Let me see if I can figure out how long Charlene will be gone," she said. "You wait right here. I'll be right back." Vera went back to her changing room, took off the store outfit, and put on her changing robe.

When she went back into the room, Ken was still standing up. Vera walked over to him and put his hands around her waist. He instinctively moved his hands down to her hips and didn't feel any underwear. "Apparently, Mrs. Harrison said she must have ten minutes of Charlene's time," Vera said. She put her hands around Ken's waist and pulled him closer.

"Time's a wasting honey," she said. She slid her hands inside his suit coat and fingered his belt buckle. "And if you want it, you got it." She reached behind her back and moved Ken's hands on her rear so he could feel the smooth satin against her bare skin. She leaned close to him, wrapped her hands around his neck, and kissed him like she really cared. He kissed her back with the passion of a man who thought he was going to get some.

"You've got to use protection, baby," she said, stepping back. She pulled a condom out of her robe pocket and handed it to him. "I'll give you a minute to get it on, and then I'll be back," she said, walking towards the dressing room door. "When you've got it on, knock twice on this door, and I'll come right in," she said. "Or should I say, *you'll* come right in." She smiled and turned as if she were on the runway and closed the door.

Ned walked up to Harrison's third floor and sat down on one of the benches at the end of the long hallway that led to the private showing rooms. When Vera ran down the hallway, embarrassed and defeated, he would be waiting.

Donny pulled Harriet's powder blue Cadillac in front of Harrison's, and one of the three uniformed doormen headed right over. Donny handed him the key, and the other doormen opened the car door for Mary and Harriet. The ladies said, "Thank you" and walked into the store, smiling.

"God, I can't wait to see her face," Mary whispered to her mother as Donny followed behind them, out of ear shot.

"Patience is its own reward, dear," said Harriet, who was expert at suppressing many emotions but couldn't suppress the smirk that started spreading across her face.

CHAPTER 30

Ken opened up the rubber, unzipped his pants, and slid it on. It went on easily because he was hard as a board. No question about it, he was going to get some before this gig was up. And the sooner he got Vera in here, the more he'd get before he would be so rudely interrupted.

"She told us to meet her outside of the Park Avenue Suite," Harriet said, walking down the hallway. Ned grew even more excited when, from his hiding place, he saw the Butchers arrive. Only a few more minutes until Vera's comeuppance.

Three overstuffed white french provincial chairs with pastel stripes were lined up outside the private showing rooms. "Let's sit here, dear, and wait," Harriet said, motioning to Donny.

"Yeah, take a load off," Donny said, pointing to the chair for Mary to sit down.

"Don't be so vulgar dear," said Harriet.

Donny looked at his watch. "I have to go to the bathroom, Mom. Be right back," he said as he walked down the hall and around the corner.

Ken walked over to the door, knocked on it twice and stood back. The force of the door slamming him against the wall almost knocked him over. When Ken saw a man coming at him instead of Vera, he fumbled to shove his very visible stuff back in his pants.

"I ought to cut it off," said Donny as he strode towards Ken who was frantically trying to zip up his pants. Just as Ken took the bottom of the zipper in his hand, Donny punched him in the jaw and knocked him over one of the French provincial chairs.

"Take that back to your friend, Ned. Tell him it's from Donny," Donny said.

Vera walked in behind Donny, now dressed in her street clothes. She looked at Ken on the floor, holding his chin as blood started to drip down on the side where Donny hit him.

She walked over to where he was lying on the floor and said, "What a shame. You were a nice looking man. I hope they paid you enough to get your jaw fixed." She smiled at him and crossed the room to where Donny waited by the door that led to the hallway.

"To hell with them," Donny said. He grabbed Vera's hand and knelt down on his right knee. Vera thought that he had to kneel down because the punch took something out of him; after all, he did hit Ken pretty hard.

Donny looked up at Vera and said, "I love you, baby. There's not another woman in the world who excites me like you do. Let's make this formal. Will you marry me?"

Vera leaned back against the wall because Donny's words took something out of her. She couldn't believe it. The day she dreamed of had arrived. A man from the 400 wanted her. No, scratch that. Many have *wanted* her. A man from the 400 wanted to *marry* her. No more Ardmore. No more waiting and wondering whether her dream was going to come true. She'd finally be a respectable woman in Negro society.

"Yes, I'll marry you," she said. She pulled him up, threw her arms around him, and squeezed him tight. "I'll marry you, alright," she said.

Donny squeezed her back with all the strength he could muster without hurting her. "Let's go," he said as he took her hand and opened the door to the hallway.

Harriet and Mary looked up in anticipation as the door opened. Harriet leaned back with a look of horror and surprise on her face, and said, "Donny! What are you doing *there*?"

"Putting an end to this shit," he said. "That stupid punk Ned bragged about your crazy scheme and his little sister heard him and told Vera, who naturally told me. We don't keep secrets from each other Mother," he said, putting his arm around Vera.

"Your little actor friend is lying in there on the floor with his jaw smashed in," Donny said, nodding in the direction of the dressing room.

Harriet and Mary jumped up.

"I don't know what happened in there, son, but this woman," she said, pointing and shaking her finger at Vera, "is a golddigger who is just after your money."

"Well, mother," Donny said, "she can have all my money because we're going to get married."

Harriet stepped back and screamed, "Oh no!"

Mary waved her arms around and said, "Oh, Donny. You can't be serious."

"Serious as a heart attack," said Donny. He took Vera's arm and said, "Now go to hell and leave us alone," as they walked down the hallway onto the escalator arm-in-arm.

A horrified Ned cowered in the corner, watching and listening to the scene down the end of the hall unfold. "Damn it," he said. "That bitch did it again."

When Donny and Vera were safely off the third floor and on the escalator going down to the second, Ned came out of hiding and scurried down the hallway to where Mary was fanning her mother, trying to revive her.

"Mary, get the smelling salts," Harriet said when Donny told her a few days later that he and Vera had gotten married in Elkton, Maryland— Philadelphian's favorite place for quicky weddings. Many an anxious young lady forced her boyfriend to drive to Elkton where a couple could marry on the spot, no blood test or waiting required.

"Oh, mother," said Donny, as he stood over Harriet with his hand in his pocket. "Don't get dramatic."

"Well, congratulations, son," said Mr. Butcher, walking towards Donny with his hand outstretched. Shaking his hand fiercely, Mr. Butcher said, "And where is the blushing bride?", as if the wedding night would give Vera anything to blush about.

"She's with her family, getting her things together," Donny said, walking over to the mahogany butler and fixing himself a drink.

"You eloped?" Mary said, yelling at him in disbelief and accusing him at the same time.

"Yea, we eloped, and there's not a damn thing you can do about it," Donny said.

Mary stood right in front of Donny with her hands on her hips and her foot sticking out like she wanted to raise it and kick him right in the balls for being so stupid. "That woman is now my sister-in-law? A part of our family?"

"That's right, baby doll," Donny said, teasing her. "Or should I say, she's now the sister you never had."

Mary turned on her heels and walked away in a huff. "The sister I'll never have. I'll never accept that woman as my sister," she said.

Mr. Butcher walked over to Mary and snatched her arm so fast that she spun around like a top. "Oh yes you will. That woman, as you call her, is now a part of our family. And if the both of you," he said, pointing to Mary and Harriet, "had stopped looking your noses down at her for two minutes you might have found out that she is a fine girl with a good heart, as I did and as Donny did. She's a part of our family now whether you like it or not." He walked around the room like a lion surveying his kingdom. "And we're going to treat her like she is."

He paced the room unrelentingly, while the force of his words sunk in. "We're going to have a reception right here to formally introduce our friends and family to Mrs. Donald Butcher, Jr."

Hearing that name used in connection with Donny and Vera, Harriet said, "Oh my God."

Mr. Butcher squinted his eyes and said his words slowly and with enough volume so that Harriet understood the force behind them. "Your God said to love one another as yourself," he said. Then he turned to Donny and said, "Son, I always wanted to see you married in a nice big wedding, but I know the wedding is always up to the young lady. So I'm going to make sure you have a reception fitting of this family."

"Thanks, Pop," Donny said, shaking his father's hand.

"Harriet, I want you to start working on the reception right away. Hold it in three weeks and spare no expense," he said. Mary frantically waved the smelling salts under Harriet's nose.

Mr. Butcher looked at Donny and said, "Son, you and your bride stay here tonight. In the morning, we'll talk about getting you all a house. I know of a beautiful one that just opened up yesterday." Mr. Butcher had the finest collection of homes of any Negro in Philadelphia. Besides the bereaved family, the undertaker was the first to know when a house became available, and Mr. Butcher frequently made an offer to purchase a house before he got the body embalmed.

Many families appreciated how quickly Mr. Butcher took those properties off their hands and gave them ready cash to pay those wretched estate taxes. Of course, many families, when they shook off the grief of bereavement, later realized that Mr. Butcher got those houses at far less than market value. By then, it was too late.

"Married?" Emma asked when Vera phoned just as she had put all the food on the table for dinner. "You've run off and gotten married?"

"Yes, yes," Vera said, screaming into the phone.

Emma blurted out her first thought, "Are you pregnant?"

"No, Mom. I'm not pregnant," Vera said. She explained how Ned and the Butcher women tried to set her up and how that only pushed Donny into marrying her. "So I figured that once he asked me, why wait? I did it, Mom. I married money, and now I'm in the 400, just like Donny."

Not just like Donny, Emma thought. He was born into it. She said, "Congratulations, Vera. I'm happy for you. I would have liked to have seen you get married at Bethel and blessed by God instead of married by a justice of the peace down in Elkton, but I'm glad to see you married. And to a decent man at that." Because Lord knows, some of those men you used to run with weren't worth two cents, she thought.

Now, the whole family gathered around the dining room waiting for Vera's return. As soon as Vera stepped across the threshold, Valerie yelled, "I want to see the ring! I want to see the ring!"

Vera held out her hand for all to see. Two overpriced carats that Donny purchased at the jewelry store next to the justice of the peace. Vera walked up to Emma and they hugged.

"How was the honeymoon?" Emma asked.

No surprises there, Vera wanted to say. But not to her mother. So she just said, "Just wonderful, Mom."

Emma decided it was best to take that at face value.

John walked up to Vera and hugged her, too. "Congratulations, honey," he said. "I could see that that boy made you happy. I'm glad you all got married."

The rest of the brothers and sisters stood in line to hug Vera. Bobby was last.

"Congratulations, sis," he said into her ear as he hugged her.

"We wouldn't have gotten married at all if it wasn't for Phyllis," Vera said.

Bobby looked at her quizzically.

She stepped back, still holding his hands. "That punk Ned and Donny's Mom and sister tried to fix me up with some other guy, hoping that Donny would catch us, not that I was interested in anyone but him," she added for effect. But she didn't have to say that for her family's benefit; they knew that as much as she loved Donny, if another man with something bigger and better came along, she would have gone with him. "Phyllis heard Ned talking about the whole thing. She called me and told me all about the plan, and I told Donny. He was so mad with all of them for trying to break us up, that after we ruined their little plan, he decided right then and there to marry me."

Everybody laughed.

Vera said, squeezing his hand this time, "And get this little brother. Phyllis said that since I helped her get her happiness with you, she was going to help me get my happiness with Donny."

Bobby looked at Vera and shrugged his shoulders. He still had a soft spot in his heart for Phyllis, and he was glad to know that she did, too, although they were going their separate ways.

"Come on, child," Emma said, as she walked over to the stairs and rested her arm on the bannister. "We've got to get your clothes packed up and get you ready. What time did you say Donny was coming?"

Vera followed Emma up the stairs. As bad as she wanted to leave there almost all her life, she felt like she didn't want to go. These were her people. She belonged here, around them, in Ardmore. What did she really know about Donny or any of those other Butchers? And as much as she wanted to be in the 400, those people weren't like her. In fact, they didn't even like her. Would Donny love her always like he did now? What if she ended up coming back to Ardmore again, in defeat?

When Vera walked inside the room, she sat down on the side of the bed and cried. Emma asked her what was wrong, and Vera verbalized every fear that played havoc in her mind.

Emma sat down next to Vera and put her arm around her. "Every bride feels the same way," she said. "Once you say I do and leave home, you're not the same. We can't be your number one family. Donny's got to be that. And it is true what they say, honey. You don't know anybody until you live with them. But you've got to step out on faith, Vera. Donny's a good man, and the good Lord brought you together—in a manner of speaking, even though you didn't get married in the church."

Vera's tears flowed as Emma went on.

"You're a smart girl, Vera," Emma said. "When I took you to Alfreda's last year, she told me something that I'm going to tell you. She said, 'If you raised her right, you have nothing to worry about.' And even though I got on you about your wild ways, I always knew that deep down inside, you had a good heart. I raised you right, honey, and I know I have nothing to worry about. Neither do you. You were my first, so you got more attention than the others, even though you never thought so."

Emma pulled Vera to her feet and said, "Come on, now. You want to be ready when your husband comes to take you home."

Vera looked up when she heard the word "home". She wiped her eyes, took a deep breath, and kissed Emma on the cheek. Then she stood up, took Emma's hand, walked over to her closet, and started cleaning it out.

CHAPTER 31

A steady stream of the 400 poured into the Butcher mansion for "A Champagne Reception in Honor of Mr. and Mrs. Donald Butcher, Jr." The women were scandalized that Donny reached so far down the social ladder to marry Vera, and the men were jealous. Mr. Butcher refused to let those matrons ostracize his daughter-in-law, so he made sure that everyone passed through a receiving line where he stood right next to Vera. He forced everyone to shake her hand. Then, he personally escorted Vera around the room as the reception got underway so that no one could escape talking with her for a few minutes. And that was really all that it took for most women to realize that even though Vera had a few rough edges, she could be charming and engaging. The men easily understood why Donny married Vera, and after the women got to talk with her, they understood, too. They were never forced to talk with her before. As long as Harriet ignored her, they figured that they could, too.

About an hour into the reception, Mr. Butcher drew Harriet away from a circle of her friends. Ordinarily, they would have been commiserating with Harriet about her new daughter-in-law, but Mr. Butcher made it clear to her that he would have none of that tonight or ever. He then asked the band to stop playing.

"May I have your attention?" he said, not really asking for their attention, as much as demanding it in his strong, authoritative voice.

As group after group stopped talking and the waiters stopped where they had served the last glass of champagne, Mr. Butcher said, "Harriet and

I want to thank all of you for coming here tonight to honor my son Donny and his bride, the former Vera Marshall. Come on up here Donny and Vera."

Vera's high heels click-clacked on the polished wooden floors as she and Donny walked through the crowd, which parted for them like they were royalty. Mr. Butcher held out his hand and wrapped it around Vera's arm, pulling her right next to him.

"Isn't she a lovely bride?" he said. The crowd answered yes and clapped, knowing that good manners dictated that they must, yet knowing that a lovely bride she unquestionably was.

"It's time to make a toast to the happy couple," Mr. Butcher said. "Waiters, see that everyone has a full glass." Waiters scurried throughout the room, pouring champagne into glasses that needed refilling and handing out glasses to those who were without.

"Harriet and I welcome Vera into our family just like she is our daughter," Mr. Butcher said. Harriet smiled broadly for the crowd and for her husband's benefit, but inside, her stomach churned. "I am certain that all of you will accept her into our circle and into your homes as you have always accepted my son. Let her feel the warmth and graciousness to which we have all become accustomed" he said, adding with a smile, "or you'll have me to deal with."

Everyone laughed, but they knew that he meant it. And from that moment on, he knew that the 400 would not snub Vera Marshall Butcher. No one wanted to be on Mr. Butcher's bad side. No one wanted to risk being cut off from the social events he provided, from the fabulous balls at his Mt. Airy mansion to the spectacular parties at his beach home in Cape May, New Jersey.

The few attorneys in the crowd wanted the clients that he referred to them to probate the estate of a now deceased loved one because the fees they made, based on a percentage of the estate's worth, were easy money. People who died without wills needed attorneys to help them through the morass at the Register of Wills office at City Hall, or at least they thought that they did, especially when Mr. Butcher told them that probate was too complex to handle without an attorney. Many an unsuspecting client didn't know that some of the estates were so simple that one of the highly qualified public servants who worked in the Register of Wills office could have told them exactly what to do—and for free.

Everyone wanted something from Mr. Butcher, and he was happy to share some of the wealth, knowing that it would only help his grow.

After the reception, Mr. and Mrs. Donald Butcher, Jr. received as many invitations to social events as Mr. and Mrs. Donald Butcher, Sr. Vera was in her glory with the never-ending round of cocktail parties, formal luncheons, and dinner dances. Mr. Butcher gave Donny and Vera a 10-room stone Tudor house on Wayne Avenue and Lincoln Drive in Mt. Airy in the bosom of the black bourgeoisie community.

And since he was now a married man with responsibilities, Mr. Butcher gave Donny an increasing number of chores at the funeral home. "This place is going to have to support two families now," Mr. Butcher said, "Yours and mine," meaning Donny and Vera and Harriet and Mary. Harriet and Mary slowly lightened up on Vera because they knew that when Donny took over the funeral home, their lifestyle would be totally dependent on his skill and beneficence.

As much as Vera liked modeling at Harrison's, she didn't have to do it anymore as Donny's wife. Unlike most men of his social and economic standing, Donny didn't demand that his wife stop working when they married. With a woman like Vera, demands were out of the question anyway. He just made it clear to her that she could do whatever she wanted—keep modeling or stay home. Vera made it clear to Donny that she wasn't going to stay home and raise children because she didn't want to have any. As the oldest girl in a family of 10, she had enough raising her brothers and sisters and wasn't about to raise any more.

"My dream has always been to open up a modeling agency and charm school," Vera told Donny. John always told her to "have something of your own." Have your own business and you'll always be working, he'd say. Vera didn't want to work for someone else all of her life. And even though Donny made or had more than enough money for the two of them, she wanted to pull her own weight and have her own money. Just in case.

Now that she had married her way into the 400, she saw that there were many more social clubs than she even imagined. The most prominent ones had their fashion shows at Harrison's, but many others had fashion shows at halls, when they could find them, and in church basements, when they couldn't. Vera figured that she could even convince some of the ladies to have small fashion shows and luncheons at their homes because they were always looking for something to make their luncheons stand out.

Donny financed Vera's dream, and with her usual fan fare, she opened the Vera Butcher Modeling Agency. Soon enough, a private fashion show arranged by Vera Butcher was every bit as prestigious as a show at Harrison's. Vera used Harrison's models on their off days and had her own string of beautiful ladies.

As the downtown department stores opened up more to Negroes, they wanted to have Negro models available for their fashion shows once they saw that Negroes spent their money just as well as whites did, and in some cases, even better. Too many Negroes thought that a dress from Wanamaker's must be better than one from Harrison's just because it was a white store and the dress cost twice as much, although that was not true. Harrison's buyers had the most exacting standards. They had to because their customers would sooner complain about merchandise at a Negro store than at a white one.

Vera was a businesswoman, and her agency had the finest Negro models available. So she supplied Wanamaker's and Strawbridge's the same as she provided fill-in models for Harrison's.

What acceptance the Butcher name didn't give her, which was precious little, her natural sense of style did. As the modeling business expanded, Vera needed more models to handle all the booking requests. Philadelphia had a lot of beautiful girls, but Vera demanded style as well as beauty. "If I can't find my own, I'll grow my own," she said. She started a charm school, training young girls to become models.

Unlike some of the other charm schools in the city that screened their students on the basis of who their parents were, the Vera Butcher School of Modeling and Beauty enrolled young women of every social class. "Just make sure that I have something to work with," Vera told her assistant who interviewed the young ladies and their parents. "Make up can't make up for everything, if you know what I mean."

Soon, girls from Vera's charm and modeling agency appeared on billboards all over Philadelphia, and in ads in *Ebony* and *Jet* magazines. Vera's girls regularly made the *Jet* centerfold and always in bathing suits from Harrison's. Mrs. Harrison appreciated the free advertising. And when Vera started doing fashion consultations that helped women improve their personal and professional wardrobes, Mrs. Harrison was even happier; Vera sent all the women to Harrison's to make their purchases.

Vera used all of her free time to build her business. "Between keeping these businesses going and keeping you happy," she said to Donny one day while they were laying in bed, "I have my hands full."

Donny didn't mind not having his own children. As long as Vera was happy, he was happy. Nothing had changed over the years except that their love grew deeper every day.

While Vera built her businesses, Bobby worked hard at building the family plumbing business, now called John Marshall & Sons. Bobby practically ran the business now. Years of damp, musty basements and carrying heavy tools took their toll on John. He was too weak to take on a lot of heavy plumbing jobs. He did mostly the light work and sometimes went with Bobby when he was called out on a complex job.

Bobby had a good head for business and was an excellent plumber with a fine reputation. He employed a number of local boys and trained them to be plumbers by working side-by-side with him. More Negroes on the Main Line bought or built their homes, and the fledgling civil rights movement opened up more business to him.

Bobby married two years out of high school to Ruby Rector, a girl from Darby, another small town right outside of Philadelphia. They met when Bobby went on a plumbing job at the Sun Shipyard in Chester, right outside of Philadelphia, where Ruby worked as a typist. After a few years of trying without success, they had four children in quick succession: Yvonne, Diane, Robert Jr. and Michael.

"Time to make your own money, son," Mr. Daniels told Ned the day he passed the bar exam. Ned agreed. It had always been his dream to open his law firm as soon as he could. He worked with another attorney from July, when he took the bar, to November, when he learned the results. Instead of Christmas cards, Ned sent the following announcement to the 400, the Howard Law School alumni, and his father's list of patients:

"Ned Daniels, Jr. is pleased to announce the December 15, 1961 opening of his law offices at Broad & Walnut Streets in Philadelphia, Pennsylvania and at Spring Avenue and Welsh Road in Ardmore, Pennsylvania."

Donny showed Vera the announcement because it was addressed only to "Mr. Donald Butcher, Jr." instead of Mr. and Mrs. Ned refused to recognize Vera as worthy of the ink it took to write her name.

"So he got his license to steal," Vera said, as she read the announcement and threw it in the trash.

"All lawyers aren't crooks, Vera," Donny said as he leafed through the rest of the mail.

"That one is, trust me," said Vera. "He didn't become a lawyer to help anybody like Thurgood Marshall and those other do-gooders with the NAACP. He became a lawyer to fleece the unfortunate and line his pockets."

Ned wasted no time proving Vera true. The Negro community in Ardmore treated Ned Jr. the way they supported Ned Sr.: they didn't much like either one, but they felt that a Negro attorney, even Ned, would treat them better than a white one. Ned's Ardmore office soon became full of people looking to beat "trumped up" criminal charges, divorce a cheating spouse, force a no-good man to pay child support, or divide up the meager possessions of a dear departed loved one. Ardmore's other Negro attorney, Randolph Jackson, had all but retired, handling only a few cases for the NAACP. He turned over his active files to Ned.

Like every attorney who handles estates, Ned learned about property that was for sale long before it was listed with any real estate agent. He knew who needed or wanted quick cash now that a parent was dead. And, like many attorneys, he took advantage of this inside knowledge to the fullest extent of the law.

Any time a family wanted to sell a home, Ned offered to buy it. Every family jumped at a quick sale because that meant quick cash and, in most cases, more money in their hands than they'd ever had. For most Negroes, the only way they got a large sum of money was when someone died. The money a bereaved son or daughter got from their deceased parents often was the only way for that son or daughter to buy his or her own home.

And if the bereaved family had any doubts about selling to Ned, he quelled them. "I want to help people buy their own homes," he'd say. "I'm going to rent the house out, but it won't be like a regular rental where the renter throws the money down the drain every month. My rentals will be lease-purchases. Every rent payment will go towards the down payment so that the renters, who may be short on cash, can buy the houses when they're able. That's the way to build a sturdy community," he said. And his clients believed him.

Ned even made sure that he got his way by double-dipping. When he drafted a will, he convinced the client to name him as the executor of the estate, the person responsible for taking care of the deceased's property. And when he became executor, he hired himself as the attorney for the estate. He collected double fees—an executor's fee and an attorney's fee, both based on a percent of the value of the estate and both perfectly legal under Pennsylvania law. As executor, he sold property to himself and even hired himself as the real estate attorney, earning a third fee for handling the house sale.

Even though Ned made a lot of money by often collecting three fees from one estate, he wasn't satisfied. He wanted more money to secure his place in the 400. Being born into it wasn't enough for him; he had to feel like he could make it in the 400 based on his accomplishments, not his father's.

A regular lease-purchase deal for all the houses he bought would never make him rich. He spent evening after evening researching lease-purchase contracts. He took the sections that were most one-sided in favor of the owner and drafted a lease-purchase agreement that assured that the occupant never would end up buying the property.

The occupants had to make their own repairs—"helps them have pride of ownership," Ned said—while, at the same time, making sure that they never missed a payment. Ned drafted the leases so that if a renter was ever ten days late on one payment, he could begin eviction proceedings immediately if the renter was ever late again. "Builds responsibility," he said.

Of course, the occupants did not realize when they signed that the lease terms were onerous. Ned wrote the agreement with as much legalese as he could complicate the English language with and then had the agreement printed in type that was small enough to cause people not to want to read it. The renters never complained, though; they trusted Ned. After all, he was an attorney sworn to uphold the law, not break it; and not just any attorney—a Negro attorney that regular Negroes thought wanted to help his people. And he was Dr. Daniels' son. Like his father, he didn't have to socialize with them, but he always treated them with a business-like respect.

Even as their situations got worse, most of the occupants of the lease-purchase houses refused to see how Ned duped them. They were hardworking, upstanding, mostly Christian folks who believed in the sanctity of the contract, that their word was their bond. They blamed themselves if they had financial difficulties, not the system. They put off repairs to keep a roof over their families' heads. If it meant being late with the rent or fixing a leaky faucet, they'd pay the rent. They'd usually patch the leak as best as they could, ending up causing more damage in the pipes from the backup or damage to the floor from the dripping water, which only was cut down, not out.

But when things got so bad that it was time to call a plumber, the occupants always called John Marshall & Sons. Sometimes John would go, but, more and more, Bobby would. Once he got inside, he shook his head at how those once well-kept homes were running down. His bills were always high because the plumbing or heating problem was severe. Even though both John and Bobby knew that it would be a long time before they got paid in full, they never refused to do the work. It just wasn't in them. Bobby & John did the work, building up their credit account at the local plumbing supply and telling their customers to pay what they could every month. Bobby and John knew these people, and they knew that they would pay their bills, even if it took years.

"It's a damn shame what's happening to these Daniels' houses," Bobby said to John one day when they were down in one of Ned's houses in a basement in five inches of near freezing water, patching up an old water heater that they patched up just a few months before.

"Forcing these folks to live like that," John said. "What's gotten into that boy?"

"He's as greedy as all get out," Bobby said. "One miss and these folks have to leave the house that they think is going to be their home. It's not right. By the time they finish paying for the house, it'll be in such bad shape that it won't be worth the money that they've already put in."

"I can't believe that Dr. Daniels approves of his boy doing that," John said.

"You can bet that he does," Bobby said. "I hear he gave Ned the money to buy those houses in the first place."

"Well," said John, "I can't believe that one Negro would treat another one like that, at least around here. He's known most of these folks since they started grammar school together."

"That doesn't mean anything to Ned. Never did," Bobby said.

"Well, believe me son," John said. "God don't like ugly."

CHAPTER 32

Bobby sat on a chair in the kitchen feeding his youngest daughter, Diane, when the phone rang. "What?" he asked. "Randolph? You can't be serious."

"Not even an hour ago," John said. "Heart attack. Right there in the office. Dead by the time they got him to Bryn Mawr Hospital."

"Good Lord," said Bobby. "And right when we got the victory." After the Rev. Martin Luther King spoke at the Main Line NAACP's annual dinner, the Negro community in Ardmore caught the civil rights fever. Randolph Jackson filed a petition with the Lower Merion Board of Supervisors on behalf of the Main Line NAACP to divide the township into electoral districts. That would allow the Negro community in Ardmore to elect one of their own to the Board of Supervisors. Just last week, the supervisors acceded to Randolph's petition, and everyone assumed that Randolph would be elected to the Board since he was basically retired and had time on his hands.

"I guess Randolph finished his work and the Lord called him home," said John.

"Maybe you're right," said Bobby, as he wiped a tear from his eye. He looked at his very-much-alive daughter, mentally said a quick prayer for her continued health, and then said to John, "OK, Pop. Thanks for letting me know."

Vera walked from gossiping group to gossiping group looking for interesting conversation at the Higgens' "Let It Snow" cocktail party, always given the second Saturday in January. The room looked like vanilla ice cream with bits of shaved dark and light chocolate mixed in. Miriam Higgens required that everyone at her party wear a white outfit, preferably with something that sparkled like ice on snow when the sun hit it at just the right angle. Her parlor was full of Negroes of all shades and complexions in ice-like white satin, whipped cream-like white crepe, and silk brocade as smooth as warm salt water taffy all stretched out. Miriam got her sparkle, all-right, as diamonds, sequins and pearls reflected off the candlelight that illuminated the room. Vera's dress outshone them all, of course, with its beaded and sequined bodice, white fur-trimmed hem, and channel set diamond choker necklace with a two carat diamond resting comfortably at the crest of her cleavage.

"Oh, Vera, dear. I must tell you," Miriam said when Vera walked over to the little group where Miriam held court. But Vera never heard what Miriam had to say. For before she could get to it, Vera turned her ears to the conversation going on behind her.

"It's mine for the taking," Ned said to the group of men puffing on cigars and drinking scotch out of heavy lead crystal old-fashioned glasses. "I've got so many people in that one-horse town beholden to me, they'll vote for me in a minute," he said.

"Who died and made you king of Ardmore," one of the men said as he laughed.

Ned looked at him and curled his upper lip. "First of all, there's those suckers living in my lease-purchase houses. I own them." He continued, "And then there's my former clients. I own them, too. I've defended half the town on criminal charges."

Vera would have flipped the champagne glass up over her shoulder if she was certain it would have landed in Ned's face. What Ned said wasn't true. Ardmore had a few bad apples, but not anything like Ned was making it out to be.

"Then for the other half, I know the secrets of too many divorces, laziness at work passed off as race discrimination, and wills forged on death beds. They won't cross me, believe me," Ned bragged. He and his friends laughed.

Miriam talked on and on, and Vera only looked at her moving mouth. She leaned back about an inch to hear Ned, although she didn't have to strain much. The more he bragged, the louder he talked.

"And when I win, we all win. I've got everything set up with the other supervisors. That township is booming, and there are construction contracts, supplier contracts, professional services contracts, contracts for everything you can think of to make money," he said. "It's 'you scratch my back, I'll scratch yours.' The only thing missing on these sweetheart deals is dry ink in the paper."

Well, I'll be damned, thought Vera. Every decent person in Ardmore fought for that seat for Randolph and now Ned thinks that he's going to step in and take that over the same as he took over his law practice. Just so he can run my home folks into the ground and give the 400 more money so they can spend it on Cadillacs and cotillions. Not if I have anything to do with it, she thought.

"That's very interesting, Miriam," Vera said, like she really gave a shit about anything Miriam said, "but I really must pee."

"Oh, Vera. You're so amusing," Miriam said with a flick of her wrist. "Right this way," she said, as both she and Vera walked away.

"You gotta do it, little brother," Vera said, as she sat in Bobby's kitchen and bounced his four-year-old daughter, Yvonne, on her knee. "If he ever becomes supervisor, your life will be hell, excuse my French, Ruby," Vera said nodding to Bobby's wife who was washing dishes. "But you know what I mean."

Vera put her hands over Yvonne's ears to shield her from the swear words she knew she was going to say. Kids repeated everything. "He'll be on your ass like white on rice," she said. "You think it was hard for Pop sometimes to get the proper licenses and go-aheads from those white supervisors? That'll be nothing compared to what Ned will do to you."

Bobby took another sip of his beer like he had something to think about. How can he be so cool, thought Vera.

"You know he hates you," she said. "Hates me, too, but I don't pay him no never mind because he can't hurt me. But you make your living here in this township, Bobby. Ned will keep you so tied up in red tape and road blocks that you won't be able to fix so much as a leaky faucet without his permission, and you know he ain't going to give you that."

Vera stood up and put Yvonne back in her high chair. Then she walked over and stood right behind Bobby and put her hands on his shoulders. "Besides that, you just can't let that boy tear down this community any more. You complain that Ned is taking advantage of the folks in those houses now. What do you think he's going to do if he's a supervisor and knows nobody in the township can stop him. Now he only *thinks* nobody in this township can stop him; if he gets on the board, he'll know for sure. He'll grease those white boys' palms so much that their dicks will slip out of their hands when they go to take a piss."

She looked at Ruby, who had put her hands over Yvonne's ears as soon as Vera said "dick."

"Sorry about the language, Ruby," said Vera, "but I only talk like that when I'm serious."

"Then you're a mighty serious woman," Bobby said, laughing because Vera talked like that most of the time.

"You got that right, Bobby," Vera said. She sat back in her chair across from him. "It's time for you to get serious, too. Nobody else around here has the brains or the popularity to win that seat if Ned runs. You know that. But everybody likes you, and you're ten times as smart as Ned. You know that, too," she said.

Bobby kept sipping. Vera was right. She usually was. Ardmore was his home and since he couldn't go to college, he knew that he would never live anywhere else. Ned didn't care diddly squat about anybody in Ardmore unless his or her last name was Daniels. But Bobby cared about his family and everyone else. He wanted to raise his children in an Ardmore that was like the Ardmore he grew up in: well-kept houses, solid families, good friends, and a fair shake for everyone. That was not the Ardmore Ned envisioned. No matter how Ned destroyed the neighborhood in Ardmore, he didn't have to look at it every day. He lived on the edge of the Negro community, far enough away from most of the homes that he owned to be bothered by them.

Bobby thought to himself that all his life, he'd never been the kind of man to seek glory for himself. He just wanted to make a good living and raise his family. But sometimes in a man's life, it was time to take a stand. Now was the time.

Bobby got up and put his arm around Ruby. "What do you think, honey?" he asked.

"For better or worse," she said, as she kissed him. "I'm with you."

Vera tapped her fingers on the table. Touching, she thought, but whatcha going to do, little brother?

Bobby turned to face Vera. "I'll do it. I'll do it," he said.

Vera jumped up and hugged him.

"That boy is like a cancer that you can't cure," Bobby said.

"Well, the doctor is in," said Vera.

Tongues wagged all over Ardmore.

"You know they never did like each other."

"Two of Ardmore's finest families fighting like that. It's a disgrace."

"I heard old Dr. Daniels has bought this election for Ned."

"I hope Bobby kicks Ned's ass."

Ned was incensed to learn that Bobby was running against him, and he went after every vote he could get. Ned's office became mighty crowded in late January as he called up former clients and had them come in to discuss some discrepancies he found in their cases. Oh, he could take care of them, all right, they were told because they could be in trouble if certain information got out. The clients who knew that they had done wrong and had made a habit of nursing their guilty consciences thanked Ned for looking out for them. And just before they left, he always said, "You know I'm running for supervisor, don't you?" He didn't have to say anything more. They got the message.

But anyone who hadn't used Ned as an attorney supported Bobby. He was related to or friendly with almost every Negro in Ardmore. Bobby had more relatives or friends than Ned had clients, so things looked good for him.

"I'll buy you a campaign manager," Vera told Bobby one day as they sat around his kitchen table talking about the election.

"What do I need a campaign manager for?" Bobby asked. He knew virtually nothing about politics except that he considered it his duty to vote in every election that the Lord sent.

"Because you're a neophyte," Vera said, using a term she heard Donny and Mr. Butcher and their friends throw around when they talked about Philadelphia politics and who the 400 was going to get to run for what office. A neophyte was a derogatory term when applied to politics; every time Vera heard the Butchers use the term, it was in connection with someone they could control.

"What do you mean?" Bobby asked.

"A neophyte," Vera said, "means that you don't know nothing, at least about politics anyhow. It's your first time out. Your first time running for office."

"So what," Bobby said. "I know what I need to know." He picked up the petitions he got from the township board of elections and said, "I get 100 signatures on these petitions, file them at the township building, get on the ballot, and get people to vote for me on election day. What's to know? I know enough people to win."

Vera rolled her eyes. Neophyte, neophyte, she thought. "It's not that easy, little brother. Not that easy at all. You got to get more than 100 signatures. Suppose someone tells you he's registered and he isn't? Then his signature is no good. Then you've only got 99 signatures, and you can't run. You've got to get more than 100 signatures to give yourself some insurance," she said.

"So I'll get more than 100," Bobby said. He wondered why Vera acted like this was such a big deal.

"I'll?" she asked. "Surely, you don't mean that you'll be out there getting all your own signatures."

Bobby looked at her like that was exactly what he meant.

Vera sighed in exasperation. She hit the petitions with her hands, emphasizing her first four words. "See what I mean? Neophyte. You've got to get you some volunteers to go out there and get you some signatures. You can't do it all alone. The more volunteers you have, the more signatures you'll get. And you need to use your time to do more than just get signatures." She walked around the room shaking her head. Help him Lord, she said silently. Even though He hadn't heard from her often, Emma always told her that God answers prayer.

"You only have about two months before election day," she said. "You need to plan your strategy. Figure out when you're going to go to what church, to which club meeting. You can't spend all your time getting signatures."

Bobby leaned back in his chair. He'd seen this before. Vera was on a tangent, and the best thing to do was humor her.

"If you want to get me a so-called campaign manager, go ahead," he said. "But I'm running my own campaign. I don't need anybody from Philly to come up here and tell me how to do things in Ardmore. But if you want to 'buy' me some help, go right ahead, because I know I can't stop you."

"No you can't," said Vera. "He'll be out here tomorrow."

CHAPTER 33

Al Stewart had no morals. That's why he worked on so many political campaigns in Philadelphia. He fit right in. He was a big man about 6 feet tall with one bad eye that made it seem like he was looking at you with one eye and watching everything else around you with the other, which he was. If the campaign was going to be a tough one, call Al. He'd dig up a speck of dirt and turn it into a mountain of the richest, filthiest manure that was ever slung at a candidate. It didn't even matter if the dirt was true. By the time Al was finished spreading the dirt about Candidate XYZ, even Candidate XYZ would think it was true.

That's why Vera wanted him for Bobby. There was enough dirt on Ned that could be slung around so that every home in Ardmore had a thick layer of it sitting right in their front rooms, a layer that would stink, a layer that couldn't be brushed away, a layer that would stick around until election day reminding every Negro voter in Ardmore what a dirty dog Ned Daniels was.

"I'm not paying you to lose," Vera told Al the day she hired him.

"I never lose," Al said. And his record proved it.

Bobby's storefront campaign office on Spring Avenue was full of people one Monday, the night before he had to file the nominating petitions. Al told every volunteer who circulated a petition to be at the office at 7 p.m. to have them notarized so Bobby could file them the next day. When a volunteer inevitably asked, "couldn't I just drop it off?", Al always answered like a broken record, "No. The circulator—that's you, the person who circulated the petitions—has to be physically present before the notary or else the signatures on the petition will not be accepted." The volunteers often grumbled that they had better things to do on a Monday night, but they'd be there, if only for Bobby.

Vera, Bobby and Al sat around Bobby's desk at the back of the office while the volunteers stayed near the front eating cookies and drinking punch with floating chunks of sherbert ice cream.

"Where the hell is she?" Vera asked a few minutes after 7.

"Calm down," said Bobby. "She'll be here."

A few minutes later, they heard scuffling at the front as people stepped aside to sounds of "Let me through. Hey. Move over. Let me through."

Edith Greene, the 72-year-old notary who worked full-time at Addit's Funeral Home and Florist Shop, pushed her way through the crowd. A black, single clasp handbag hung from one arm and a tattered carpetbag of equal size hung from the other. Edith worked at Addit's for the past 50 years, never missing a day. Lou Addit kept her on even though her eyesight was failing and her vanity stopped her from wearing her glasses as much as she should.

As long as Edith wanted to work, she had a job with Lou Addit. She was the only Negro notary in Ardmore, too. There was no sense in anybody else in the neighborhood becoming a notary as long as Edith was; everybody knew they would find her at Addit's, 9 a.m. to 5 p.m. on weekdays and from 9 a.m. to 12 p.m. on Saturdays, without fail. She made house calls, too, and notarized many a deathbed signature on a will.

Edith acted like she was the only Negro notary, too. Cantankerous, some people called her. But the folks who needed the stamp of approval that Edith's notary seal provided usually had no choice but to wait on Edith and do what she said or go to a white notary, but nobody wanted to give a white notary power over their official affairs.

"Too many damn people in here for me," Edith said, as she walked over to the desk. Bobby quickly got out of his chair and said, "Good evening, Mrs. Greene. Have a seat right here. Thank you so much for coming."

Edith placed her carpetbag on the table and her handbag on the floor under her feet. Never could be too careful, she thought, especially with people she didn't know, like that big man with the bad eye hovering over the desk.

"Hello, Mrs. Greene," Vera said.

"Oh, so you're back," Mrs. Greene said, moving her head to look at Vera from head to toe. "I thought you were living the high life in Philadelphia with the 400."

Help me hold my tongue, Lord, Vera said in silent prayer. She knew that it would take the strength of God to keep her from saying something smart to this woman who they so desperately needed. Vera took a deep breath and said, "You know I have to come back to help my little brother, Mrs. Greene."

Mrs. Greene looked around the room. "Looks like he's doing just fine without your help," she said.

Bobby stood behind Vera and held her hands to restrain her from getting up and putting either of those hands on her hips and telling Mrs. Greene a thing or two. "Mrs. Greene, let me introduce you to my campaign manager, Al Stewart," Bobby said, tilting his head toward Al because he felt Vera's arms shaking in anger.

"Pleased to meet you, Mrs. Greene," Al said.

"Likewise," said Mrs. Greene. "Now let's get down to business. What do you have for me to notarize today, Bobby?" she said as she pulled her notary seal, stamp pad and record book out of the carpetbag.

"My nominating petitions," Bobby said. He let go of Vera, opening his eyes wide and silently mouthing to her "behave." He walked around next to Mrs. Greene to show her exactly what needed to be done. "I need you to notarize the circulator's affidavit. These people," he said, waving his arms at the crowd gathered out front, "collected all these signatures. I need you to notarize each affidavit that says that the circulator personally appeared before you and swore that they collected the signatures."

Mrs. Greene picked up the petitions and thumbed through them. There were about 40 of them. "If I get each of them to swear to this, we'll be here all night," she said.

"They don't have to say what's printed there," Al said. "They just have to appear before you."

Mrs. Greene adjusted her glasses and looked up at Al. "What makes you think that you know how to notarize documents, young man?" she said.

Bobby stepped in. "He doesn't, Mrs. Greene. Certainly not like you, but he's worked in a lot of campaigns in Philadelphia."

"But this isn't Philadelphia," she shot back. Then she sat back in the chair and looked at Bobby. She always did like him. Hard working young man, very much like his father. Then she looked over at Vera. Nothing like that sister of his.

"Why don't you call out the circulator's name on the petition, have them come over, and then you can notarize it," said Bobby. "That might make things flow a little smoother. And a little faster. I know I promised to get you home in time for Gunsmoke."

That was right, Edith thought. I'm not missing Festus for any of these folks. "All right, son," Mrs. Greene said. "I think that would be all right."

Al went over to the volunteers and explained what they should do.

Mrs. Greene picked up the first petition and called out, "Paul Burton?"

"Over here, Mrs. Greene," Paul said.

"Fine," she said. "Tell your Momma I asked about her, hear?"

"Sure will, Mrs. Greene," Paul said, as he went back to talking with the others.

Edith picked up her notary seal, squeezed the petition between it, signed her name, stamped the stamp on the pad and then on the petition. "Where's Regina Climers?" asked Edith.

"Here I am, Mrs. Greene," Regina said, raising her hand.

"OK, sugar," said Mrs. Greene.

And on it went. Much too slowly for Vera. After about 20 minutes of this, when Mrs. Greene called out the next name, Vera lost it. If only she'd just notarize the damn petitions, Vera thought. But no, she couldn't do that. She had to get into a conversation about everybody's momma and daddy and who shot John. "They're all over there, Mrs. Greene. You know that. You know everybody. Can't you just notarize the rest of them so we can all go home?"

The moment Vera said it, she was sorry. Bobby quickly tried to smooth over the rough words. "What Vera really meant to say, Mrs. Greene," he said, looking at Vera like he wanted to kill her, which he did, "was that with all the rest that are left, you'll never get home in time for Gunsmoke."

"Yeah, that's it," said Vera. "I meant that if you notarize the rest of them, you can go home and watch Gunsmoke."

Mrs. Greene whipped around and looked at Vera. "I know very well what you meant young lady," she said. She rolled her eyes and said to everyone and no one in particular, "Always was too big for her britches." Then she said to Bobby, "That sister of yours is going to get you in trouble one day. If it wasn't for your dear sweet mother and father, I'd walk out the door right now, young man."

Bobby looked at Vera and then at Mrs. Greene. "I know that Mrs. Greene, and I'm sorry. Please don't leave. You do know everyone here though," he said. "You know everyone in Ardmore."

Mrs. Greene looked at her watch. If she didn't leave soon, she would miss Gunsmoke. And Bobby was right; she knew everyone in the room because she knew everyone in Ardmore. She made a point of snatching the first petition off the desk, throwing her notary seal down and stamping the stamp pad so hard that a few drops of ink flew up in the air and landed on Al's hand.

She snatched, squeezed and stamped the next 18 petitions, not calling out any names, and barely even looking at the circulator's name. "Finished," she announced. Then she pushed the petitions across the desk to Bobby.

Bobby picked them up before Mrs. Greene changed her mind about giving them to him, touched her arm and sincerely said, "Thank you, Mrs. Greene. I don't know what I would have done without you. Let me drive you home."

Mrs. Greene didn't say a thing. She just put her seal, record book, and stamp pad back in her carpetbag and picked up her handbag. Then she pointed her finger at Vera and shook it. "That mouth of yours is going to get you into trouble one day, young lady," she said, as she turned to walk away. "And I use the term loosely."

Vera started to say something, but Bobby put his hand up as if to silence her. Al held his hand over his mouth to stifle his laughter, and Bobby hung his head to try to hide his.

The week after Bobby filed the petitions, he campaigned hard, going to churches, club meetings and walking door-to-door. On Tuesday, Bobby was in his campaign office running off flyers on a mimeograph machine when a delivery boy from the Township Board of Supervisors made Bobby sign for a hand delivery.

Bobby opened up the envelope and pulled out the paper. It read, "COMPLAINT—CHALLENGE TO THE NOMINATING PETITIONS OF ROBERT MARSHALL." Bobby continued reading. He didn't understand all of the legal language, but he made out some of the more important points.

"COUNT 1. In violation of Section 202 of the Pennsylvania Election Code, the signatures of 62 electors are invalid, being that the electors used ditto (A) marks instead of writing out the complete date, or complete town name or address."

"COUNT 2. In violation of Section 203 of the Pennsylvania Election Code, the signatures of 53 voters are invalid in that the electors did not sign their names exactly as they appear on their voter registration card" being . . . and it listed each elector's name.

"COUNT 3. In violation of Section 204 of the Pennsylvania Election Code, 11 electors signed Robert Marshall's nominating petitions after signing the petition of Ned Daniels, a candidate for the same office."

Count 4, the last paragraph charged that 43 of the signatures on 9 petitions were improperly notarized because the circulator did not personally appear before the notary and, thus, were invalid.

The Complaint closed with the statement "leaving Robert Marshall with 84 valid signatures out of the 253 he filed. Therefore, Robert Marshall has failed to file the 100 valid signatures necessary to qualify as a candidate for Supervisor."

Bobby couldn't believe what he just read. Then he turned to the last page and saw an affidavit signed by Al Stewart attesting to the irregularities in having the petitions notarized. It read, "On February 15, I was an eyewitness to the fact that the following circulators did not personally appear before the notary, Edith Greene . . ." and it identified the petitions that Mrs. Greene hurriedly notarized after Vera's outburst. Al's affidavit went on to say that the names listed on five of the petitions were not even real people because he faked all the signatures and the name of the circulator.

"What?" Bobby said out loud to no one because he was alone. "Al? Testifying against me? I can't believe it." He read the petitions again, trying to understand every word. Then he called Vera.

"That punk ass motherfucker," she said, slamming her fist on the mahogany desk in her office. "And that two-timing, double-dealing, one-eyed bastard," she said. "Ned must have paid Al off. Mother fucking Philadelphia political consultants. Wait 'till I spread the word on him. He doesn't know who he just fucked with."

"That's not helping any, Vera," Bobby said. All he could think of was that his dreams were going up in flames, again. First, college, and now this. He took a stand and got knocked over.

"Wait right there," Vera said. "I'll be right over. I want to see this shit for myself."

CHAPTER 34

Vera and Bobby sat at his desk trading papers. He read one and then handed it to her to read. Then they talked about what it meant.

"It means that I'm out," Bobby said, shaking his head and pacing around the campaign office.

"Only if Ned is right, which I refuse to believe," Vera said. "Just because he makes the argument, doesn't mean it's right. You know that. God knows, he has no problem lying."

"Well," Bobby said, "neither you nor I understand this mumbo jumbo enough to know whether he's lying or not. I need a lawyer." He reached for the phone book on the desk. "And I'm going to get one."

Bobby didn't know any of the other lawyers in the township, so he started at the top of the alphabet. He explained the case to the first lawyer he talked to, and he turned him down. So did the second. So did the third. Nobody would take the case. When they heard he was talking about the race against Ned Daniels, all Bobby got was: "I can't help you."

It didn't take him long to realize that no attorney in the township wanted to take the case against Ned. In fact, one of the attorneys, Carlton Stevenson, remembered Bobby from chemistry class at Lower Merion. He told him, "Save yourself the trouble, Bobby. Nobody around here is going to take that case. As much as I like you, there's an unwritten rule: the attorneys stick together. And Ned has the white attorneys in town thinking that money is going to fall from Heaven if he gets elected, and he's pretty close to right."

Vera got the same response from the lawyers in town that she knew. "Now you know I couldn't take a case against one of my brethren," one of the attorneys told Vera. "No self-respecting Negro attorney would."

"You guys stick together like white on rice. But like that rice at Wing Chung's Chinese Restaurant, your ass is going to get fried," she said as she banged down the phone.

"Ned has those boys in town all tied up," Vera told Bobby. "Nobody wants to touch this thing, but it figures. When one of them gets in trouble, they circle the wagons, and if you're not in the circle, they leave you out to get shot up and die."

Bobby leaned back in his chair and sighed. "It looks like I'll just have to represent myself," he said. "I'll give it my best shot, and if I don't make it, then it wasn't for me."

Vera hated to admit that maybe Bobby was right. Ned's ties with all the lawyers they knew ran too deep. Those old boys stuck together. But then she thought: the boys stick together, but maybe the girls don't.

"Let me make one more call, little brother," Vera said. She picked up her purse and walked out.

Susan Vanderpool leaned back in her black leather club chair and looked at the two documents on the wall of her 10' x 10' office. The first was her diploma from Georgetown University Law Center. She didn't understand any of the words on it because they were all written in Latin, but she understood how hard she worked to earn it. Three years of torment from men, both white and Negro, and even one Asian, who thought that women should be barefoot and pregnant instead of learned in jurisprudence and competent to stand before the bar of justice. The second document was a certificate from the Supreme Court of the Commonwealth of Pennsylvania informing the world that she was a member of its bar and permitted to practice law in any courtroom under its jurisdiction.

Then she looked at the letter in her hand from the landlord notifying her that the rent was 20 days past due. A license to practice law was not a license to make money, as every non-lawyer she knew assumed. Especially not for a woman.

It wasn't because she didn't look the part. She still looked on her fashion consultation with Vera Butcher as an investment.

"Dress like you've got it honey, or you never will—get it, I mean," Vera told her.

Out went the dowdy, ill-fitted blazers and skirts she wore during law school.

"Show your shape, honey," Vera said. "When you're in court, you want them to hear every word you're saying, right?" Susan answered, "of course." "Then make them look at you, girl," Vera said. "Draw their attention with your body, then hold them with your mind."

Susan now owned five matching suits, tailored by Harrison's alterations to fit her perfectly. While the suits still were grey, navy blue, and black, they fit like a second skin and always had a dash of style—a white lace collar, contrasting color piping around the waist or neckline, or velvet collar or cuff. She had the clothes of a confident, successful attorney and the papers on the wall to prove that she had the brains of one. Now all she needed to do was get the clients.

Susan took out her appointment book and looked again to see if she could get a retainer from any new clients coming in that day so she could at least give the landlord something. The few appointments she had were follow up meetings with clients whose money she had already spent.

The phone rang, and she hoped it wasn't another bill collector. "Susan Vanderpool speaking," she said.

"Good morning, Susan. This is Vera Butcher."

"Good morning, Mrs. Butcher," Susan said. "It's nice to talk with you again." Or at least I think it is, thought Susan. Don't tell me my check bounced with her, too. "What can I do for you?" Susan asked, holding her breath, expecting the worse.

"Glad you asked," Vera said. She explained Bobby's case and ended by saying, "None of the men will take it. You know how they stick together. I was wondering if it was different for you lady lawyers?"

It sure is, Susan thought. When she graduated from law school, none of the Negro male attorneys would hire her. "As soon as you get married, you'll leave," they said. "And a lawyer has to be tough. That's no kind of work for a nice young lady."

Undaunted, Susan told them that she was committed to practice, and that if they didn't hire her, she would open her own practice. Not a threat, but a fact. She asked them, as most young lawyers do, to just refer to her the cases that they didn't want, the ones that didn't pay the high fees or that required a lot more work than they were willing to do. They even refused to do that. Especially Ned Daniels. He barely agreed to talk with her. And when he did, he just leaned back in his chair, chewed on a pencil, and said, "I don't think I can help you, Miss Vanderpool. When I look for a young lawyer, I look for two things without question. A man. And a Howard University Law School graduate. You, Miss Vanderpool, are neither." He stood up, opened the office door, and said, "Good day."

Susan didn't take two seconds to think about Vera's request. "I'd be happy to take the case. When can I meet your brother?"

"Marshall campaign," Bobby said when he answered the phone at the campaign office.

"Is that you little brother? I hardly recognized your voice," Vera said. "I haven't heard you sound that sad since you and Phyllis broke up."

Bobby realized that was true. He couldn't sound anything but sad when he'd lost one of his dreams.

"When it rains, it pours, Vera," he said.

Yea . . . and . . . tell me something I don't know, thought Vera.

"What are you talking about?" she asked. But before Bobby could answer, Vera went on, "I got you a lawyer. A lady lawyer at that."

"Well," Bobby said. "Tell her not to waste her time. A messenger from the Courthouse just left here. The case is assigned to Judge Davis. Only Negro judge in Montgomery County and they have to give the case to him. At least with one of the white judges I might have had a chance."

You got that right, little brother, Vera thought.

All the Negroes in Montgomery County cheered when Governor Remick appointed Attorney T. Jefferson Davis to fill a vacancy on the county Court of Common Pleas. Bobby normally would have been happy to have a case in front of Judge Davis. He was tough on criminals, but fair to everyone else, especially to other Negroes. His sense of justice wasn't far from those NAACP lawyers that made everyone proud.

But he was 400, too, just like Ned.

And just like Ned, he belonged to the Talented Tenth Club, an exclusive group of Negro professional men who met monthly for dinner and who permitted their equally exclusive wives to meet with them twice a year— once in the summer and once again at a gala at Christmas, where they perpetrated the illusion that the gala really was given in honor of their wives, not in their continuing quest to create an exclusive social event that would show how really special they were.

"That'll make it harder, little brother," Vera said. "No question about that. But this girl's a fighter, and she's not afraid of any of those men. You just work with her and see what you can come up with. I'll send her over this afternoon."

Vera quickly hung up. She didn't want to wallow in despair on the phone with Bobby. He felt bad enough already. No sense in dragging him down any further. Susan would have to come up with an airtight argument to get Judge Davis to rule against Ned. Those Talented Tenth bonds were like blood, thicker than water and hard to wash out once they were set.

She leaned back in the swivel chair and chuckled, rolled her eyes and shook her head. That 400 sure had everything sewn up. The average working Negro didn't stand a chance to get ahead playing it straight, let alone the poor ones who weren't working. No wonder the numbers runners and the gambling joints were so popular, she thought. And then she thought of the fun that she had when she hung out with Alfreda and that crowd at places like Velvet's and the Nile.

Near the end of the day, Vera called Donny and said, "I'll be home late, baby. I've got some business to take care of." She opened up her desk drawer, grabbed her purse and walked out of the office smiling. She told her secretary, "I'll see you tomorrow, Marsha. Right now, I need a drink." She was chuckling and talking to herself like somebody who needed to be committed when she got into her Cadillac and drove down Lancaster Avenue to her favorite club.

The temperature in Courtroom 309 was 10 degrees warmer than any other courtroom in the Montgomery County Courthouse. "Too many Negroes in one place," Alfreda said to Vera and Emma as they looked behind them at a courtroom full of Marshalls and their relatives, friends and neighbors and Negroes from all over Montgomery County who just wanted to be among the first to see two Negro lawyers, and one a woman at that, fighting each other in front of a Negro judge. Race pride gone wild.

Bobby and Susan worked in her office until the last possible moment, going over the names, the arguments, the cases and the strategy. They walked into the courtroom with a stack of papers and a gaggle of witnesses following behind them like geese to a row of seats that John had reserved.

Susan laid the papers on the counsel's desk and took a legal pad out of her briefcase. She was prepared to argue the law. She found plenty of cases to attack Ned's technical challenges. She figured that the acerbic Mrs. Greene would provide strong testimony that, after 72 years of living in Ardmore, she knew every circulator and saw every circulator in the room and could overcome the notarizing challenges, except for the five petitions that Al Stewart faked. The way Susan figured it, those arguments would get her 121 signatures, not much room to spare over the 100 that Bobby needed, but enough to get by.

Ned sat at his counsel's table, twirling a pencil in the air. He had one yellow legal pad, one copy of the Pennsylvania Election Code, and one witness—Al Stewart, who sat behind him.

At 9:05, Judge Davis walked into the courtroom. At 6'2", 200 lbs. and swathed in black, he made an imposing figure. The bailiff called the court to order and announced the case.

"Good morning, counselor," he said, nodding his head and looking at Ned.

"And good morning to you, too, Miss Vanderpool," he said, looking at Susan. Damn him, she thought. He knows he ought to call me counselor, too, but he won't because I'm a woman. She held her tongue and said what she knew she had to say, "Good morning, your Honor."

The judge flipped through the pleadings and raised his head to look at Ned. "You may proceed, counselor."

Ned stood up and paced around the front of the courtroom as he explained, in detail and without notes, how Bobby Marshall had almost gotten away with committing a fraud on the good people of Lower Merion Township by submitting nominating petitions with so many flaws that the didn't even have the nominal 100 signatures to get on the ballot. The flaws were so evident and egregious, he said, that the signatures must be stricken on their face; witnesses were not even necessary. Then he introduced the petitions in question into evidence, the signatures that must be thrown out having been previously marked.

"Thank you, counselor," said the judge. He looked over at Susan. "Miss Vanderpool. Have you any argument?"

"Yes, your Honor," said Susan, brushing off the judge's insult in her mind as she brushed off a piece of lint from her sleeve, the mind control game she learned in law school.

Susan started attacking Ned's challenges on the law. "As you can see from my pleadings, your Honor," she began, explaining how other courts have upheld the validity of signatures on election petitions calling the technical challenges—like the elector's use of ditto marks, failure to write out their occupation, or failure to sign their name exactly as it appears on their voter registration card—insignificant details that do not invalidate an otherwise valid signature.

Judge Davis let Susan go on. "As you are aware, Miss Vanderpool, the Pennsylvania Supreme Court has not ruled on these issues."

Susan interrupted. "I am aware of that, your Honor, but the majority of the Courts of Common Pleas in the Commonwealth have, and they have followed the law exactly as I have argued it."

"Well, then, Miss Vanderpool," Judge Davis said, taking off his glasses for effect, "you must also be aware that I am not bound to follow the decisions of another Court of Common Pleas, especially when you are talking about fraud involving 126 of 253 signatures."

"Yes, your Honor, but . . ." Susan said.

"No buts, Miss Vanderpool," Judge Davis said. "Your arguments are without merit in this courtroom. The signatures will be stricken. You may be seated."

Susan cringed. That left only 127 signatures, and she had just made some of her strongest arguments. She never figured that he would strike all of the signatures on the technical challenges. She wrote meaningless notes on her legal pad, trying to hide her disappointment.

Bobby couldn't hide his. He lowered his head into his hands.

The observers in the courtroom murmured.

Vera looked at her watch. It was 9:25.

Judge Davis looked over at Ned, whose lips quivered as he tried to hold back a smile. "Counsel, you may proceed with your arguments, which I believe go to fraud in notarizing these petitions.

"Yes, your Honor," Ned said, as he stood up and confidently strode over to the witness stand to call his first witness.

"Al Stewart," Ned said. Al stood up, pushed his chair back, and whispered to Bobby as he walked past, "Money talks."

Bobby looked at Al, too dispirited to say what he really thought, which was "And your bullshit fat ass can barely walk."

As soon as Ned asked Al to tell the court his name, there was a commotion at the courtroom door. People were standing in front of the door and in the aisles, and someone was trying to get through. "Excuse me. Excuse me. Coming through, ma'am," said a male voice. Bodies moved from side to side, grumbling.

When the sea of bodies parted, Vera smiled. "Thank God," she said to no one in particular. "Move down," she said to Alfreda, moving her hips in her direction. "We've got to make room for him right here."

CHAPTER 35

Velvet walked down the aisle. He wore a black fedora with a black and red feather that was attached to the hat with a gold medallion in the likeness of Julius Caesar. He accented his black and white pinstripe suit with a red silk scarf in the pocket. His black leather shoes shined like patent leather.

He looked for Vera on the front row and walked over to the space she had just pushed free for him.

"I sure am glad to see you, honey," Vera whispered, "although I thought you'd never get here."

"You give some bad directions, girl," he said.

"Can we have order in the courtroom?" the bailiff asked, thinking that this crowd of mostly Negroes had behaved much better than he expected. "Order. Order," he said.

Everybody who was looking at Velvet looked at the bailiff as he called out again. When the courtroom settled down, Ned said, "May I proceed, your Honor?", but he got no answer. "May I proceed, your Honor?", Ned repeated, more firmly this time.

Judge Davis looked over at Velvet, who nodded his head at the judge in recognition. The judge took off his glasses, rubbed his eyes, and then put the glasses back on, looking over the rims in Velvet's direction.

"Your Honor?", Ned repeated, as he looked at the judge and expected, as did everyone else in the courtroom, an answer.

"Uh," said the judge, unable to find the words. "Uh," he pulled a handkerchief out of his pocket and wiped his sweaty brow. "Fifteen minute recess."

He banged the gavel and hurried out of the courtroom.

Ned, mouth wide open, looked at Al. Vera put her arm around Velvet's and squeezed it. Bobby looked at Susan and shook his head.

The judge closed the door to his chambers and took off his robe. He was sweating profusely, and his wife had just gotten the robe cleaned. He didn't have the money to get it cleaned again that week. He sat at his desk and let his mind race, wondering what interest a Philadelphia night club owner would have in a small time, Lower Merion election case. Just as he poured himself a glass of water, there was a knock on the door. His special assistant came in.

"I hate to interrupt you, Judge, but a gentleman gave me this note and said that it was imperative that you receive it as soon as possible," he said.

"Thank you, Morris," the judge said, extending his hand to take the note. "You can leave now."

The judge opened the note. It read, "100+=3,000-". It was signed simply, "V".

Ten minutes later, Judge Davis returned to the bench. Ned stood up and motioned for Al to follow him as he walked toward the witness stand.

Judge Davis interrupted. He looked at Ned and said, "Counselor, there's no need to call your witness. I took the recess to review the pleadings and do further research to determine whether the challenge to the notarizing process can be determined on the pleadings or whether testimony is necessary."

He continued, "I have determined that no further testimony is required. The pleadings speak for themselves. It is quite clear that, except for the five petitions referred to in Mr. Stewart's affidavit, which amount to 19 signatures, Mrs. Greene properly notarized the remainder of the petitions. Therefore, discounting the signatures on Mr. Stewart's petitions, the Defendant, Robert Marshall, has 109 valid signatures and qualifies as a candidate for Supervisor of Lower Merion Township."

Ned yelled out, "But Jeff...," then caught himself and said, "I mean, Your Honor."

Vera jumped up and hugged Velvet. "Thank you," she whispered in his ear as she handed him an envelope with $3,000 cash inside.

"Anything for an old friend," he said as he took the envelope and walked out.

Bobby jumped up and hugged Susan, who thought that her legal arguments really were that good.

Then Vera ran over to Bobby, who gave her the biggest hug of all.

"Don't tell me now, but why do I think that Velvet had something to do with this?" he asked, laughing between words.

"You have to use what you've got to get what you want," Vera said. Then she gave Bobby another hug and said, "I'll take over your campaign now."

She left Bobby to the congratulatory hugs of others and walked over to the counsel table where Ned stared off in space as Al Stewart asked, "what happened?"

Vera stood directly in front of Ned and said, "See you election day. I'm running Bobby's campaign now."

She leaned over to Al and said, "Don't forget our campaign office phone number—MI3-5555. You'll need it on election night when Ned wants to call to concede."

Vera laughed and walked away. Who would have thought that all that hanging out in Velvet's club would have come to some good? The vats of bourbon and ginger ale had clouded her memory, so she was a little slow remembering that Judge Davis, who was just an attorney in private practice back in her party days, frequently visited Velvet's back room. And if she knew those gamblers, and she knew enough of them, she knew that they never changed. They didn't get older and wiser; they got older and poorer.

The judge stayed in debt to Velvet. Velvet didn't mind letting Vera pay off the man's $3,000 debt because he knew that the judge's losses would be back up to that in no time. And Velvet knew that the judge would rule the way he told him to if he thought that would get him out of debt.

Shorty Lane's band was vibrating the windows at the American Legion Hall on Welsh Road on election night. Bobby and Vera felt a rush of heat from all the bodies packed inside when they opened the door. It took 15 minutes to work their way to the small platform that Shorty was using as a bandstand.

When Bobby and Vera made it to the front, Vera took Shorty's microphone and announced to everybody, as if they didn't know, "I have the honor of presenting the next Supervisor of Lower Merion Township, Bobby Marshall."

Over the applause and cheers, Vera held Bobby's hand in the air in a victory sign, and said, "Go get 'em, little brother," as she handed him the microphone.

THE END

READER'S GUIDE
Discussion Questions

1) What does "Chasing the 400" mean to the reader?

2) Does "the 400" really exist? Is there a Harriet Butcher type in your town?

3) In the novel, the upper class African Americans lived in the city and the working class African Americans lived in the suburbs. Is that the case today?

4) Is Harrison's based on any particular store?

5) Did Bobby make the right decision about college? Should he have tried another way?

6) Vera starts out the novel as a very grown, confident, sassy and sexy 17-year-old. Do you think that was typical for girls her age in the 1950s? Is it true today?

7) Ned thinks that the Daniels are better than the Marshalls because of their economic and social status, while his sister, Phyllis, doesn't. Do you think the Daniels are better or just different? And what does "better" mean anyway?

8) Is the African American community still as economically and socially stratified as in the novel?

9) Vera becomes the first dark-skinned model at Harrison's. Do color-line issues still exist today?

10) Alfreda left Ardmore to live the way that she wanted to. Would she have to leave home today?

11) On the same night, Phyllis went to a ball with members of the 400, and the Marshalls went to a big dance with members of their social group. Were the 400 and the working class groups on the Main Line really that different?

12) Discuss your experiences with social and economic barriers in the past and present.

13) The novel does not give many details about the first few years of Vera and Donny's marriage and Vera's early years in the 400. What type of experiences do you think they had?

14) This novel concerns class distinctions in the African American community. Do other ethnic groups have the same distinctions? Do they handle them the same?

15) Today, is it easier or more difficult to move back and forth between the worlds of the upper class and working class than it was during the time period depicted in the novel?